$\mathcal{P}$aige clinked her glass against Anthony's. "To us! And the best year ever!"

"That includes finding ourselves boyfriends," Anthony added.

"But if we don't, then we're the other's date for the Senior Prom, right?"

"Right!"

Just then the doorbell rang and Anthony's eyes lit up. He took a sip of his drink and then grabbed Paige by the hand, dragging her with him to the front door.

"Let's get this party started!" he exclaimed.

is he

or isn't he?

JOHN HALL

AVON BOOKS

AN IMPRINT OF HARPERCOLLINSPUBLISHERS

This book is for my cousins:
Michael, Theresa and Gina; Nancy and Diane;
John, Lisa (aka Mona) and Frank (aka Cheech);
Maria (who used to live next door!)
and especially Donna

Thanks for making growing up so much fun
and thanks for so many great memories!

chapter one

*I*t had been the worst summer of her life.

But her best friend didn't need to know that.

Of course, it was never easy keeping things from Anthony. He was always able to detect when something was wrong or when she was keeping a secret from him.

Seventeen-year-old Paige Crane took a deep breath and rang the doorbell of Anthony's penthouse apartment. A few seconds later she could hear the sound of approaching footsteps. She pasted a smile on her face as the door began to open.

"So what do you think?" she exclaimed, throwing her arms up in the air and twirling in front of Anthony. "Do I look like I just spent the summer in Los Angeles?"

Anthony blinked in disbelief, rubbing his eyes. "Who are you and what have you done with the real Paige Crane? The

Paige I know hates the sun." Anthony gave Paige a huge hug and then inspected her from head to toe. "I almost didn't recognize you! Where did you get that great tan?!"

"It's a fake bake!" Paige exclaimed, walking into Anthony's apartment. The icy air-conditioning that greeted her felt great after the steamy humidity of Manhattan's city streets. "I went to this Brazilian spa on Madison and 81st. You strip down to your underwear and step into a chamber that's about the size of a locker. Then they spritz your body with this liquid that makes your skin golden brown."

"The other girls are going to be *so* jealous." Anthony gazed at himself in a hallway mirror. "What do you think of my tan? It's not fading, is it?"

"Please! If I know you, you spent the entire summer lying on the beach." Paige followed Anthony into the kitchen and hopped up on a stool next to the breakfast bar as he began pulling carrots, celery and other veggies from the stainless steel fridge, placing them in front of her.

"So where's Ian?" she asked, reaching for a cutting board and knife. She began slicing a zucchini into thin strips. "I thought he'd be helping set up."

"Who?"

"Ian. Tall, dark and handsome Ian. Remember him? Your boyfriend?"

"You mean *ex-boyfriend*."

"What?!"

Anthony held up a hand, silencing Paige. "You don't want to hear the details. Trust me. Let's just say he's ancient history and leave it at that. Now, tell me all about your summer in La-La Land."

Paige put down the knife she'd been using. "Oh no you don't, Mr. DeMarco. I want *details* and I want them *now*. We'll get to my summer later."

Anthony opened a package of onion soup mix and added it into a bowl of sour cream. "I'm single again."

"Obviously. What happened?"

Anthony sighed. "You're really going to torture me by making me relive the entire nightmare, aren't you?"

If there was one thing Paige knew Anthony loved, it was talking about himself. Especially when something dramatic had happened to him. Telling her about his break-up with Ian was *not* going to be torture.

"Yes, I am. Now spill!"

"Okay, I'll tell you but we're not talking about it at the party," Anthony said. "Deal?"

"Deal."

"He broke up with me in Provincetown after a week. He gave me the 'It's not you, it's me' speech."

"You didn't believe him?" Paige asked while slicing a green pepper and arranging it on a platter.

Anthony shook his head. "I didn't believe him. Ian got a look at all the guys in P-Town and suddenly decided he could do better than me. You should have seen it, Paige. Everywhere you looked there were hunks. On the beach. In the water. Riding the bike paths. We're talking *GQ* material. Ian's head was spinning around in so many different directions, he didn't know where to look first. He was like that possessed girl from *The Exorcist*."

Anthony began stirring the sour cream furiously. "One day we were at the beach and there were some guys tossing around a Frisbee and they asked Ian if he wanted in on the game. Do you think he asked me if I minded if he went off to play with them? No! He ran off, leaving me alone on our blanket."

"What did you do?" Paige asked, knowing there was more to the story. And if she knew Anthony, there was going to be plenty of drama.

"I left and went back to the beach house. Ian followed after me because he knew I was mad. Of course, I had also taken their Frisbee after it had landed on our blanket and they couldn't continue the game without it."

"And then?"

"When we got back to the house, that's when Ian gave me his speech and asked if we could be friends."

"What did you tell him?" Paige asked, even though she was sure she knew the answer.

"I told him no!"

Paige had been right.

"Who wants to be friends with their ex? Especially one who's a cheater."

"You think he cheated on you?" Paige gasped.

"If he hadn't, he was going to. It was only a matter of time."

"Where did he end up spending the rest of the summer, then? Wasn't he staying at the beach house with you?"

"That's right, he *was*. After dropping his little bombshell, he took back the Frisbee and went off to join his new friends. You'll be proud to know that I didn't lose my temper. After Ian left I put a note on his bedroom door telling him I wanted him out of the house by the end of the day."

"That's it?" Paige asked skeptically. "That's all you did?"

Anthony stuck a finger in the bowl of onion dip he had finished making and took a taste. "Delish!" He held out the bowl to Paige. "Want a taste?"

Paige dipped in a carrot. "You didn't answer my question."

Anthony gave Paige a wicked grin. "Did I forget to mention that I *accidentally* left a bottle of cologne open in one of his drawers?"

Paige giggled. "You didn't."

"I did." Anthony put the bowl of dip into the fridge and began taking bags of potato chips and pretzels out of the grocery bags that lined the granite counter. "It was the latest fragrance from the L & F line. Expensive stuff."

"Where did he stay after you kicked him out?"

"I don't know. He probably came back to the city. Or maybe he bunked with one of his new friends. I never saw him again after that day."

"Really? P-Town's a pretty small place."

"I didn't spend the rest of the summer in P-Town. I spent it on Martha's Vineyard by myself. Call me a coward, but I didn't want to run into Ian. It would have hurt too much. My folks have friends who own a house on the Vineyard and I knew they were in Europe so I asked if we could go out there. My dad wasn't too happy about losing the money we spent renting the house in P-Town, but my mom worked her magic. During the day I went to the beach with my folks, and at night I either read, listened to CDs or watched TV."

"That's it?" Paige asked in disbelief. "You didn't try to meet someone else?"

Anthony shrugged. "I didn't want to."

"Why didn't you call me?!"

"I didn't want you feeling sorry for me, okay? I know I could have called and believe me, I was tempted—I even picked up the phone a couple of times—but I was feeling sorry for myself. Enough for the both of us."

Anthony sighed as he began opening bags of potato chips and pouring them into bowls. "I needed to be alone. Ian was my first real boyfriend. Okay, we only went out for like three months and yeah, he'll be at Boston University this year, but I thought it was the beginning of *something*, you know?"

The expression on Anthony's face was so sad that at that moment all Paige wanted to do was give him a hug and tell him everything was going to be alright. Anthony DeMarco had been her best friend since the seventh grade. She had been the new girl in school and notoriously shy. Her first week in class, she'd kept to herself. Then, during a field trip to the Metropolitan Museum of Art the following week, she'd been paired with Anthony. Secretly, she'd been pleased. The dark-haired, blue-eyed boy with dimples had caught her attention the first day she arrived at Peppington Prep, a private school on the Upper East Side. He looked so adorable in his oversized navy blue blazer and loosened burgundy striped tie and it seemed like everyone in their class was his friend. Paige instantly knew she wanted to be friends with him, too.

During the field trip, they were supposed to be studying Modernist paintings. But after an hour, all the canvases started to blur together.

"This is soooo boring," Anthony whispered to Paige, his first words to her that afternoon, looking up from his notebook where he'd been taking notes. He took off the headphones he'd been wearing during the museum lecture and pushed his straight black hair off his forehead. A second later it flopped back down on his forehead. Paige had to resist the urge to push it away. She'd seen some of the other girls in her class do it on various occasions, but she hardly knew Anthony. "We can buy one of these tapes on the way out and learn everything we're supposed to. Why don't we cut out?"

"But we're supposed to stay here," Paige whispered back, afraid one of her classmates would overhear their plans and possibly snitch on them. But Anthony was asking *her* to do something with him! And wasn't that what she wanted? "We could get in trouble."

Anthony rolled his eyes. "It's the last class of the day. Nobody will miss us."

"But what will we do if we leave?"

"The Museum of Television and Radio is showing the first five seasons of *The Simpsons*. That's way more fun than this. And we can stop at Serendipity for a frozen hot chocolate on our way down. My treat."

Paige's eyes lit up. "*The Simpsons*? A frozen hot chocolate? D'oh! Those are two of my favorite things!"

Anthony smiled and put his notebook in his backpack. "Then I guess you're coming with me."

After that, Paige and Anthony were joined at the hip. From the second they left the museum, they started talking and never stopped. They had lunch together every day at school, hung out at each other's homes after classes ended and spent as much of their free time together as they could. Sometimes there were fights—Anthony was always more adventurous than Paige, wanting to take risks and try things that were different, and she was more of a scaredy cat, always afraid of what could go wrong—but they never stayed mad for long and always made up. Why wouldn't they? They were best friends, and that's what best friends did.

In the early days of their friendship, Paige never once considered Anthony boyfriend material. When she thought of Anthony, she thought of him as a friend—someone to hang out with, have fun with and confide in. And she'd never gotten any sort of vibe from Anthony that he was interested in dating her (of course, there had been a reason for that, but at the time, she didn't know it). She didn't think of him as a possible boyfriend because if she wanted a boyfriend, she could have one. Easily. Like most of the girls in their class, she had started dating and there was always a guy calling to invite her to a movie or school dance. Usually the dates were a disaster—seventh grade boys didn't have a clue about what to do on a first date, although they all seemed to think the date was supposed to end with an open-mouthed kiss. Not!— and the best part was when she got home and called Anthony to give him a recap.

Paige nibbled on a potato chip while Anthony began cutting up blocks of cheese and arranging them on platters with crackers and grapes.

"You do that so well," Paige pointed out. "I can't even make a decent-looking peanut butter and jelly sandwich."

"It's a skill I'm going to need if I don't make it as a screenwriter in Hollywood. Professional cater-waiter. At least the one perk of the job will be meeting cute guys. All cater-waiters are either aspiring actors or writers. And let's not forget the most important thing. Many of them are gay!"

It never failed to amaze Paige how at ease Anthony was with being gay. It was no big deal. Just part of who he was. She could still remember when he had told her he was gay three years ago. It had been a snowy afternoon and they'd been at her apartment, flipping through issues of *Teen People*. Anthony had held up a page featuring Leonardo DiCaprio.

"Leo's so cute."

Paige glanced at the photo with mild interest. Unlike her other female classmates, Leo didn't do much for her and she hadn't seen *Titanic* ten times. "I can see that."

Anthony flipped to another page in the magazine. "God. So is Christian Bale."

"*That* is definitely true," Paige agreed.

"Oooh! Now here's a real hunk." Anthony held up a page with Brad Pitt wearing a pair of faded jeans. "I wonder what it would be like to kiss him."

"Excuse me?" Paige wasn't sure if she'd heard Anthony correctly. Then the light bulb went on over her head. "Are you trying to tell me something?"

Anthony went back to his magazine. "I just did."

And just like that, Anthony had told her he was gay. It was no big deal. For a while, Paige had suspected that something was up. When they were shopping at department stores, Anthony always made a point to linger in the men's fragrance department, talking to the cute older guys holding cologne bottles and gathering free samples.

"What's going on in here?" a deep voice asked.

Paige turned around on her stool to see Anthony's older brother, Paolo, walk into the kitchen. Paolo was two years older than Anthony and starting his sophomore year at NYU. While Anthony wore his dark hair long and had blue eyes, Paolo had lighter hair that he wore in a buzz cut and his eyes were more of a blue-green. He was wearing shorts and a T-shirt with cut-off sleeves. Unlike Anthony, Paolo was a major sports buff. Cradling a basketball under one arm, he wiped a sheen of sweat off his forehead with the back of his hand while sticking his head in the refrigerator. Seconds later he emerged with a bottle of Gatorade that he began drinking directly from the bottle.

"Ugh!" Anthony exclaimed. "Must you share your germs? And you're dripping sweat all over the kitchen."

Paolo looked around at all the trays of food on the counter.

"Not another party?" he groaned.

"Don't worry, this isn't one of my usual extravaganzas," Anthony said, throwing ice cubes and strawberries into a blender as he prepared to make nonalcoholic daiquiris. "I'm saving that for Halloween. I just invited a few friends over for an end-of-summer party."

"How many is a few?"

"Around twenty or thirty." Anthony put the lid on the blender and pressed a button. Soon the sound of crushing ice filled the kitchen. "I can't remember," he shouted over the din.

Paolo slapped himself on the forehead. "Mom and Dad would flip if they knew how many people you were having over."

Anthony gave his brother a pointed look. "They won't know unless someone tells them."

Paige loved Anthony's parents. They were both so glamorous and she never tired of hearing how they fell in love when they were both students at the Fashion Institute of Technology. Anthony's parents were Lorenzo and Francesca DeMarco, fashion designers who were known around the world. The L & F logo—which first appeared when they were students and Lorenzo had carved a heart on a tree with an L & F inside of it—appeared on everything from jeans, shirts, dresses, underwear, shoes, and perfume bottles to sheets and housewares. If there was a spot on an object where the L & F logo could be stamped, it was!

Because they were constantly opening up boutiques across the country and overseeing the production of their merchandise in Europe, Anthony's parents were rarely in New York. They made an appearance at least once a month and Paolo was usually responsible for taking care of Anthony, although one of their many aunts usually stopped by to make sure the refrigerator was well stocked with food and the penthouse was still in one piece.

Paige's home life was no different. Her mother was the soap actress Camille Crane. She starred on the daytime soap opera *The Yields of Passion*, where she played the much-married and much-divorced Priscilla Foxworth—not much of a stretch from Camille's own life. Fans of the show *loved* Camille and the wicked character she played.

Paige wished she had a closer relationship with her mother, who lived year-round in Los Angeles, where *The Yields of Passion* was taped, but the only person Camille seemed to care about was herself. Even though her mother had let her down in the past, Paige had hoped that this year things would be different. She had so been looking forward to spending the summer with Camille. She figured that she and her mother could spend a lot of time together. She would hang out on the set of the soap, they'd go shopping and maybe even take a car ride down the coast for a long weekend, stopping in cute little towns along the way. Camille would ask what was new in her life and she'd tell her.

None of that had happened.

With the exception of a once-a-week phone call with Camille, Paige hardly had any contact with her mother during the school year; it was no different in July and August. First, Camille forgot to pick her up at the airport. Then, when she arrived at Camille's house, she wasn't there. When her mother finally put in an appearance after three days—she'd been rejuvenating herself at a health spa—she apologized for her forgetfulness and then flew off to the Bahamas, where *The Yields of Passion* was filming some episodes on location (Priscilla had been kidnapped by a voodoo priest who was obsessed with her and was preparing to sacrifice her on his altar of love unless she married him). When Camille finally returned from the Bahamas after three weeks, she still didn't have time for Paige. She was either busy taping her show or running off to some party with her latest boy toy. Paige had kept herself busy with shopping and movies, but she didn't have any friends in California and by the end of July, she was bored out of her mind. When August finally rolled around, Paige couldn't stand it anymore. She left her mother a note and hopped a plane back to New York.

She hadn't heard a word from her mother since leaving.

Paolo put the bottle of Gatorade back in the refrigerator. "I'm going to be in my room doing some reading. Classes have already started for me and my professors have really doled out the work. Try to keep the noise level down, okay?"

"Okay, okay," Anthony promised, pouring a daiquiri for Paige and adding a swirly straw. "Now beat it. Your anti-party buzz is destroying the mood."

"Bye, Paolo," Paige called, taking a sip of her daiquiri as Paolo left the kitchen. "Mmmm. Good."

Anthony poured himself a daiquiri. "Now that you've heard all about my depressing summer, it's my turn to hear all about your fabulous one. Cheer me up! Confess! I want to hear *everything*. Did you meet any hot young actors? Dance on table tops? Make a naughty video? Paige Crane in *Girls Gone Wild Part Thirty*! Go to any fun parties? Camille must get tons of invitations."

"Yes, she does, but she didn't share any of them with me."

"How come?"

"She never asked me. She either went by herself or with whoever the latest boyfriend of the week was. I think the new one's name is Bruno, but that could have changed since I left."

"Did you ask her if you could tag along?"

"No."

"Well, duh!" Anthony took a sip of his daiquiri. "How would she know that you wanted to go if you didn't tell her?"

"Why should I have to ask? Besides, the parties don't matter. I just wanted to spend time with her. That's why I flew out there!"

"Did you tell her that?"

"Why should I? She should know. She's my mother!"

"Paige, sweetie, I've met your mother. She's *such* a diva. So over the top. Big hair. Big clothes. Big jewelry. Big ego. She's into herself and the character she plays on TV. I think she just needs to be reminded that she's supposed to be doing Mom-like things."

"Next time she calls I'll tell her I need a dozen cupcakes for the school bake sale," Paige said dryly. "I can just see her becoming the new Betty Crocker. Not."

"Look, I know Camille is never going to be Mother of the Year, but cut her a little slack. She's not that bad."

"I suppose you're right," Paige grudgingly admitted. "It's just that I'm still mad at her! I spent the entire summer by myself."

"Then why didn't *you* call *me*?" Anthony demanded. "Misery loves company. We could have consoled each other."

"I didn't want to spoil things for you and Ian. I knew you'd be worried about me and probably insist that I fly out."

"That's exactly what I would have done." Anthony shook his head. "We're both two of a kind. Here I thought we were going to be like Sandy and Danny in *Grease*, telling each other about our hot summer nights. Instead they were lonely summer nights. Okay, new promise. You ready?"

"Ready."

"When we go off to college next year, we talk or e-mail each other *every* day. Deal?"

"Deal!"

"So you want to take a look at the outside?"

Paige nodded and followed Anthony out of the kitchen,

daiquiri in hand, eager to see his decorations. Anthony's parties always had some great theme.

"What do you think?" Anthony asked, throwing open the French doors that led outside to the penthouse deck.

"Wow! I thought you said this wasn't going to be one of your usual extravaganzas."

"I lied."

Anthony had transformed his deck into a Hawaiian paradise. There were palm trees with coconuts, pineapples and bananas on their branches, lush orchids and other tropical-looking flowers, thatched huts, tiki torches and piles of white sand everywhere. There was even a roasted pig turning on a spit!

"How did you do all this on such short notice?" Paige asked.

Anthony flipped out his cell phone. "There's a prop shop that my parents use when they have their fashion shows. I gave them a call and told them I needed whatever they had that was Hawaiian."

"They even had the pig?"

"The caterer provided that. I'm good with putting together munchies, but that's about it. You know I can't cook to save my life. We're going to have a chef who's going to barbecue burgers and hot dogs and chicken. And he'll also slice up the pig."

"Is that the ocean I hear?" Paige asked, still amazed by what she was seeing.

"It's a sound machine. I figured we could listen to some lapping waves and the screech of seagulls before we switch over to music." Anthony glanced at his watch. "I better go change before everyone gets here. You better go change, too."

"Into what?"

Anthony's mouth dropped open. "Paige Elizabeth Crane! You're not telling me you didn't bring a swimsuit, did you?"

"What's wrong with what I'm wearing?" Paige was wearing a short-sleeve hot pink cotton blouse tied in a knot at her waist with white shorts and flip-flops. Her light brown hair was worn in a ponytail tied in a matching pink ribbon and she had a pair of sunglasses perched on top of her head.

"Nothing, but you don't look like you're going to the beach. You look like you're going to a family barbecue out in the suburbs."

"I do not!"

Anthony grabbed Paige by the hand and dragged her back into the apartment. "Come with me."

After depositing Paige in his parents' bedroom, Anthony returned with a box filled with brightly colored fabrics. He handed the box to Paige.

"What's this?" she asked suspiciously, knowing Anthony was up to something.

"Swimsuits from this year's L & F line. My parents have a whole storeroom full of stuff next to the kitchen. You should be able to find something that fits in there."

Paige fingered through the string bikinis. "These don't leave much to the imagination."

"They're not supposed to!" Anthony huffed in exasperation. "You've got a great body, Paige! Show it off! Use it to find yourself a boyfriend."

Paige's lack of a boyfriend was a sore point and a topic she didn't like discussing. She was seventeen years old and still hadn't had a serious boyfriend. Sure, there had been dates and a few kisses here and there, but she still hadn't had a deep, feel-it-all-through-your-body-toe-curling kiss from the one guy who you know is *the one*. Of course, one needed to be asked out on a date in order to acquire a boyfriend, and for the last few months her phone hadn't been ringing. Hopefully that would change with the beginning of senior year.

"I'll meet you outside in fifteen minutes," Anthony said. "Make yourself into the gorgeous babe I know you can be!"

After Anthony left, Paige went through the box. There had to be something in here that she could wear. After digging through the tiny bits of fabric, she finally found something she could live with.

"Leave it to you to find the only one-piece swimsuit,"Anthony sighed fifteen minutes later when Paige joined him back outside wearing a one-piece L & F swimsuit in neon yellow.

"You said to find something in the box," Paige said with an innocent smile.

"Okay, you win this round, but I'm not giving up. One of these days I'm going to unleash the sexy babe that I know is inside you."

"If it's any consolation, you look like you could star on the WB."

Anthony was wearing a pair of boxer-cut swim trunks with a lime green and yellow diagonal stripe pattern. Around his neck he had a white shell necklace on a thin leather strap and he was wearing a white tank top.

"If we had more time I'd do something about your hair

but we don't," Anthony said.

Paige reached up to her ponytail in a panic. "What's wrong with my hair?"

"Nothing! But straight guys love chicks with long flowing hair."

Paige raised an eyebrow at Anthony. "And how would you know that?"

Anthony raised an eyebrow right back at Paige. "Gym class. Locker room. Straight guys. You do the math."

"Gotcha." Paige plopped herself down on a chaise lounge. "When is everyone supposed to start arriving?"

"Eight o'clock. I'm sure the place will be packed by nine. Have you spoken to anyone since you've been home?"

"Colleen and I have been playing phone tag and I haven't heard from Bianca and Rachel."

"I wonder what kind of mischief those two have been getting into. They sent me an e-mail, saying they were coming."

"I'm sure they were auditioning all summer long."

"For what?" Anthony asked. "You know I love them both, but when are they going to get a clue?"

Bianca and Rachel Torres were identical twins and heiresses to the Torres Taco fortune, which included a line of frozen Mexican dinners. Bianca and Rachel were two of the richest teenagers in Manhattan, but there was one thing their family fortune couldn't do for them: make them stars.

Paige didn't want to be mean, but Bianca and Rachel were *desperately* untalented. They were constantly trying to find a way to claim their fifteen minutes of fame, often with disastrous results. First they tried to be models (they were bored walking down the runway and didn't like the constant changing of clothes), then actresses (they couldn't remember their lines and asked if it were possible to have cue cards made) and then pop singers (dogs AND cats howled when they heard the twins sing). Now they were determined to claim their fame via reality TV and were always trying out for shows.

Anthony glanced at his watch. "They'll be here soon enough, so I'm sure they'll let us know what they've been up to."

"Why can't they be happy running for something like Homecoming Queen?"

"Don't even suggest that! We're only allowed one homecoming queen. Can you imagine what would happen if one of them lost?"

"We'd have one pissed-off runner-up," Paige said.

"You think? Anyway, let's forget about Bianca and Rachel," Anthony said, raising his daiquiri glass. "How about a toast?"

Paige clinked her daiquiri glass against Anthony's. "To us! And the best year ever!"

"That includes finding ourselves boyfriends," Anthony added.

"But if we don't, then we're each other's date for the Senior Prom, right?"

"Right!"

Just then the doorbell rang and Anthony's eyes lit up. He took a sip of his daiquiri and then grabbed Paige by the hand, dragging her with him to the front door.

"Let's get this party started!" he exclaimed.

chapter two

*A*nthony DeMarco loved throwing a party.

There was something creative about the whole process. Putting together a guest list, coming up with a theme, ordering the food, deciding what you were going to wear, then watching as your guests arrived and seeing how they interacted with each other.

It was kind of like directing a movie. In your mind, you saw how the movie needed to be set up before being filmed. From the sets to the costumes to the actors. All the elements were pulled together and put into place. And then action!

Anthony *loved* movies. What he wanted more than anything else was to work in the movie business after college.

Like the best movies, the best parties always had some sort of drama. Either a couple had just broken up and they were seeing each other for the first time or someone's ex-boyfriend showed up with a new girlfriend and the ex-girlfriend pretended she didn't care but she really did and either tried to make her ex-boyfriend jealous with another guy or started a catfight with the new girlfriend.

Tonight's party was a little low-key. Everyone was reconnecting from being away for the summer. Most of the girls were showing off their summer tans in outfits that left little to the imagination. Lots of short shorts, miniskirts, halter tops and cropped T-shirts that bared midriffs and exposed toned tummy muscles.

The guys were exposing just as much skin as the girls. There were skimpy tank tops and tight T-shirts to display buff summer chests.

Confidence was in the air. Everyone knew they looked good and they were all checking everyone else out. Looking to see who was free and available. There were lots of smiles, winks, and waves over sipped drinks.

Anthony wished he could join in the games, but as usual, there was no one for him.

He smothered a sigh. It wasn't easy being a gay seventeen-year-old when most of your male classmates were straight with a capital S. Anthony's close friends knew he was gay, but it wasn't something he advertised to the world. And that world, for another year, was Peppington Prep. The last thing he wanted was one of his jock classmates to think he was looking too closely at him.

Sure, he'd met gay guys in the past. Hello! His parents worked in fashion and some of the most famous designers in the world were gay. The gay guys he'd met over the years at his parents' office were handsome and cool and he wanted to be just like them. But older guys were off limits because of the whole age difference. Either they saw him as the boss's kid or—and this *really* irked him because he was already cast in the part, thank you very much—a little brother.

Anthony knew there was a whole gay world out there—a world where there were guys just like him—but it wasn't within reach. At least not yet. Not until he was a few years older.

Anthony knew he only had to wait another year. Once he was in college, things would be different. He'd be in a world where being gay wasn't a big deal. But he was getting tired of waiting.

He wanted a boyfriend *now*.

How could he have been so stupid?! He'd had a boyfriend until he'd let his jealousy get in the way. Maybe he shouldn't have been so quick to jump to conclusions. Maybe Ian had only been looking. Maybe he wasn't going to cheat on him. Maybe . . .

No! No, no, no, no, no! He wasn't going to think about Ian. It still hurt too much. And he wasn't going to start beating up on himself or doubting his decision. This wasn't some Lifetime movie. He didn't need a guy—well, at least not a guy who was a two-timing louse. Ian was old news. Over. Done with. It was time to move on. To think about the future and the Mr. Right who was waiting for him.

If only he could find him!

Paige grabbed Anthony's arm and gave it a squeeze, shaking him from his thoughts. "Hey! Great party!"

"You think?"

Paige nodded, sipping from a glass of punch. "Everyone's having a blast."

"Anthony!"

Anthony turned around to see Colleen O'Brian headed his way. She was carrying a plate filled with two cheeseburgers, ribs and a baked potato loaded with butter and sour cream. Unlike the other girls, Colleen ate what she wanted when she wanted. No carrot sticks and celery for her. She wasn't a slave to her scale and it was the reason why she was one of Manhattan's top plus-sized teen models.

Colleen had curves. Lots of curves. She also had a *great* chest. Anthony might be gay, but he knew what the straight boys liked and Colleen had dressed for battle tonight, showing off her cleavage in a hot orange bikini top that matched the sarong around her waist. She also had a great head of hair. It was shoulder length, in a gorgeous shade of red, shot with strands of gold and toffee. Tonight she was wearing her hair pushed back with a wide white headband with orange polka dots.

"Kiss, kiss," she said, brushing cheeks with Anthony and sitting down at a patio table. "So Paige filled me in about Ian."

Anthony glared at Paige. "Oh she did, did she?"

Colleen nodded, biting into a cheeseburger. "What a rat."

"She asked where he was," Paige explained. "What was I supposed to do? Lie?"

"Yes."

"You guys broke up," Colleen said. "Big deal. It's nothing to be embarrassed about."

"I'm not embarrassed. It still hurts, okay? And talking about it brings back all the unpleasant memories. Change of topic, please."

"Okay." Colleen finished off her first cheeseburger and

started on the second. "Did I tell you I'm taking singing and dancing lessons?"

"You are? How come?"

"I'm getting tired of modeling. I've been doing it for two years. I'd like to maybe try some acting."

"Tell him the truth," Paige urged, sitting down next to Colleen and swiping one of her ribs. "Tell him, tell him, tell him!"

Colleen swatted at Paige's hand. "Hey! Go get your own."

Paige ignored Colleen and began nibbling on the rib. "Tell him or else I will."

"Tell me what?" Anthony asked.

"Colleen wants to audition for *Hairspray* next year when the actress who's playing Tracy Turnblad leaves the show."

"Don't you think I'd be perfect for the part?" Colleen asked, her emerald-green eyes lighting up.

"Absolutely," Anthony said and meaning it. "Everyone loved you last spring at the Talent Show when you sang that song from *Dreamgirls*."

"What was it again?" Paige asked.

"'And I Am Telling You I'm Not Going,'" Colleen said.

"Did you know they're making it into a movie?" Anthony asked.

"No!!!!" Colleen squealed excitedly. "That's fabulous. Another plus-sized girl on the big screen. Effie is a role I'd kill for."

"You better keep your career plans to yourself," Anthony advised, "or a certain set of twins will suddenly decide to start overeating."

"Huh?"

24

"Shhhh." Anthony put a finger to his lips as Bianca and Rachel Torres joined the table.

As usual, the twins looked gorgeous. Like they had just stepped off the cover of a fashion magazine. Of course, Anthony knew they'd had a little help from their stylist. And makeup artist. And hairdresser.

Even though the twins had identical features—from their wavy jet-black hair, brown eyes and light brown skin—they differentiated themselves by the clothes they wore. Bianca usually went for a sexier look, showing off a lot of skin, while Rachel showed less.

Tonight Bianca was wearing frayed denim shorts that barely reached the top of her legs, high-heeled sandals and a T-shirt that said: TELL YOUR BOYFRIEND TO STOP CALLING ME! She'd also given herself big hair, teasing out her waves. Anthony thought she looked deliciously trashy. Rachel, on the other hand, had gone for a more subdued look. She was wearing a white tennis skirt and sleeveless red blouse with her hair in a French braid.

Anthony had been friends with the twins since kindergarten. One day he'd forgotten his lunch on the school bus and when it was lunchtime, no one would share with him. Except the twins. Bianca had offered him half of her tuna fish sandwich while Rachel had shared her potato chips and given him sips of milk from her Thermos. From that day on, Anthony had sworn his allegiance to the twins. Yes, they were airheads and they drove him batty with their schemes to become famous, and sometimes they were a little selfish and self-centered, but deep down, they had hearts of gold, and that meant something to Anthony.

He'd never forget the time in the sixth grade when a representative from Toys for Tots had visited Peppington Prep, explaining about the program and how it provided Christmas gifts for underprivileged children. After they'd selected names from the Christmas tree provided, Bianca and Rachel had asked what happened to the names that weren't picked. When they were told that sometimes not all the children received a Christmas gift, the twins had been horrified and had instantly taken all the names off the tree.

To this day, every December, the twins still gave an abundance of gifts to Toys for Tots.

"You'll never guess where we were today!" Bianca exclaimed. "You'll never ever guess!"

"We were at MTV!" Rachel screamed before anyone could answer. "Auditioning for their new reality show, 'Working Girl.'"

"'Working Girl?'" Anthony asked. "What's that?"

"It's this show where rich girls are going to be put in *horrible* situations," Bianca said. "Like working as a waitress in a diner or washing clothes in a laundromat."

"Not only that, but we're going to have to *live* like working girls," Rachel said. "You know, with their *families* in *tiny* apartments where there's only one bathroom."

"And probably no running hot water!" Bianca chimed in.

"Or elevators. We'll have to take the *stairs* to reach our apartment."

"And we won't be able to bring any of our own clothes. We're going to have to wear outfits that are *mass-produced*." Bianca shuddered. "Can you *imagine*?"

"How ever will you survive?" Colleen commented while

licking barbecue sauce off her fingers.

"What happens to the working girls?" Anthony asked. "Do they get to live your lives while you're living theirs?"

Bianca shook her head. "Oh, no. Can you imagine? It would be too much of a shock. All that luxury. I think they get sent to a spa or something."

"Maybe a trip to Disney World," Rachel said. "Or wherever they film those *Girls Gone Wild* videos."

"Ooooh! An opportunity for them to get some extra work!" Colleen exclaimed.

"They don't pay the girls in those videos," Bianca said. "Duh!"

Colleen gave Bianca a sly smile. "But it's *great* exposure. Some of those girls have even gone on to be stars."

"I think you're wrong, Colleen," Anthony said, knowing what his friend was up to and giving her a *shut up* look. If Bianca and Rachel thought they could be stars by doing a *Girls Gone Wild* video, they'd be on the next plane to Cancun.

"You're definitely going to be on the show?" Paige asked.

"We met with the producers today and they *really* liked us," Bianca said.

"Especially when we told them we'd never done a hard day's work in our *entire* lives," Rachel added.

"They got really excited when we told them we had maids and personal assistants who do everything for us."

"I'm going to go get some more ribs," Colleen said, leaving the table.

Anthony decided to follow after Colleen and fix a plate for himself but stopped in his tracks when he saw who was on the opposite side of his penthouse deck.

"What's wrong?" Paige asked, noticing the pissed expression on his face.

"Who invited *him*?"

Anthony glared at his uninvited guest. It was Felix Fennimore.

"Didn't you?" Paige asked.

Anthony gave Paige a *get real* look. "When have I *ever* invited Felix to one of my parties?"

"Never," Paige said. "I still don't understand what the problem is between the two of you."

The problem went all the way back to first grade when Anthony ran against Felix for class president and won. Felix, sore loser that he was, spread a rumor that Anthony ate his snot. Not to be outdone, Anthony started his own rumor. Only it was a rumor that was true.

That Felix played with Barbie dolls.

The part of the rumor that Anthony left out, though, was that when he and Felix had play dates, they *both* used to play with Felix's older sister's Barbies.

From that point on, Anthony and Felix had been rivals, always competing against each other. For grades. For friends. For awards. They *pretended* to like each other, but really didn't.

And then there was the gay factor.

Felix was also gay.

Anthony had discovered that fact in eighth grade when he was down in Chelsea one Saturday and spotted Felix buying a copy of *Out*. Deciding that maybe it was time to mend fences, Anthony walked over to Felix and told him he had just finished reading the same issue.

"Am I supposed to be impressed or something?" Felix had asked coldly, slipping the magazine into his Louis Vuitton backpack. (Years later, Anthony would come to realize that Felix was a label queen. Everything he owned or wore had to have a designer label on it.) "Is this supposed to *bond* us? Sorry, I'm not the bonding type."

With those final words, Felix had walked away, leaving Anthony alone on the corner.

Out of all the guys at Peppington Prep who could possibly be gay, why Felix? *Why?* Why couldn't it be someone he liked? And not like-*like*—as in wanting to make out with a guy you like because you think he's cute and you're attracted to him. But *like* as in "I like you as a person and want to be your friend."

"He's probably here to get some news for his gossip column," Paige said.

Felix penned Peppington Prep's school gossip column *In the Know*, writing all about the social lives of his classmates. Often there were also blind items in which secrets that were meant to be kept were exposed. That was the main reason why the column was a favorite with everyone at Peppington Prep and got Felix invited to all the best parties.

It also didn't hurt that Felix's father was head of programming at the Cooking Channel. He was responsible for bringing such hit shows as "Yummy for Your Tummy," "Everything Chocolate" and "Hot Italian Mamas" to the air. His latest success was a TV show featuring celebrity chef Steve Coulter. *People* magazine had recently named Steve their Sexiest Man Alive.

"I know you and Felix don't get along," Paige said, "but he's always been nice to me."

"That's because he's waiting for the two of us to have a huge fight!" Anthony exclaimed. "When that happens he'll move in for the kill, hoping you'll spill all my secrets so he can print them!"

"You know, this is going to sound crazy, but I think Felix might like you."

"What?!"

"Think about it. He's always worming his way into your life. Why else would he do that?"

"Because he likes making me miserable. It's what he lives for."

Paige shrugged. "If you say so."

"I say so. Me and Felix? A couple?" Anthony shuddered. "Brrr!"

Felix had caught sight of Anthony and waved to him. There was no mistaking the smug smile on his face. He knew he hadn't been invited to the party and he knew that Anthony knew he knew that.

"What are you going to do?" Paige asked, nervously biting her lower lip.

Well, he'd wanted a party with drama. And now he was going to get it.

Anthony turned back to Paige. "I'm going to go tell my uninvited guest that the party is over for him."

"You can't throw him out!"

"Just watch me."

Anthony left Paige's side and went across to the other side of the deck. There was no mistaking Felix. From his sun-streaked blond hair to his rich dark tan and blue eyes, to his sky blue tie-dyed shorts and white tank top (all designer names, of course), he had the California beach boy look down pat. Anthony was pleased to note that, unlike some of the other hotties at the party, Felix didn't have the muscles to fill out his tank top. He was as skinny as a string bean.

"Felix! What are you doing here?" Anthony was smiling, but the smile didn't reach his eyes.

"Tony!" Felix gushed. "Fab party! Love the eats."

Anthony gritted his teeth. If there was one thing he absolutely hated, it was being called Tony. And Felix knew that. *No one* called him Tony. It was so Brooklyn-sounding—like John Travolta's character in *Saturday Night Fever*—and he was a Manhattan boy!

"I'm surprised to see you."

"You are?" Felix plunged a toothpick into a chunk of cheese and popped it into his mouth. "I tagged along with Bianca and Rachel. We ran into each other at J. Crew and they mentioned coming over. My invitation probably got lost in the mail."

"It didn't get lost," Anthony said. "It was never . . ."

The rest of the words died in Anthony's throat. Felix was totally forgotten. Instead, Anthony's attention was completely focused across the terrace on one of the *cutest*, most *adorable* guys he had ever seen. He was wearing jeans and a loose baseball jersey with the number 10 on the front. It was probably some famous baseball player's number, but Anthony knew zip about sports. On his head was a baseball cap that was worn backwards. How had he missed noticing this guy all night?!

"It was never what?" Felix asked.

"Huh?" Anthony asked, feeling like he'd just woken up from a deep sleep. He tried to focus on Felix's face but he kept looking over his shoulder at Baseball Jersey Guy.

"My invitation?" Felix prodded.

All Anthony wanted to do at that moment was make a bee-line across the terrace and find out the name of the new guy. But he couldn't do that until he got rid of Felix. Quickly. If Felix got a look at this cutie . . . well, Anthony suddenly had a vision of the Big Bad Wolf drooling over the Three Little Pigs!

"It didn't get lost," Anthony said, wondering how he could steer Felix in the direction of the front door.

Felix speared another chunk of cheese. "It didn't? Then I guess I should leave. I wouldn't want to be accused of being a party-crasher."

Anthony couldn't believe what he was hearing. Felix *never* gave in. He had to be up to something.

"Let me just find Max and we'll leave."

"Max?"

"You haven't met Max? Oh, you have to! He's a great guy!" Felix scanned the deck of partygoers and then his blue eyes lit up. "There he is."

Anthony followed Felix's pointed finger and his mouth almost dropped open. *"That's* Max?"

"That's Max," Felix proudly stated. "Not bad to look at, is he?"

No! Anthony wanted to wail. *No!!!* Max was the cutie across the terrace. Baseball Jersey Guy. His future boyfriend! Was Cupid laughing at him? Was this some sort of cosmic practical joke? There couldn't be any other explanation. The one guy he was interested in had come to his party with Felix!

Felix waved to Max, who waved back and walked over in their direction.

There was something vaguely familiar about Max but Anthony couldn't put his finger on what it was. He felt like he'd already met him but that was impossible. There was no way he'd forget a cutie like this! Where had Felix met this guy? He wasn't a student at Peppington Prep. Could he be Felix's boyfriend? Anthony bit back a groan. Life couldn't be that unfair!

Felix noticed the puzzled expression on Anthony's face. "You feel like you've met him before, but you don't know where, right?"

"Right," Anthony admitted.

"You haven't been reading your *Teen People*, have you, Tony? Max is the son of Steve Coulter. You know who Steve is, don't you? My father gave the greenlight to his TV show, 'Delicious.'"

That's who it was! Max was a younger, less sculpted version of his muscular, macho father. Unlike other TV chefs, who advocated healthy cooking, Steve used only the most fattening ingredients in his dishes and owned a restaurant in Los Angeles. The catch-phrase on his show, which was now known from coast to coast, was: "It's supposed to taste *good*." Female—and male—fans were known to throw their underwear at him (along with hotel room keys).

"Max's father is opening a new restaurant in New York," Felix explained. "He's going to be here for at least a year, overseeing things, and he decided to bring his entire family.

He's also writing his first cookbook and wants to be close to his publisher. Max is living in my building and he'll be going to Peppington Prep. When I heard about your party from the twins, I didn't think you'd mind if I came along and brought a guest. You know, to help him fit in and feel welcome."

So he *wasn't* Felix's boyfriend. If he was, he was sure Felix would have dropped that little tidbit. Over the last year, Anthony had run into Felix on more than one occasion outside of school and he was always with a hot-looking guy who he made a point of introducing to Anthony as his boyfriend. Anthony *always* felt like one of Cinderella's ugly stepsisters when that happened.

"Hey Felix!" Max said, joining his side and wrapping an arm around his shoulders. "What's up?"

"We have to leave, Max."

"Leave?" A puzzled look washed over Max's face. "But we just got here."

Anthony was relieved to notice that up close, Max was just as adorable as he had been from far away. Phew! Some guys suffered from FAB syndrome. They were Far Away Beauties who looked good from a distance but when they got closer . . . yikes!

Like his father, Max had chocolate brown eyes and a chiseled cleft in his chin. He took off his baseball cap and ran a hand through his dark brown hair. Despite wearing a baseball cap, it was perfectly styled and fell neatly into place. His face was totally smooth and . . . was that cologne he was wearing? Anthony took a tiny step closer to Max and sniffed discreetly. Yes, it was! And expensive stuff, too!

"Are we leaving for another party?" Max asked.

Anthony couldn't believe what he was hearing. "Leave?! You can't leave!" 🔊

"But I didn't get an invitation to the party," Felix pointed out.

Anthony's mind scrambled for an answer. "You weren't on the guest list because you're not a guest. You're one of my oldest friends. You didn't get an invitation in the mail because I was going to call and *personally* invite you."

Felix looked at Anthony skeptically. "Oh, you were?"

"Of course! How could I have a party without you, Felix?"

"You have in the past."

"Only because you're always off at some better party."

"That's true," Felix agreed. "The other parties are always better than yours."

Anthony ignored the dig and kept smiling. No way was he going to lose it in front of Felix.

"It's because he doesn't like me," Felix whispered into Max's ear. "Never has. Never will."

Anthony laughed. "You're such a kidder, Felix." Anthony turned to Max with a smile. "Felix and I have been friends since first grade. We're like brothers."

Felix gave Anthony a smirk. "Don't you mean *sisters*?"

Anthony ignored the comment and held his hand out to Max. "Hi, I'm Anthony DeMarco. I live here."

Max reached for Anthony's hand and gave him a huge smile that lit up his entire face. "Max Coulter. Nice to meet you."

Anthony's heart began racing madly. He did *not* want to let go of Max's hand. At that moment Anthony felt like he was going to melt into a puddle. Was this what they called love at first sight?

Whoa, whoa, whoa! Where had *that* thought come from? He had just met Max and he didn't know a thing about him. Time to hit the brakes.

Anthony let go of Max's hand and smiled back at him. "I hope you're having a good time."

"A blast."

"I'll bet there are lots of people you still haven't met. I'd be happy to introduce you."

Felix wrapped an arm around Max's waist and drew him closer. "That's nice of you, Tony, but I'm sure you're busy hosting. I'm taking care of Max tonight."

There was no mistaking Felix's message. *Back off!* Max was *his*. Fine. This round went to Felix. But Max was a big boy, and eventually he was going to want to play with others.

"Hey, Felix!" A blond girl wearing a coconut shell bra and grass skirt ran over, grabbing Felix by the hand. Anthony didn't recognize her; she must have come with someone he invited. "You have to come with me. Sherry's confessing all about her summer vacation in Maui. There's at least three columns' worth of stuff. Come on!"

It was clear to Anthony that Felix was torn. He could see he wanted to leave for some juicy dirt. But at the same time, he didn't want to leave Anthony and Max alone. Jealousy, perhaps? Was Max gay and Felix was hoping to make him his latest boyfriend? Gay or straight. That was the question. Anthony's gaydar, which was usually quite reliable, wasn't working. With just a look, he could usually tell if a guy was gay or straight. If someone asked him to explain what gaydar was, he wouldn't know how. When you're gay, you just know when someone else is. You could recognize it by their style. Or flair.

Or a unique sense of individuality. It might be the fact that their hair is dyed or the clothes that they wear are over the top or it's the amount of jewelry they have on. Or it could be the way they walk and talk. Gaydar was an instinct that was inside you and allowed you to identify with others who were just like you.

But Anthony couldn't figure out if Max was gay or straight. Despite the casual outfit Max was wearing, it was in perfect condition. It wasn't grungy and wrinkly the way it would be if a straight guy was wearing it. And he was groomed to perfection.

But that didn't mean anything. Ever since the arrival of the metrosexual—straight guys who care about their appearance—Anthony had been having problems with his gaydar. On more than one occasion he'd pegged a guy as gay and been proven wrong when the guy's girlfriend came along. He knew there were some gay guys who couldn't dress to save their lives, but the ones with money usually could, and since Steve Coulter was Max's father, he probably had a wallet full of credit cards and a closet full of designer clothes.

And he did come to the party with Felix. And Felix had been awfully touchy-feely with Max. Maybe tonight was their first date. For a second, Anthony had a flashback to his first official date with Ian. He felt a huge wave of sadness approaching, but immediately blocked it off, looking over his shoulder for Paige.

Anthony saw Paige staring at him and Max from across the deck with wide, excited eyes. She pointed to Max, who had his back to her, and opened her mouth. It wasn't hard to figure out the word she was saying.

"Yum!"

"Felix? Are you coming?" Coconut Girl asked, tugging on his arm.

Reluctantly, Felix allowed himself to be dragged off, leaving Anthony and Max alone.

After Felix left, there was an awkward moment of silence. Anthony didn't know what to say. He knew what he wanted to say, but couldn't. *Can I hug you? Can I kiss you? Will you please be my boyfriend?!*

"How are you liking New York City?" Anthony finally asked.

Max shrugged. "It's okay. It's strange not having a car, though. Back home in L.A., I used to drive around everywhere. Here, I just hop on a subway or bus. Or I walk."

"You must miss your friends."

Max nodded. "Yeah, I do. But I'll make new ones." Max gave Anthony a smile. "Can I ask you something personal?"

"Sure. Anything." *He's going to ask me if I'm gay. Or he's going to ask me if I have a boyfriend and if I don't would I want to go out on a date. Maybe catch a movie some night. Or maybe . . .*

"Does everyone call you Tony?"

Anthony's bubble popped. So much for his overactive imagination. "Felix is the only one who calls me that. And he knows I can't stand it. Everyone else calls me Anthony."

"Mind if I call you Ants? I have a friend out in California called Anthony and you remind me of him. I used to call him Ants."

You can call me anything you want, Anthony wanted to say. *Is California Anthony gay? Is that why I remind you of him?* "Ants is fine. Some of my cousins call me that. And my brother."

"What's it like having parents who are famous designers?"

"No different than having a father who's a famous chef, I guess. Does he cook at home the way he does on TV?"

"Just about. He's the only one in our family who can cook. My mom and I are hopeless in the kitchen."

"I guess that means you're not planning to follow in his footsteps?"

Max laughed. "Are you kidding? I can't even boil water. Felix's father had the idea of having me guest on the show with Dad. You can call it the lost episode of 'Delicious.' It never aired, it was such a disaster. I almost bled to death slicing a tomato."

"You're kidding!"

"I'm not. I nicked my wrist with a carving knife and it wouldn't stop bleeding. And then I burned the turkey in the oven. No, I'll be ordering take-out for the rest of my life. Unless I become a famous actor and then I can have a live-in chef."

"You want to be an actor?"

"Uh-huh."

"Peppington Prep has a great drama club." Anthony waited to see what Max would say. Most straight guys avoided the drama club at all costs. Unless they were looking to score with the girls who joined.

Last year Anthony had toyed with the idea of joining the drama club, but in the end decided not to. He didn't want to be an actor and he didn't have much interest in plays or musical theater; he preferred film—less room for mistakes. Not a good place to find a boyfriend if you didn't have the same interests.

"I'll have to check it out," Max said.

Ooookay, Anthony resolved, this situation would *definitely* involve further investigating. A straight guy *willingly* joining the drama club and not being blackmailed into it by a teacher? Then again, Max could be devoted to his craft. Hmmm. Maybe he'd have to rethink his own interest in the performing arts.

After all, if Max did "play for the same team," he was going to need a boyfriend who could support him. Root for him. Encourage him as he pursued his acting. Right?

And he could do *a lot* better than having love 'em and leave 'em Felix Fennimore for a boyfriend.

In fact, a nice Italian boy like himself would be perfect!

chapter three

"What a mess!" Paige exclaimed.

It was after midnight and Anthony's party was over. The penthouse deck was a disaster area. Everywhere she looked there were empty plates and glasses. Crumpled napkins were tossed on the floor and the buffet table, which had been heaped with tons of food hours earlier, had nothing but picked-over remains. White sand was scattered everywhere, smoke was wafting from the turned-off barbecue and all the tropical flowers Anthony had decorated with were drooping.

"A big mess," Anthony said. "And I'm the lucky one who gets to clean it all up."

"Don't worry, I'll help."

"I'll tackle it tomorrow." Anthony plopped down on a chaise lounge. "I'll get my big brother to help me," he said as

Paolo came out onto the deck and began searching the buffet table for something to eat. "Right, bro?"

"Don't look at me, Ants," Paolo said. "Your party, your mess." He poked around a few platters and came up empty-handed. "Did your friends eat *everything*? The refrigerator inside is empty. All that's left is a jar of mayonnaise."

"Don't you just love my brother, Paige? Always ready to help out his baby brother."

"Hey, I wasn't invited to your party, remember?"

"That's because you locked yourself away in your bed-room, Bookworm. If you had asked if you could come, I would have said yes. There were lots of hot girls here tonight. You could have scored."

"High school girls," Paolo pointed out.

"Oooh. Big Man on Campus only goes out with College Girls now."

"What's wrong with high school girls?" Paige asked, sliding onto the chaise lounge next to Anthony.

"I didn't say there was anything wrong with them."

"But you implied that there was."

"There's a difference between high school and college, that's all."

"Are you saying high school girls are *stupider* than college girls?"

"No, that's not what I'm saying. High school girls just take things way too seriously. Especially when it comes to guys. College girls are much more laid-back. They've got other stuff going on in their lives. Romance isn't their top priority."

"But it *is* a part of their lives," Paige said. "Everyone wants to fall in love!"

"All I'm saying is that there's no reason to get super serious about someone, especially at a young age."

"Unless the person you meet is your soulmate," Paige pointed out.

"The one," Anthony chimed in.

"No one has any control over when they're going to fall in love," Paige said. "It just happens. And when it does, you have to go with the flow. You could be sixteen or sixty."

"I can see I'm not going to win this argument, so I'm going to leave." Paolo grabbed a can of soda from a cooler and headed back inside. Soon the sound of the TV wafted out onto the deck.

Anthony grinned at Paige. "I think you scared Paolo."

"Good." Guys, especially older guys like Paolo, thought they knew everything when it came to girls. But what was wrong with a little emotion? What was wrong with sharing feelings? Most guys only had one thing on their minds, and it wasn't saying *I love you*. Although they would say it just to get what they wanted and think nothing of it. She'd seen it happen to too many girls at Peppington Prep and she had gone out with too many guys who'd pulled the "You would if you loved me" line. Did they think she was stupid? Please! The second they zipped up, they would lose her cell number and move on to the next conquest. She wasn't saying all guys were like that, but most were and, unfortunately, they still went to high school. Not going all the way had cost her more than one boyfriend but, in the end, she realized the guy hadn't been worth it. Otherwise he would have respected her decision. And in the end, it all came down to self-respect.

"Earth to Paige! Earth to Paige!" Anthony snapped his

fingers in front of her face. "Come back, Paige!"

"Sorry."

"You were a million miles away. Were you thinking about Max?"

"Max?"

"Max!!!!!" Anthony exclaimed. "The hottie that Felix brought along tonight."

"Max!" Paige squealed, clapping her hands excitedly. "My new reason for living!"

Anthony pulled his legs up under him and leaned forward eagerly. "Mine too. Did you get to talk with him? Find anything out?"

"We only spoke for a few minutes. He told me about his dad and moving to New York."

"That's it?" Anthony asked, a disappointed look on his face.

"I don't know if you noticed, but practically every girl at the party was surrounding him."

"I know," Anthony complained. "They were all like sharks circling prey. I hardly had a chance to talk with him after Felix let him out of his clutches. What did you think of him?"

Paige had liked Max. A lot. Often she was shy when she met someone new, but she hadn't felt shy at all with Max. The conversation had flowed and they had even exchanged phone numbers. But she was getting the sense that Anthony liked Max, too. And that might cause a problem . . .

"I hate to burst your bubble, sweetie, but I saw Max talking to a lot of girls tonight." She pointed to her chest. "And his eyes were focused straight ahead."

"That doesn't mean a thing. All the girls were spilling out of their tops tonight. How could he not notice? *I* even noticed!

Besides, he came to the party with Felix, and Felix took every opportunity he could get to drape himself all over Max. No straight guy would stand for that."

"Maybe he was being polite. Like you said, Felix brought him to the party. Maybe he didn't want to offend him."

"What other evidence do you have?"

"We exchanged phone numbers," Paige reluctantly admitted, knowing that the info was going to bum out Anthony.

"So did we!" he exclaimed. "What else have you got?"

Paige shook her head. "I don't have anything else." She laid back on her chaise lounge and gazed over at Anthony. "You really think he could be gay? The thought never even crossed my mind."

"Maybe. But maybe not. I'm not so sure myself."

"What happened to your gaydar?" Paige teased.

"It wasn't working tonight."

"I suppose it could be a possibility, but I hope not."

"Why?"

Paige shrugged. "No reason."

"You're holding back on me. I can tell. It's like that time freshman year when you had a crush on Dylan Hollis and wouldn't admit it until I found your notebook with little hearts drawn all over it with 'DH's scribbled everywhere. Spill!"

"I like him."

"I like him, too."

"I like him *a lot*. I don't want him to be gay. I want him to be straight."

"Well, I like him a lot, too. And I don't want him to be straight. I want him to be gay!"

Paige sat up, wrapping her arms around her knees. "Where does that leave us?"

"It leaves us with a question."

"What question?"

"Is he or isn't he? And how are we going to find out?"

"Did you notice how kissable his lips were?" Paige asked. "All plump and soft. It was all I could do not to throw myself at him and start kissing."

"His lips? What about the rest of him? Did you see how big his arms were? That boy spends serious time in the gym."

"I'd love to have those arms wrapped around me in a hug," Paige said. "Wouldn't you?"

"Okay, time out! All this drooling over Max isn't getting us anywhere. We still don't know if he's gay or straight. We're going to have to come up with a plan."

"What kind of plan?"

Anthony began pacing around the deck. "Obviously he likes both of us and wants to be friends, otherwise he never would have given us his phone number."

"True."

"That means we'll be spending time with him. Hanging out together. Getting to know him. Makes sense, right?"

"Right."

"Eventually, he'll have to say or do something that will give us an answer."

"And then what?"

"If he turns out to be gay, you do all you can to help me land him. And if he turns out to be straight, I do everything I can to keep the rest of Peppington Prep's divas away from him while you make your move. What do you think?"

"It sounds like a plan."

Paolo's voice called out from inside the penthouse. "Not that I was eavesdropping since the two of you are so loud, but there's a simpler way to find out if he is or isn't."

"There is?" Paige asked. She walked inside, followed by Anthony.

Paolo nodded while channel-surfing in the dark. The light from the big-screen TV gave his face a bluish glow. "Uh-huh."

"Well, don't keep us in suspense," Anthony urged. "Tell us! Our love lives are at stake!"

"Why don't you just ask him if he's gay or straight?"

"That's your answer? That's your solution?" Anthony threw his hands up in disgust. "That's the stupidest thing I've ever heard!"

"Why's it stupid? What do you have to lose?"

"Our self-respect!" Anthony proclaimed, making a face at his brother. "We've got to let Max make the first move. That way, if he's not interested in one of us, we haven't exposed too much of ourselves to him. He doesn't need to know that we're both drooling over him. Plus, if he *isn't* gay, it could make things uncomfortable between him and me."

"It could?" Paolo asked. "How?"

"The answer is so obvious! What is it about him that made me think he might be gay? You straight boys always have that problem when gaydar gets scrambled. It's like suddenly you start questioning your masculinity. It'll drive him batty and I'll always be a reminder of it. If that were to happen, why would he want to hang out with me? It would ruin the friendship."

"Then you should ask yourself what's more important . . .

having him as a friend or a boyfriend."

"You know, I don't remember asking for your opinion," Anthony snapped.

Paolo rolled his eyes and went back to channel-surfing. "You don't have to bite my head off. I'm just giving you my advice. You don't have to follow it."

"I don't think we will. Come on, Paige. Let's go back outside. We need to start strategizing."

"You two are worse than Lucy and Ethel," Paolo called out. "I smell disaster in the making. Mark my words. Whatever you two come up with is going to blow up right in your faces."

Paige followed Anthony onto the deck and sat on her chaise lounge. "Maybe Paolo is right. Maybe we should just ask him."

"Forget my brother's dum-dum advice. He scored really low on his SATs and he's gone to summer school more than once. I'm the brains of the family and we're going to figure out a way to land Max for one of us." Anthony began pacing. "We need to get as close as we can to him. What do we know about him?"

"He wants to be an actor."

"Do you think Camille could get him a part on *The Yields of Passion*?"

Paige laughed. "Now who's the dum-dum? When it comes to her soap, the only person Camille looks out for is herself. And the show tapes in California, remember?"

The only reason Paige was living in New York was because when she was thirteen, her mother had gotten a role in an Off-Broadway play. Unfortunately, the play closed sooner than expected, but by that point Paige had already gone through most of her school year. The ratings for *Yields* had plummeted since Camille's exit nine months earlier and the writers quickly went to work fixing things. As a result, Priscilla, who had gone missing in an avalanche, was now alive and well, but had amnesia. She was selling cherry pies in a small town hours away from Harmony Hills and mistakenly believed she was a nun! But Paige decided she wanted to stay in New York and live with her father, Brandon (he was hubby number three of Camille's five ex-husbands— so far), an investment banker. He was around more often than Camille and also had a live-in housekeeper, Justine. Camille hadn't offered much resistance when Paige told her she wanted to live with her father.

"We want Max to stay here in New York," Paige said. "Besides, we don't even know if he can act."

Anthony nodded. "Good point. He needs to start out small and work his way up to bigger things."

"Oooh! What about your screenplay?" Paige suggested. She knew Anthony was working on a screenplay and she'd read parts of it last spring. It was all about a sixteen-year-old Italian boy named Michael living in Brooklyn and working at his family's pizzeria who realizes he's gay.

"What about it?"

"Aren't you going to film it as part of your admissions package for UCLA?"

"So?"

Anthony wasn't getting where she was going. Sometimes he could be really slow.

"You're going to have to *cast* the roles. You're going to need *actors* and Max is an *actor* . . ."

Paige could see that Anthony had finally connected the dots.

Anthony ran over to Paige and gave her a hug. "Paige, you're a genius! I'll offer Max the lead!"

"And having him play Michael could help us figure things out."

"How do you mean?"

"Well, Michael, your main character, is gay. Maybe Max will have a problem playing a gay guy."

"Good point. If he turns down the part, then that will tell us something. But what if he doesn't? What if he decides to take the part? That still won't tell us anything. A lot of straight actors have played gay. Kevin Kline in *In & Out*, Tom Hanks in *Philadelphia*, Robin Williams in *The Birdcage* . . ."

"You're saying he'll be secure enough in his masculinity to take the part and will see playing a gay guy as a challenge."

"Yes. But the real test will come when it's time to do the kissing scene."

"Kissing scene?"

"Oh, that's right," Anthony said, as if suddenly remembering something he'd forgotten. "You haven't read the rest of the script, have you? I've added this great kissing scene between Michael and Dominick, the guy he falls in love with."

Anthony wiggled his eyebrows at Paige. "Guess who's going to be playing Dominick!"

chapter four

"*I* can't believe I don't have any classes with Max!"

Anthony slammed his locker door shut and waved his class schedule in Paige's face. "Seven periods a day and not one class!"

"You *do* have gym with him," Paige reminded.

"Gym doesn't count. You can't do any socializing in gym class."

"Girls can," Paige said smugly. "All we have to do is say we've got our period and we're suffering from cramps. Then we can sit in the bleachers and gossip."

Anthony stuck his tongue out at Paige. "Lucky you. Unfortunately, I don't have that option. The guys in my gym class are too busy grunting and throwing some sort of ball at each other, although in my case, I'm usually running away from it. And *nobody* looks good in gym class. You get all hot and sweaty and wrinkly. I look my worst in gym! At least you've got a real class with Max."

"A.P. History. My toughest class with the toughest teacher at Peppington. What was I thinking?" Paige groaned, leaning against Anthony's locker. "Practically all my classes are A.P. or College Introductory. I should have taken no-brainer classes like Bianca and Rachel are doing."

"We talked about this last spring," Anthony said. "All those advanced classes will look good on your college applications, remember?"

"I know. I know. I just don't think I'll be passing any notes to Max. I'll be too busy *taking* notes!"

"So you won't have time to flirt with him in class. There's got be some way you can get closer to him." Anthony's eyes lit up. "I know! You can arrange some after class study sessions with him. You can pretend to be dumb and ask him to explain stuff to you because Mr. Owling's lectures are so dry and boring."

"I'm *not* going to dumb myself down for some guy."

Anthony ignored Paige's comment. "And we can make sure you always look good!" He stuck a finger in his mouth and began nibbling on it as he started strategizing. "Maybe come up with a theme for each day of the week. Tropical Tuesdays. Fantasy Fridays. Yeah! We could even dress you up like a biker chick! Why don't I come over to your place later this week and we can go through your closets. Come up with some outfits that will catch Max's eye. Better yet! We can go to the Bryant Park Fashion Show next week. I'm sure I can score some passes from my parents. Maybe we can get you some clothes from the new collections. You'll be one step ahead of all the other girls!"

"That's awfully sweet of you, Anthony, but I don't need any new clothes," Paige said. "Besides, I want Max to like me for me. Not for what I look like."

Anthony placed a hand on Paige's shoulder and looked deep into her blue eyes. "Paige, honey, that's all very hearts and flowers, very Hallmark, but listen very carefully. If Max turns out to be straight, chances are he's got a copy of *Stuff* or *Maxim* under his bed and it ain't for the articles!"

Paige's mouth dropped open and she shoved Anthony's hand off her shoulder. "You're saying I should dress like a tramp?!"

"Of course not! But what's wrong with using what you've got?" Anthony checked out Paige's school uniform of a gray plaid pleated skirt, white blouse and gray vest. "You know, if you loosened a few buttons and raised up the hem of your skirt, you could have that naughty schoolgirl look."

Paige swatted Anthony on the chest as the bell for first period rang. "Hopeless. Absolutely hopeless. Are you sure you're gay, because you've got the mentality of a straight frat boy. Come on, we're going to be late for homeroom."

Anthony followed Paige down the crowded hallway.

"Obviously you've been figuring out my strategy for landing Max, but what about yours?" Paige asked over her shoulder.

"Other than my screenplay, I don't have a strategy, so I really hope he takes the bait."

"You haven't spoken to him since your party?"

"Nope."

Anthony couldn't explain why, but suddenly he'd become very shy around Max. Their paths had crossed more than once in the days leading up to the first day of school, giving Anthony more than one opportunity to talk to him. Last week there had been Senior Orientation and Anthony had sat two rows behind Max in the school auditorium. Another day they'd seen each other in the school library when they were both picking up their textbooks. They'd waved and smiled across the crowded library, but that was it. Max didn't come over to talk to Anthony and Anthony didn't go over to Max.

Part of him was waiting for Max to seek him out. He was waiting for a sign. Something that he could grab on to. To make him believe that Max liked him and wanted to be with him. He hadn't told this to Paige—he was too embarrassed— but he couldn't stop thinking of Max. He was the first thing he thought of when he woke up in the morning and the last thing he thought of when he went to sleep at night. And the rest of the day he was constantly daydreaming about things like their first date or their first kiss.

Why hadn't Max called him? Didn't he have a good time at his party? Didn't he like talking with him?

Anthony shook his head. Maybe he was deluding himself. Hoping for something that wasn't going to be.

But attraction was a two-way street, he reminded himself. How could someone know you were interested in them unless you let them know it? For all he knew, Max was waiting for him to make the first move. Maybe he'd never had a boyfriend before. Maybe he still hadn't come out.

"So why haven't you spoken to him?" Paige asked again.

Anthony shrugged. "I don't know. I'm having a hard time figuring him out. Maybe he's had his heart broken and he's afraid of falling in love again."'

"If that's true, then you're perfect for each other."

"Huh?"

"What you said about Max could also be said about you. Are you scared of putting yourself back out there? Is that why you're staying away from Max? You can't be afraid. Not every guy you meet is going to be like Ian."

Anthony's mouth dropped open.

"How did you know?"

Paige gave Anthony a smile. "I'm your best friend. Give me a little credit. And I know what you're going through, remember?"

"Jeremy Lacter," Anthony said.

"Jeremy Lacter. You know how he broke my heart sophomore year the day before the Spring Fling when he got together with his ex-girlfriend, Sheena Wolverton, and told me he was taking her to the dance instead of me. I locked myself in my bedroom for a week, cried nonstop, and wouldn't see or talk to anyone."

"How could I forget? When you finally emerged from your bedroom it looked like raccoons had nested in your hair! And let's not talk about your face!" Anthony shuddered. "I thought I was going to faint! We had to get you an emergency visit to my mother's salon. Thank God Jorge had an opening."

"Do you remember what you said to me when my hair was being shampooed? You told me that Jeremy was a jerk."

"I also told you that looking good is the best revenge," Anthony quipped. "You should have listened to me and gotten those blond highlights!"

Paige ignored Anthony's wisecrack. "You told me that I

had to forget what had happened and move on because if I didn't put myself back out there, if I didn't start dating other guys and trusting them, Jeremy would be winning. You have to do the same thing."

"I know, I know. You're right. But it's hard."

Paige squeezed Anthony's hand. "Trust me, it gets easier."

Anthony and Paige walked into their homeroom and took two seats at the back of the room. Hopefully they'd have a homeroom teacher cool enough to let them sit where they wanted instead of an anal-retentive one who would insist on having everyone sit in alphabetical order. The fact that their homeroom teacher hadn't show up yet was a good sign.

"Guess who's in almost all of Max's classes," Anthony said.

Paige looked up from the notebook she was writing in. "Who?"

"Felix."

Paige bit down on the end of her pen. "It makes sense. Felix probably helped him pick his classes."

"And made sure he wasn't in any of mine."

"Felix would do that?"

"All's fair in love and war."

Anthony wondered what Felix had told Max about him. Felix's style wasn't to publicly trash someone. Oh, no, he was too smart for that. Felix liked to cover his tracks. That way he always looked innocent and nothing could be traced back to him.

Could Felix have told Max that he was gay? Was that why Max was keeping his distance? But that theory didn't make sense. Max was hanging out with Felix and Felix was gay.

Plus, if *Max* were gay, Felix probably wouldn't want him to know that Anthony was gay. Why help out the competition?

And if Felix knew that Anthony had the slightest interest in Max, well, he'd do everything he could to sabotage things.

Anthony knew he'd have to be careful around Felix.

Very careful.

Just then their homeroom teacher entered the room. It was Pamela de la Vega, who taught Spanish to sophomores and juniors. The late-twentysomething teacher was laid-back, but she didn't take any bullshit from anybody. The year before she'd given the Torres twins Fs on their year-end term papers. The theme of the assignment had been to do a biography on a noted Hispanic figure in popular culture. Ms. de la Vega had been thinking along the lines of Frida Kahlo, Carmen Miranda or even Ricky Martin. Instead, Bianca's paper had been on Speedy Gonzalez from the Warner Brothers cartoons while Rachel had chosen to write about Bumble Bee Man from *The Simpsons*.

Paige leaned over her desk to whisper in Anthony's ear as Ms. de la Vega started taking attendance. "Can I give you some advice?"

"Sure."

"Today's your first gym class with Max. Find a way to talk with him."

"I don't know if I'll be able to," Anthony whispered back.

Paige pointed her pen at Anthony. "Do we have a question that needs answering or don't we?"

Anthony chuckled, and Ms. de la Vega looked in their direction. "You're right, we do!" he whispered.

chapter five

"Only seventy-five more school days until Christmas vacation," Bianca said, tossing her Gucci shoulder bag onto the floor while taking a seat next to Paige in the school auditorium for afternoon assembly.

"Are you counting down the days already?" Paige asked in disbelief.

"Aren't you?"

"It's only our first day back!"

"I wish it was still summer vacation."

"Look, I chipped a nail," Rachel said, taking a seat on the opposite side of Paige.

She pulled out her cell phone and dialed a number. "Hello, Ling? I need to make an appointment this afternoon. It's an emergency. You have to fix a nail." Rachel examined the rest of her nails. "Actually, why don't we do all of them.

My pinkies are looking a bit ragged and I could use a new color. Something autumny."

"Can't you just do that yourself?" Colleen asked, joining the group and taking the aisle seat next to Bianca.

"It never looks as good as when it's done professionally," Rachel said.

Colleen rolled her eyes. "Whatever."

Paige stifled a giggle. Rachel and Bianca were such girly-girls, always worrying about the way they looked, while Colleen went with the flow. If she needed to dress up, she did, but she was usually dressed casually. Bianca and Rachel, on the other hand, always looked ready for a fashion spread in *Elle* magazine.

It was strange how the four of them had become friends. Separately, they had nothing in common, yet as a group, they seemed to click.

Paige had become friends with Colleen first. It was Paige's first day at Peppington Prep and no one had gone out of their way to make a place for her at their table as she'd walked into the cafeteria with her lunch tray. Except Colleen.

Every day after that, they had lunch together. They didn't get to hang out much after school, though, because Colleen's mother had her signed up for every kind of lesson imaginable. But when they were able to get together—for a movie or a trip to a museum or just a day of shopping—they always had a fun time.

What Paige loved about Colleen was her confidence. Yes, she was larger than the other girls in their class, but that didn't matter to Colleen. Nor did the catty comments about her weight; about how she could be such a pretty girl if she only lost a few pounds; of how she could get a boyfriend if she were thinner. Colleen ignored it all—she liked what she saw when she looked in her mirror. If no one else did, tough.

And Paige knew there was more to the twins than met the eye. Yes, they were pampered princesses, but that was because they were treated that way by their father. When Paige was at their house, she'd heard their dad say things like: "You don't need to worry about working. All you have to do is look pretty and one day get married. Your husband will take care of you and manage all your money someday."

No wonder the twins paid more attention to their clothes, and boys, than to school!

Paige felt that that was also why they were so obsessed with trying to become celebrities. She felt like they were trying to prove themselves to their father and that made her sad.

Because she knew what it felt like to have a parent who ignored you. It was one of the reasons why she had bonded with the twins. But they were also very funny, and sometimes you just needed to have a friend who was silly and made you laugh.

"Think Ling can squeeze me in?" Paige asked Rachel. "We'll have a girls' afternoon."

"Not a prob!" Rachel said reaching for her cell phone.

"So, have you checked out some of the hot new guys?" Colleen asked.

"High school boys!" Bianca sniffed disdainfully. "So immature! We need to start expanding our horizons! And I know *exactly* how we can do that." Bianca looked around to make sure she wouldn't be overheard. "There's a keg party at one of the fraternities this weekend up at Columbia."

"No! No more keg parties!" Paige said firmly. "Remember what happened the last time we went to one? You drank too much beer and I wound up holding your hair back from a toilet."

"I only had one beer!" Bianca exclaimed. "It was food poisoning! I had some bad mayo that day. Come on, don't be such a spoilsport. Think of it as a sneak peek of what we can expect next year!"

Colleen shrugged. "I could be up for a little college excitement. How about it, Paige? I'll go if you go."

Now it was Paige's turn to look around to make sure she wasn't overheard. "If I tell the three of you a secret, do you promise to keep it to yourselves?"

"Swear," Rachel said, crossing her heart.

"I'm interested in one of the new guys."

"Which one?" Bianca asked.

"Max Coulter."

"Isn't he the one who's buying new uniforms for the cheerleading squad?" Rachel said.

"Where did you hear that?!" Paige exclaimed.

"One of the girls in my Web design class told me. Max had a free period this morning and was watching the squad practice. He noticed how crappy the uniforms are and said that his father would be happy to make a donation to the school."

"Sounds like Max knows how to score with the ladies," Bianca said. "I bet he walked away with at least ten phone numbers."

"It does, doesn't it?" Paige murmured.

Rachel nodded. "Girls were throwing themselves all over him. Hugging and kissing him. *Including* Sheena Wolverton."

"Oooh, we hate the She-Wolf," Bianca hissed, using the nickname Sheena had been given for her ability to devour and discard boyfriends that belonged to other girls.

"If you're interested in Max, you better make your move," Colleen advised as the auditorium lights dimmed and a slide show presentation began. "Sounds like you might have some competition."

Paige was at her locker after assembly getting her books for her afternoon classes when she heard a voice calling her name.

"Paige. Hey, Paige!"

Paige turned around and looked around the crowded hallway. Her whole face lit up when she saw who was calling.

Max!

She waved. "Hi! I didn't recognize your voice."

Max leaned against the locker next to Paige's. "Guess we'll have to do something about that."

Like what? Paige was tempted to ask.

"Sorry I've been out of touch. Busy with back to school stuff, ya know?"

Paige tossed a thick textbook into her backpack. "I know. Me too."

"I wanted to ask you a question."

"Sure."

"How easy is it to cut a class?"

"What?!"

"You know. Skip out. Are the teachers really firm about taking attendance?"

"Uh, yeah. For what our parents pay to send us here, they better be."

"Ugh! I thought so."

Paige slammed her locker shut and began walking down the hall to her next class. "Why do you want to cut class?"

"I don't feel like hanging around here," Max said, walking with her. "It's a beautiful day outside. I feel like going to Central Park and tossing around a Frisbee. Can't toss a Frisbee by myself. What do you say? Let's be bad together."

Oooh! That sounded *so* sexy. Who would have thought that Max was not only possible boyfriend material, but also *bad boy* material. But she couldn't! It was the first day of school. This was when their teachers were most diligent about taking attendance and college transcripts were still being put together.

"Maybe in the spring."

"Come on," Max pleaded. "Pleeeeease . . . I promise to show you a good time."

How good a time? Paige was tempted to ask. Her heart fluttered as she imagined herself alone with Max and she felt herself wavering.

Then she remembered all the phone numbers he'd collected from the cheerleading squad.

But he was asking *her* to go with him to the park.

He hadn't asked the She-Wolf, had he?

"You're tempting me, Max. You really are. But I can't. I've got a ton of A.P. classes and I can't mess up."

"Yeah, I'm taking A.P. History. It should be a piece of cake."

"Piece of cake? History's my hardest subject. I always have a tough time remembering all those names and dates."

"Really? When it comes to names and dates, I kind of just absorb that stuff like a sponge. Plus I love watching the History Channel. Just think, hundreds of years from now, students will be reading about our lives and thinking *we* lived in the Stone Age!"

He's good-looking and smart, Paige thought to herself. Could it get any better than this?

"Maybe we'll have to have a private tutoring session," Max suggested. "How does that sound?"

Paige felt tingles going up and down her spine. "Sounds like you know your stuff."

"You'd be surprised at what I could teach you."

He said the words with such *sexiness*! The tingles traveled all over Paige's body and she found herself speechless.

The bell for the next class rang and Max sighed. "Well, since I guess there's no escape, I might as well head to my next class."

"Which is?"

"Gym." Max gave Paige a wink. "Talk to you later."

"Bye," Paige whispered, as she watched Max disappear down the crowded hallway, wishing she could switch places with Anthony. If she wasn't such a goody two shoes, she'd be the one spending the next forty-five minutes with Max. Instead, it was going to be Anthony.

Don't say I've never done anything for you, Mr. DeMarco!

chapter six

Anthony couldn't wait until gym class was over.

He was being tortured.

Tortured!

Anthony struggled to finish his push-ups as Coach Harris kept counting. "Forty-eight. Forty-nine. Fifty!" Coach Harris blew on his whistle. "Okay, that's it for today. Everybody head for the showers."

Anthony collapsed on the floor, struggling to catch his breath as he mopped his sweaty face with the bottom of his T-shirt.

Anthony *hated* gym class.

It was the one class where he always felt inferior. He'd never had any interest in sports so he didn't know the rules of any of the games. And gym class was nothing but games. Baseball, football, basketball, volleyball. All he knew was that the balls came in different shapes and colors.

Yet because he was a guy, he was supposed to *love* sports. He was supposed to want to spend hours in front of the TV watching groups of guys running after a ball.

Ugh!

He had better things to do with his time.

Okay, some of the players did look good in their form-fitting uniforms, but that wasn't enough of a reason for him to watch.

Gym class was a breeze in September because they often went out to Central Park and jogged. In October and November, they played football and basketball. Those games were never a problem. He could just run away from the ball—making it look like he was running *after* the ball, of course—and let his teammates who were into the game handle it.

December was the month he hated most. That was when they played volleyball. Anthony shuddered. Volleyball was the one game where you couldn't run away from the ball. If the ball was headed your way, you better hit it. Or else.

Anthony knew about *or else*.

On more than one occasion, he had missed hitting the ball when it came in his direction. Or he'd cringed at an approaching ball, afraid of getting hit, using his hands to shield his face. He'd had more than one irate teammate scream at him, "Are you *blind*?! Hit the frigging ball!"

"Hey, Ants!"

He looked up at the sound of Max's voice. Anthony had gotten to class late and found a spot at the back of the gym. Max must have been hidden out of sight in one of the front rows.

Anthony did a double take when he got a look at Max.

Okay, it was time to rethink gym class.

Max looked fine.

Mighty fine.

Unlike Anthony, Max's gym uniform fit him perfectly. His shorts weren't baggy and his T-shirt, instead of being loose and flowing, was tight and form-fitting.

Like Anthony, he was drenched in sweat, but his sweat wasn't in big messy patches. He looked cool and comfortable, like someone who had just stepped out of a TV commercial, and his hair was all in place, yet slick with moisture.

Did this guy ever *not* look good?!

Anthony shuddered to think what he looked like. Not his best. And definitely not cover model material. He wasn't a ninety-eight-pound weakling, but he wasn't buff and muscular the way Paolo was; his older brother had gotten all those family genes.

Max punched Anthony playfully on the shoulder. "This guy's pretty tough. I haven't had a workout like that in ages."

"Coach Harris knows how to crack the whip."

"He's better than my personal trainer."

"You have a personal trainer?"

"Only three times a week." Max looked around, then leaned in close to Anthony. "I'll let you in on a little secret. When I was younger, I was kind of chubby. No, that's not true. I was fat. Kids at my old grammar school used to call me Maximum because I was so big. I had the worst sweet tooth. Still do."

"You're not fat any more. You're all muscle."

Max lifted his T-shirt and slapped a hand across his abs.

"That's 'cause I work at staying in shape."

Oh my god, he has a six-pack!

"A couple of years ago, it was all flab," Max said. "Exercise made the difference, but I outgrew some of it, too. How about you? You look like you're pretty fit."

He thinks I look fit?!

Calm down, Anthony. He's only making an observation. It's not like he's declared his love!

Much to Anthony's disappointment, Max pulled down his T-shirt, hiding his mesmerizing abs. But their disappearance helped. Anthony no longer felt like a powerless mouse being hypnotized by a hungry snake. He was able to focus again.

"I'm not an exercise junkie, but I try to watch what I eat," Anthony said. "Sometimes I go to the gym to lift weights."

Like on Tuesdays and Thursdays when I know that cute personal trainer with the barbed wire tattoo on his right bicep is working. Girls aren't the only ones who can play dumb when it comes to figuring out how to use exercise equipment.

Max squeezed Anthony's arm. "It shows."

Tingles shot up Anthony's arm and he could feel his cheeks turning red.

"You okay?" Max asked.

"Just need to get some water," Anthony croaked, walking in the direction of the locker room. "Still recovering from the Harris workout."

"Sorry I've been out of touch," Max said. "Felix's been taking me everywhere. I hardly have five minutes to myself."

"Felix is great," Anthony lied, leaning over a water fountain.

He's a great big scheming conniver who wants you all to himself!

"Anyway, I was wondering if you wanted to hang out together one afternoon. You know, so we can get to know each other better. I'd like to start making some friends of my own. That way Felix doesn't have to feel like he's baby-sitting me."

This is your chance, Anthony. Do it, do it, do it! Invite him over this afternoon!

Anthony took a sip of water and wiped his mouth. "We must be psychic twins or something, because I was going to ask if you wanted to come over to my place this afternoon."

"You were?"

"I wanted to run an idea by you."

"Shoot."

"At my party you told me you wanted to be an actor. Well, I'm trying to become a screenwriter and I've just finished a screenplay. I'm going to be including it with my admissions packet to UCLA and I'm going to shoot it this fall—just on a video camera. I'm casting some of the parts and I think you'd be great as Michael, my lead character."

"What's it called?"

Anthony paused and then said, *"Not All Italian Boys Are Straight."* He waited to see if the title had any effect, but Max just looked like he was listening. "It's a gay coming of age comedy set in Brooklyn."

Anthony held his breath. This was it. The moment of truth. Either Max was going to say yes or he was going to run screaming for the hills.

"Sounds interesting. I'd love to read it."

"Really? You would?"

"Absolutely. What time do you want me to come over?"

"How does four sound?"

"It's a date."

Date? It's a date? Okay, Anthony, calm down. It's just a figure of speech. He didn't mean date in a romantic way. He meant it as in a time and a place kind of thing.

But what if he didn't?

Concentrate, Anthony. Concentrate. Stay focused!

"Okay, I'll see you later."

After changing back into his clothes, Anthony whipped out his cell phone and called Paige.

"It's about time you called!" she exclaimed.

"Gym's now my favorite class. You would not *beee-lieve* the bod he has. Jealous, much?"

"If you were standing in front of me, I'd scratch your eyes out. So you talked to him?"

"I did more than just talk to him. I invited him over this afternoon. And he's coming!"

"Whoa! You didn't waste any time."

"You sound bummed."

Paige sighed. "I had an opportunity for a little alone time this afternoon with Max, but I blew it."

"Enlighten me."

"He wanted to cut class and spend the afternoon together in Central Park."

"And you said *no*?!" Anthony was horrified. "What are you, crazy?!"

"I know, I know. Don't remind me. Anyway, what are you planning?"

"He's coming over to read my screenplay."

"Did you tell him the plot?"

"Uh-huh."

"You told him *everything* about the story?"

"Everything except the kissing scene."

"The kiss is nothing."

"I wouldn't be too sure."

"Tell him he doesn't have script approval," Paige teased. "What are you going to wear?"

"Yikes! I forgot all about that." Anthony glanced at his watch. "And I don't have time to do any shopping. I'm going to have to find something in my closet. Gotta go!"

"I want a full report," Paige called out before Anthony disconnected her.

Anthony had a huge walk-in closet.

There was rack after rack of leather jackets, suits, sport jackets, dress pants, jeans, khakis and sweatpants.

There were shelves of sweaters, T-shirts, cotton shirts, silk shirts, tank tops and vests in a variety of colors.

There was pair after pair of shoes, sneakers, boots and sandals.

With so much to choose from, you would think he could find one perfect outfit.

Yet there was nothing to wear! Nothing!

Anthony didn't want Max thinking he'd dressed up for him Then again, he wanted to look good, of course.

Anthony pulled out a pair of black leather jeans and a Dolce & Gabbana shirt with a wild polka dot pattern.

Too gay.

He threw the outfit to one side.

A pair of olive khakis and a plum-colored Ralph Lauren polo shirt came out next.

Too preppy.

They fell on top of the leather pants and the D&G shirt.

Everything he pulled out had a problem.

Too loud.

Too quiet.

Too tight.

Too baggy.

Too dated.

A pile of clothes was building on the floor. After pulling out each outfit, Anthony would hold it in front of himself before his full-length mirror. Then he'd discard it. As impossible as it was to believe, he was starting to run out of clothes. What was he going to do?!

"What's going on in here? I could hear you rustling through your hangers all the way in the living room."

Paolo stood in the doorway of Anthony's closet, gazing at the scattered outfits.

"What are you doing here?" Anthony asked. "I thought you lived at the dorms during the week."

"There's an Italian soccer match on this afternoon and our dorm TV doesn't get the channel."

"You and your sports! Is that all you live for?"

"That and making your life miserable."

"Max is coming over at four. He's going to read my screenplay. I'm trying to decide what to wear."

"Hmmm. I'd go casual."

"You think?"

Paolo shrugged. "That's what I always do. At least on the first date."

"It's not a date."

"Are you sure?"

"No."

Paolo sighed. "Look, Ants, you didn't want to take my advice the other day, but I'm serious."

"Fine. What?" Anthony said impatiently.

"Take things slow with Max."

"Why, because you think he's straight and I'm setting myself up for humiliation?"

"No, it's just . . . even if he is gay, or whatever, you might want to get to know him as a person first. That's all."

"Are you speaking from experience?"

"It wouldn't hurt for you to learn from someone who's actually been in more than one relationship."

"Don't worry, Max isn't going to go all *Fatal Attraction* on me the way some of your girlfriends have."

"Hey! That was just Linda. And she had issues."

"Whatever. Now get lost. And stay lost when Max gets here!"

Paolo balled up one of Anthony's T-shirts and was getting ready to throw it at him, when he took a closer look at it. "Hey! This is mine!" Paolo took another look at the clothes scattered around the floor of Anthony's closet and his eyes widened. "And so's that striped shirt. I've been looking for it for months! I thought the dry cleaners had lost it. And those jeans!" Paolo's face turned red. "What have I told you about wearing my clothes?" he screamed.

"Calm down, Pow," Anthony said, using his childhood

nickname for Paolo. When he was a baby, he'd never been able to say Paolo. Instead, all he'd been able to say was Pow. "I only borrowed your stuff. I was going to put it back."

"When? You borrowed it around a year ago!"

Paolo angrily began snatching clothes up off the floor. "I'm warning you for the last time, Ants, stay out of my closet! If it wasn't for your sticky fingers, I wouldn't have had to buy all those new clothes last month."

After Paolo left, Anthony mulled over his brother's words. The ones of advice, not the ones banning him from his closet. He knew that Paolo was only looking out for him, but his words bugged him. His brother—and all straight guys—had it so easy. If they saw a girl that they liked and wanted to go out with, they could just walk up to her, start a conversation, see how it went and then ask her out. He couldn't do that. Everything was so much more complicated for him. If he met a guy that he liked and started steering the conversation in a more romantic direction, he'd better be sure the guy was gay. Otherwise he was going to get insulted, get punched in the nose, or worse.

Anthony gave up on his closet. What was he going to do? He didn't have anything to wear.

Unless . . .

He knew he was taking his life into his own hands but Paolo *had* mentioned buying some new clothes last month. Knowing his brother, who always wore the same three T-shirts and jeans, the clothes were probably still in the shopping bags they'd come in.

And they were probably very ordinary.

But ordinary might just be what he needed.

Anthony left his closet and stuck his head out into the hallway. He could hear the sound of the TV in the living room.

Good. That meant Paolo was occupied.

The coast was clear!

He tiptoed down the hallway to Paolo's bedroom. When he opened the closed door and stepped inside, he wrinkled his nose. Pew! What was that sour smell?

Wrinkled clothes were thrown all over the floor, the bed was unmade and there were empty pizza boxes on the dresser.

His brother lived like a pig! He could only imagine what his dorm room looked like.

Anthony headed straight for Paolo's walk-in closet. When he opened the door, he saw two shopping bags lined against a wall. He took a peek inside of one and inhaled the scent of fresh, new clothes. Yes!

As Anthony rummaged through the bags, he knew he shouldn't be doing it but he wouldn't even be raiding his brother's closet if Paolo hadn't mentioned the new clothes he'd bought. It wasn't *his* fault. Paolo was the one to blame for tempting him!

After finding what he wanted, Anthony left the closet. He had just closed the door and turned around when he saw Paolo standing in the bedroom doorway. Paolo's mouth dropped open in shock at the sight of Anthony.

And then his eyes fell on the pile of clothes in Anthony's hands.

"What do you think you're doing?" Paolo asked in a deadly whisper.

Uh-oh. Caught!

And it wasn't good that Paolo was whispering. No way.

When Paolo whispered, that meant he was *really* angry.

Anthony shrugged innocently. "Just borrowing something to wear."

"What did I just say no more than five minutes ago? Stay out of my stuff! I don't want you borrowing my clothes." Paolo held out a hand. "Hand them over."

"Come on, Pow," Anthony pleaded. "Just let me borrow this one outfit and I'll never go through your things again. I promise."

"No! I haven't even worn it yet. Besides, you'll stink it up with your cologne."

"That's better than your unwashed jock smell."

Anthony clasped a hand over his mouth. Ooops!

"Oh, you are so going to regret that, Ants." Paolo began advancing toward Anthony, a determined look on his face. Anthony remained frozen in place, but then, just as his brother neared, he zigzagged around him and raced back to his bedroom, locking the door behind him.

Yes, success!

Paolo began pounding on the locked door.

"I'm going to count to five and if you haven't opened this door by then, I'm going to break it down. One . . ."

"Calm down, Pow. Take a chill pill. I promise I won't wear any cologne and after Max leaves, I'll wash and iron your outfit, okay?"

"No! Not okay! You're a spoiled brat who thinks he can do whatever he wants and I'm sick of it!"

"Go away, Pow. I have to get dressed."

"You're going to have to come out eventually, and when you do . . ."

"Aren't you missing your soccer game?" Anthony called out.

"Shoot!" Paolo pounded on the door one last time. "I'll deal with you later."

Anthony listened as Paolo stomped back to the living room. As long as the soccer game was on, he was safe. He'd worry about Paolo's revenge later.

In the end, Anthony was pleased with the way he looked. He was dressed casually in a pair of Diesel jeans and a white T-shirt trimmed with navy blue at the neck and sleeves. So the jeans were designer, the T-shirt wasn't, and the sneakers he wore were Keds (his own, not Paolo's). It all balanced out.

The doorbell rang right at four o'clock and Anthony's heart began thumping madly as he went to let Max in.

Get a grip! This isn't a date. We're just going to be hanging out.

As he walked past the living room, he could hear the sound of the soccer game blaring and Paolo yelling excitedly at the TV. That was a relief. One less thing to worry about.

"Right on time," Anthony said, opening the front door. Max was wearing a pair of white jeans, flip-flops and a bright blue short-sleeved shirt. "Cool outfit. You look like you should be headed to the beach."

Max shrugged, tossing the backpack he was carrying over one shoulder onto the chair next to the front door. "You can take the boy out of California, but you can't take California out of the boy."

"Want a snack?" Anthony asked.

"What have you got?"

Anthony led the way into the kitchen and began poking

around the stainless steel freezer. He brought out a container of vanilla ice cream. "How about hot fudge sundaes?"

Max grinned and slapped his stomach. "Sounds good, but I don't have these abs because of hot fudge sundaes. Got anything else? Like yogurt or fruit?"

"Sure." Anthony put away the ice cream and stuck his head in the refrigerator, quickly scanning the shelves.

Why did I offer him a hot fudge sundae? Now he's going to think I'm a junk food junkie!

"There's some sliced honeydew and strawberries."

"That sounds good."

After fixing them both a bowl of fruit, Anthony and Max headed to his bedroom. Max flopped himself down on Anthony's bed while Anthony took a seat at his desk.

I don't think I'm ever going to wash that bedspread again!

"Who's in the living room watching TV?" Max asked.

Anthony rolled his eyes. "My brother Paolo. He's watching some soccer match."

Max's eyes lit up. "The one from Italy?"

"Yeah . . ." Anthony slowly said. "I think that's the one."

Max abandoned his bowl of fruit and jumped off the bed. "Would he mind if we watched with him? I'm a huge soccer fan."

"You are?"

An hour later Anthony was sitting on the couch in the living room, bored out of his mind while Paolo and Max were glued to the TV, screaming every time a goal was made or missed. And then during the commercials, they bonded over football, baseball, basketball, hockey and every other sport known to man.

Who would have thought that Max would be such a jock?

Finally, the game ended, much to Anthony's relief.

"Thanks for letting me watch with you," Max said when Paolo turned off the TV.

"Any time you want to watch a game, just give a call," Paolo said. "Any friend of Ants's is a friend of mine."

"Don't you have a college paper to research or write?" Anthony asked while glaring at Paolo.

Paolo settled deeper into the couch, putting his feet up on the coffee table. "Nope."

"Hey, Paolo, are you a Knicks fan?" Max asked.

More sports talk? Anthony mentally wailed. *Nooooo!!!!!*

"Of course!"

"I have courtside seats for the season. You wanna go one night?"

"You bet I would!"

Anthony couldn't believe what he was hearing. Max was asking *his brother* out? What about him?!

"You too, Ants," Max said, turning to Anthony.

Sure, treat me like an afterthought!

"I'd love to go," Anthony said, hoping he sounded excited.

"Anthony? Go to a basketball game?" Paolo howled with laughter, clutching his sides. "That I've got to see!"

"I think I hear the phone in your bedroom ringing," Anthony growled between gritted teeth.

Paolo tilted his head in the direction of his bedroom and listened. "I don't hear a thing."

"I do."

"Are you sure?"

Anthony jumped off the couch and shoved Paolo's feet off the coffee table. "Yes, I'm sure. You better go answer it. *Now.*"

"Temper, temper, Ants," Paolo whispered into Anthony's ear as he got off the couch. "See you later, Max," he said as he left the living room.

"Your brother is really cool," Max said.

"I guess, but he's a total pain," Anthony complained.

"So where's the screenplay?" Max asked.

"In my room. Let me go get it." Anthony returned and handed Max a freshly printed out screenplay. "You can take it home with you. Or you can read it here."

Max began flipping through the pages. "Wow, I can't believe you wrote this."

"They're just words."

"No they're not." Max held up the screenplay. "You've created a whole world here. Characters who live and breathe and think. Not everyone can do that."

"Thanks."

Max started reading a few pages.

"Are you sure you want to do this?"Anthony asked.

"Why wouldn't I?"

"Some actors won't take . . . gay roles," Anthony explained. "You know, because they're afraid people are going to think they're gay in real life. Or that it might hurt their career. And then there are actors who really are gay, but they don't want the rest of the world knowing and so they pretend to be straight."

"A good part is a good part," Max said. "Actors who turn down roles because they're afraid of what other people are going to think or say are stupid."

"Do you want to run some scenes together?" Anthony suggested.

Max glanced at his watch. "Oh, wow! I don't know. I'm actually supposed to meet my mom at six." Max held up the screenplay. "But I'm going to take this home with me. Start learning my lines. You can definitely count me in."

Anthony walked Max from the living room. At the front door, he grabbed his backpack off the chair where he'd left it and unzipped it to put in the screenplay. As he did, a jumble of papers fell out.

"I'm not the most organized guy in the world," Max said, as he started gathering the fallen papers and tossing them into his backpack.

"Let me help," Anthony offered.

"That's okay. I've got it."

"Guess I'll see you at school tomorrow," Anthony said, holding the front door open.

"Yeah, let's have lunch together," Max said, tossing his backpack over one shoulder. "I really had a great time today. Bye!"

"Bye," Anthony said.

After Max left, Anthony stormed into Paolo's bedroom where he found his brother on his bed, spinning a basketball on his finger.

"You ruined everything!"

"Oh, I did, did I?" Paolo asked, keeping his eyes on the basketball.

"Yes, you did! This afternoon was supposed to be about me and Max getting to know each other better. Instead, what happens? You steal him from me!"

"What?!" Paolo stopped spinning the basketball and started laughing hysterically. "I didn't *steal* him from you.

Can I help it if Max and I have a lot in common? Stop being such a baby."

Anthony stomped his foot. "I'm not being a baby!"

"Yes, you are." Paolo began singing, "Baby, baby, stick your head in gravy. Wash it out with bubblegum and send it to the navy! Baby, baby!"

"You're impossible!" Anthony shouted, leaving the room and then storming back in. "You're not going to that basketball game with him!"

"I'm not?"

"No, you're not! If anyone is going out with Max, it's going to be me!"

"Can I help it if your boyfriend likes me better than you?"

Anthony picked up a pillow at the foot of Paolo's bed and started pounding him on the head with it before Paolo grabbed the other pillow on the bed and started pounding back. Within seconds the brothers were wrestling on the bed and Paolo had pinned Anthony down.

"Listen to me *very* closely, Ants, because I'm going to say this once and only once," Paolo warned. "You listening?"

"Ahg! I'm listening!" Anthony said, struggling to break free.

"You've got five minutes to march yourself down to your room and change out of my clothes. *Five* minutes." Paolo released his grip on Anthony and got off the bed. "Or else."

"Or else what?"

Paolo reached into the drawer of his nightstand and withdrew the electric hair clipper he used when he gave himself buzz cuts. "Or else I'm going to shave your head the next time you go to sleep!"

"You wouldn't!" Anthony gasped.

Paolo gave Anthony an evil smile. "Down to the scalp and you know it."

Anthony jumped off the bed and ran all the way back to his bedroom.

"He didn't want to rehearse," Anthony told Paige five minutes later. He was lying on his bed in a yellow polo top and blue jeans, talking on his cell phone after dumping Paolo's clothes back in his bedroom. He kept running a hand through his hair, as if wanting to make sure it was all still there. Paolo didn't make idle threats. Tonight he'd be sleeping with his bedroom door locked. Maybe he'd even push a dresser in front of the door.

The scent of Max's cologne was still on his bedspread. Anthony buried his face in it and inhaled. "What do you think that means?"

"Maybe he's one of those Method actors. You know, he has to immerse himself into the character first."

"I suppose," Anthony grudgingly admitted.

"Why do you sound so down?"

"Because as much as I hate to admit it, I think my big brother may be right. Max might be straight. You should have seen him watching that soccer game."

"Lots of gay guys like sports."

"The one you're talking to doesn't."

"Ever hear of opposites attracting?"

"I guess."

"Don't forget that he agreed to play Michael! You're overreacting."

"Maybe . . . but maybe not."

"You know what?" Paige said. "You need a sugar fix. Right now I'm getting a mani and pedi with Rachel, but I shouldn't be here much longer. Why don't we meet at our usual spot?"

"Okay."

After getting off the phone with Paige, Anthony left his bedroom. As he was walking to the front door, he noticed a slip of paper under the chair where Max had left his backpack. He must have overlooked it when he was putting everything back into his bag. Yay! A reason to call Max!

But when Anthony picked up the slip of paper and saw what was written on it, he stared at it with disbelieving eyes.

No! It couldn't be. It just couldn't be!

But it was.

Undeniable proof that Max was straight.

chapter seven

"How bad should we be?" Paige asked Anthony.

They were at the Frosted Cupcake, their favorite hangout in Greenwich Village. The Frosted Cupcake was a coffee bar/bakery well known for its homemade cupcakes and desserts. The interior of the shop was warm and cozy, the walls painted a creamy caramel and decorated like a family room with plush couches and oversized armchairs. There was a fireplace in one corner that was often roaring in the fall and winter, framed movie posters on the walls and end tables covered with newspapers and magazines for customers who wanted to read them.

Paige loved the Frosted Cupcake because of their yummy banana bread while Anthony loved their red velvet cupcakes. But Paige knew the real reason Anthony liked coming there was because it was so close to Chelsea, the neighborhood where most of Manhattan's gay community lived. Besides the yummy treats *behind* the counter, there was plenty of free eye candy *in front* of the counter for Anthony to drool over.

On the weekends it was often impossible to get a seat inside the Frosted Cupcake and there was always a line out the door and around the block for their cupcakes. But during the week the bakery was much quieter and there was never a problem getting a seat.

"Let's be bad. Very bad," Anthony said, staring at a menu as they settled into two armchairs covered with colorful suede patches. "Hmmm. Decisions, decisions. Am I in a chocolate or vanilla mood?"

"Do you guys know what you want?"

Paige looked up and gave a smile to Roger, their waiter, who had been working at the Frosted Cupcake for the last year. He was about the same age as them, with dirty-blond hair that he wore in a shaggy cut and piercing blue eyes. She'd never once seen him clean-shaven, but always with a five o'clock shadow. Paige liked the way his darker beard contrasted with his light hair color and how his wardrobe usually consisted of T-shirts, plaid shirts with the sleeves rolled up and jeans. He always wore a chunky silver bracelet on one wrist and a watch with a wide black leather band on the other. Roger's overall style was laid-back, but it suited him.

"I'll have a latte and two chocolate cupcakes," Anthony said. "And I want the ones with sprinkles on top."

Roger looked up from his order pad. "Tough day?"

Anthony returned his menu to Roger. "It started out good, but quickly went downhill. You don't want to know the details."

"Gotcha." Roger turned to Paige. "And what would your sweet tooth like?"

"I'll have a slice of banana bread," Paige said.

Roger tucked the menus under his arm and slid his pen behind one ear, which was pierced with a small silver hoop earring. "Be right back."

"So let's recap the Max situation," Paige said once they were alone. "Don't you think you're overreacting a bit?"

"Am I?"

"He wants to do the movie."

"But when I suggested we rehearse, he found a reason to leave."

"Maybe he really did have to leave."

"Maybe. But then I found this." Anthony placed the slip of paper he had found on the table. It had a name and a phone number on it.

Paige glanced at it. "Sheena Wolverton's phone number?"

"What's Max doing with the She-Wolf's phone number?!"Anthony wailed. "If we were looking for an answer to 'Is he or isn't he?' well, guess what, we found it!"

"Calm down and I'll fill you in."

"You knew about this?" Anthony gasped.

Paige squirmed in her seat. "Kind of. Max is buying new uniforms for the cheerleading squad. A lot of the girls were hugging and kissing him, including Sheena, as a way of saying thanks. I guess Sheena must have slipped him her number."

"Only a straight boy would buy new uniforms for the cheerleading squad," Anthony moaned.

"Not necessarily. I mean, Max is new. Maybe this is his

way of trying to fit in and make friends. Get everyone to like him. As for the She-Wolf's phone number, just because he had it doesn't mean he was going to call her."

"You're right. He's not." Anthony ripped the slip of paper into tiny shreds.

"Anthony!"

"What? She's the competition and with the way things are shaping up, *your* competition."

Paige studied Anthony closely. He was down in the dumps and that was rare. And when he did get down, it usually took a couple of days to happen. Something else was going on. "This isn't about Max. Something else is bothering you."

Anthony sighed. "I'm just tired of . . . I don't know . . . being different, Paige."

"What do you mean?"

Anthony looked around the bakery. "Sometimes I wish I wasn't gay. Sometimes I wish I was just like everyone else."

"Oh, sweetie." At that moment, all Paige wanted to do was give Anthony a huge hug. Which she immediately did, jumping out of her seat and wrapping her arms around him, squeezing as tightly as she could.

"Being gay is a part of who you are. It's what makes you special."

Anthony hugged Paige back. "Thank you."

"I didn't know you'd switched teams," Roger said, placing their order on the coffee table in front of them.

"Ha ha," Anthony said, reaching for a cupcake and taking a huge bite. "I'm just getting a little TLC from my best friend."

"Where's the boyfriend?"

Paige knew that Anthony and Ian had often come to the Frosted Cupcake when they were dating and had been served by Roger. The fact that he didn't have a problem with Anthony being gay made him very cool in Paige's book.

"You mean ex-boyfriend," Anthony said. "Probably off breaking someone else's heart."

"His loss."

"Thanks," Anthony said, perking up. "Hey, nice jeans. I love how faded out they are."

"You do? Thanks."

"Where'd you get them?"

"The 23rd Street flea market. Only twenty-five bucks, which was a steal for a pair of Levis."

Anthony tried not to look horrified. "You bought a *used* pair of jeans?"

"They're not used, they're vintage."

Anthony held up a hand. "You might like digging through piles of dirty clothes, but I want my clothes to be fresh off the rack and never before worn."

"Fashion past influences fashion future," Roger said. "Didn't you know that?"

"No. How do you?"

"I'm taking a design class. I'd love to chat some more, but I've gotta get back to work. If you need anything else, I'll be behind the counter with Candy."

"Wasn't last week's girlfriend named Nina?" Paige whispered as Roger walked away.

Anthony shrugged, finishing off his first cupcake and already removing the paper wrapper of his second. "Who knows? I've lost track of Roger's glamazons."

The glamazons was the nickname Paige and Anthony had given to Roger's girlfriends. It seemed like every other week, Roger had a different girl draped over his arm. They were always tall and leggy, with the type of gorgeous hair you'd see in a shampoo commercial. When Roger wasn't busy serving customers, he and his latest glamazon were usually huddled together at the counter doing homework. Roger was always the one doing the talking and pointing at their textbooks while his study partner listened, but Paige didn't think Roger's glamazons had much in the brains department. They usually had a blank expression on their faces, as if they didn't understand a word he was saying, although their makeup was *always* flawless.

Today's glamazon—Candy—was a redhead with a short pixie cut that Paige wished she had the courage to try.

"Why can't I be like Roger?" Anthony asked.

"Roger likes girls," Paige pointed out.

"That's not what I mean. Roger always has a girlfriend. Why can't I always have a boyfriend?"

"I don't know. But trust me, once we're in college you're going to have so many guys interested in you, I'm never going to see you."

"Let's hope so," Anthony grumbled.

Paige took a bite of her banana bread as a blond guy in his early twenties walked into the bakery. "He's cute."

"Don't get your hopes up," Anthony said, sipping his latte.

"Huh?"

"He's gay."

Paige took another look at the guy and shook her head.

"He is not. Look at how conservatively dressed he is."

Anthony sighed. "Must you doubt me?"

"He's not gay," Paige insisted.

"Observe the clues, Miss Paige. Even though he's wearing a navy blue suit, he's wearing loafers without socks. Second, note the color of his tie. It's pink. Sherbert pink! Third, his clothes are immaculately pressed; there's not a wrinkle on him."

"Maybe he's a metrosexual. Did you stop to think of that?"

"Yes, he *could* be a metrosexual, but he's not." Anthony sat back in his arm chair, a smug smile on his face. "And I have proof."

"What kind of proof?"

"There's the backpack tossed over his shoulder. Note the key chain attached to the zipper."

Paige took a closer look at the guy, noticing all the things Anthony had pointed out. Then she zeroed in on the key chain and knew she was wrong and Anthony was right.

It was a Hello Kitty key chain.

"And if you need any further proof," Anthony continued, "let's listen to his voice when he orders. That should be the icing on the cake. Or considering where we are, the icing on the cupcake."

Paige listened; the blond man had a slightly effeminate lisp.

"Okay, okay," she sighed. "I admit defeat. You're right. He's gay."

"Yes! Victory!" Anthony exclaimed. "That's another round of 'gay or straight' to me!"

"Gay or straight" was a game that Paige and Anthony sometimes played. Basically, it was just people watching, but trying to figure out if someone was gay or straight. Paige was amazed at how Anthony was always able to win the game. He could usually tell from a guy's haircut, backpack, type of eyeglasses he was wearing, shoes—the list went on and on— if he was gay or straight.

Paige's cell phone rang. When she looked at the incoming number, she groaned. "It's my mother."

"Are you going to talk to her?"

"I guess I should. Who knows when I'll get another chance?"

"When was the last time you spoke to her?"

"This summer. Out in California."

"Ouch."

Paige pressed the phone to her ear, trying to sound cheerful. Something was up. The only time she heard from Camille was when she wanted something. Or when there was a crisis in her life. "Hello, Mother."

"Paige!" Camille wailed over the line. "Have you seen the latest issue of *Soap Opera Insider*?"

"No, I haven't. Why?"

"You're not going to believe what's happening."

Paige sighed. She'd been right. Something was going on in her mother's life. Something not good. "What's happening?"

"They're going to age my daughter on the show!"

"But didn't you give birth to Ivory two years ago?"

"Yes! It's a plot, I tell you. A plot!"

"A plot?"

"The new producer hates me! She's trying to push me off the show. She feels we need a younger audience so they're going to age Ivory so she can start wreaking havoc in Harmony Hills. She's going to go off to nursery school on Friday and come back home as a sixteen-year-old on Monday! *I'm* the one who's supposed to be wreaking havoc in Harmony Hills, not my daughter!"

"Maybe—"

Camille cut her off. "Don't you see what's happening? They're going to backburner me! I'm not going to get any story line! And then when my contract comes up for renewal, they're going to drop me from the show."

Where was her mother's agent? Isn't this what he got paid his fifteen percent commission for? Better yet, where was her therapist?!

"Mother, calm down. You're overreacting."

But Camille wasn't listening. Her voice was becoming more and more hysterical. *Not* a good sign. Anthony leaned closer to Paige, trying to listen in, but she shooed him away.

"What happens if they fire me? What will I do then? No other show will want to hire me. I'll be out of work. Penniless! You know how I live, darling. I spend like crazy— and I don't have anything in the bank."

But you do have ex-husband number five who pays you monthly alimony, Paige thought. *I doubt you'll be hungry or homeless. Or you can always find hubby number six.*

"My career is over. Over!" Camille wailed.

"Mother, listen to me," Paige ordered. "Listen to me!"

Anthony stopped in mid-bite of his cupcake, eyes wide open at Paige's firm tone of voice.

"Are you listening?" Paige asked.

There was silence at the other end of the line.

"You're the star of *The Yields of Passion*. The show's not going to fire you. They can't. The fans would revolt and the ratings would tumble. You're the reason everyone watches. Just like Susan Lucci on *All My Children*."

"You think so?" Camille asked in a tiny voice.

Paige gave a sigh of relief. Apparently her words had calmed Camille down.

"Yes. The fans love to hate you."

Just like I sometimes do in real life.

"I suppose you're right. The fans *do* love me and *Soap Dish* magazine named me outstanding villainess for the fourth year in a row."

"Have you seen any scripts yet with a teenage Ivory in them?"

"No."

"Then maybe it's not going to happen. You know how those magazines are. They hear a rumor and they print it. Maybe Ivory won't be turning sixteen for another five years."

"I feel much better, darling. Talking to you always helps."

Then why don't you do it more often, Paige wondered. *I'm your daughter, after all.*

Still, it was nice that Camille *did* turn to her. Maybe this could be the start of them rebuilding their relationship. Maybe . . .

"How are things in New York?" Camille asked, interrupting her thoughts. "Classes just started, right? Junior year or senior year?"

What?! Paige almost dropped her phone. Was Camille for

real?! Did she not know her own daughter was a senior?

"Did you buy some new clothes?"

"New clothes?"

"I meant to say something when you were visiting this summer. You need a new look, Paige. Something less dowdy and more sexy."

"Sexy?"

"Yes, sexy."

The warm and fuzzy feelings Paige had started to feel again for Camille were disappearing. Quickly. Now she was starting to get mad. Very mad.

"What's wrong with my wardrobe?"

"Maybe it's an East Coast thing, that conservative look."

"Are you saying you want me to dress like a hoochie?"

"Of course not! But if my fans saw us together, well, they'd never believe you were my daughter."

And how likely is that to happen, Mother, when we're so rarely together!

"And you need to do something with your hair," Camille continued. "It needs more color. Have you considered going red?"

"Red?" Paige squeaked, her throat tight with anger. "You want me to become a redhead?"

"Being a redhead hasn't hurt that young actress with all those hit movies. What's her name? It starts with an L. She's the one who supposedly got breast implants."

"Do you want me to get those, too? Is that what you're saying? Because if you are then you can go straight—"

Anthony, sensing she might say something she would regret, snatched her phone out of her hand.

"Camille! It's Anthony! How are you? I am *loving* you on the show. Priscilla is being *so* wicked these days!"

Paige grabbed what was left of Anthony's second cupcake off his plate and stuffed it in her mouth while he talked to her mother.

When Anthony finished his conversation, he turned off her phone and gave it back to her.

"Your mother said to tell you she loves you."

Paige glared at Anthony until he squirmed.

"Okay," he admitted. "She didn't say it, but she would have if she'd remembered. They were calling her back onto the set."

"I need another cupcake," Paige said.

Anthony went to the counter and came back with two more cupcakes, one with chocolate frosting and one with vanilla. Paige chose the vanilla cupcake.

"She makes me so mad sometimes!"

"That's Camille for you."

"Don't you mean *Priscilla*?" Paige's voice dripped with scorn. "She cares about that stupid character more than she does me!"

"You know that isn't true."

"Do I?"

"Yes, you do."

Paige sighed. "I don't want to talk about my mother anymore."

Paige and Anthony were distracted when a group of teenage guys came into the bakery and stood around the counter, pointing at various desserts.

"Now that's what I call sweet!" Anthony exclaimed.

"Why don't you go over and introduce yourself? Don't tell me you can't figure out which ones are gay and which ones are straight?"

"My gaydar never works when it comes to guys my own age. You know that. Look at the situation we're in with Max."

"We forgot all about him."

"For a full five minutes!"

Paige licked the vanilla frosting off her cupcake. "What are we going to do?"

"What can we do? Just keep proceeding according to plan so we can get closer to him and figure out what's what. But I think the next move is yours, Paige. I've laid some ground-work with the movie, but you have to come up with something to test him. Got any ideas?"

"A couple. Don't worry, we're going to figure this out. And when we do, one of us is going to have a boyfriend!"

After leaving the Frosted Cupcake, Anthony and Paige headed back to his apartment to do their homework together. When they got there, they found Paolo in the living room, lounging on the couch in a pair of navy blue shorts and a gray tank top, watching TV.

"Are you *still* here?" Anthony grumbled.

"Didn't I tell you?" Paolo gave Anthony a wicked grin. "I'm sleeping over tonight." He hit the mute button on the remote. "Hey, Paige, don't you think my brother needs a hair-cut? His hair's getting way too long."

Paige glanced at Anthony's head. "I suppose he could use a trim."

"Don't you think he should try something different?

Maybe get a buzz cut?"

"Don't even think about it," Anthony warned, eyeing his brother nervously. "I held up my part of the deal."

"What are you watching?" Paige asked.

"Female boxing."

"Female boxing?!" Paige screamed in outrage. "Are you serious?"

"You've got a problem with female boxing?"

"It's wrong. Wrong, wrong, wrong!"

Paolo gave Paige an amused smile while putting his feet up on the coffee table. "Why, why, why?"

"Because women shouldn't be going around beating each other up, that's why!"

"Are you saying women can't do the same things that men can do?"

"Of course not! Women can do anything."

"Then what's your problem with female boxing? Female wrestlers have been around for years."

"Wrestling is different than boxing."

"How so?"

"Well, first of all, it's fake! It's scripted. Boxing is real. It's ugly. It's dangerous. People bleed! And boxers have been known to die from injuries they've gotten in the ring. It's just not something a woman should do!"

"This conversation is boring me," Anthony announced. "I already got my daily dose of Jock 101. I'm going to my room."

"So, Paige, back to female boxing," Paolo said. "Are you saying that women should just be pretty things? Taken care of and adored?"

"No, I'm not saying that!"

"Then what are you saying?"

"Boxing is a *male* sport. Plain and simple."

"Boxing is a game of skill," Paolo countered. "You have to be one step ahead of your opponent. You have to think on your feet."

"And if you don't you get a fist in your face! There are some things that women shouldn't be allowed to do and boxing is one of them! What woman in her right mind would want to get pummeled?"

"Maybe the challenge of the sport is in making sure you *don't* get pummeled," Paolo stated. "Ever think of that?" Paolo didn't allow Paige to answer. "Let me ask you a question. Do you have a problem with male boxing?"

"Huh?"

"Should men not box?"

"If men want to box, they should box."

"Then why can't women?"

"I just told you why! Weren't you listening?"

"I was listening. I just don't agree with you."

"And I don't agree with you. I don't want to talk about this anymore!"

"Why? Because you can't back up your argument?"

"No! I think *all* boxing is wrong, alright? Why would anyone want to watch two people beating each other up? Possibly even killing each other! And when it comes to female boxing, the only reason you and all guys like watching is because you want to see two women fighting with each other."

"That is a plus," Paolo agreed, taking a sip from his can

of 7-Up. "Hey, the commercial is over. Wanna watch?"

Paige shook her head at Paolo in disbelief. "You can't be serious."

"Come on, give it a shot," Paolo urged, patting the seat next to him. "You might change your mind. You might even want to give it a try!"

"Not in this lifetime!" Paige said as the sound came back on the TV. "Enjoy yourself."

"Don't worry, I will!" Paolo exclaimed. "Whoa! These girls are *hot*!" He started fanning himself with a magazine. "I think I'm going to need some AC to cool off!"

"Your brother is *so* infuriating," Paige fumed as she stormed into Anthony's bedroom.

"Tell me something I don't know," Anthony said.

"Sometimes I think he argues with me on purpose."

"He likes pushing your buttons. And you let him."

"I do not."

"Do too."

"Don't!"

"Do!"

"You're just as bad as your brother!" Paige exclaimed. "Always wanting to get the last word!"

Anthony shrugged. "What can I say? It's a DeMarco family trait. Who would have thought I'd have something in common with my jock brother?"

chapter eight

"Tell me one more time what a good-bad movie is," Max said.

It was Saturday night and Anthony had invited Paige and Colleen over to his apartment to watch videos. He'd also invited Max.

Max was the first to arrive.

"A good-bad movie is a movie that's originally made with the intention of being good, yet somehow turns into a disaster. When it's released, it gets horrible reviews and disappears. But then, over the years, it starts to develop a cult following. Even though the movie is bad, it's fun to watch. There's something over-the-top and campy about it. The acting. The dialogue. The directing. Everything! I can't explain it. Once you've seen enough good-bad movies, you'll know what I mean."

"What are we watching tonight?" Max asked as he plopped down on the couch.

"A camp classic. *Valley of the Dolls*. Have you ever seen it?" Max shook his head.

"It was made in the late '60s," Anthony said. "It's based on the best-selling trash novel of all time. I have a copy if you ever want to read it. It's brilliant! Jacqueline Susann wrote it. Anyway, the story focuses on three single gals who try to make it in Hollywood and they become hooked on booze and pills. The pills are called dolls. What's also interesting about the film is the way the characters toss around the word *fag*."

"What do you mean?"

"They just constantly use that as an insult."

Max raised his eyebrows, but before he could respond, the doorbell rang.

Shoot! Just when things were starting to get interesting! Anthony cursed whoever was at the door as he went off to answer it. It was Colleen, who was loaded with bags of Chinese takeout. Anthony scowled at her.

"Why the face?" she asked.

"Your timing couldn't be more off," Anthony whispered, looking over his shoulder to make sure he wasn't overheard. "I was making some progress on the 'Is he or isn't he?' front. Now I'm back to square one!"

Colleen rolled her eyes, handing Anthony a bag. "Paige filled me in. Don't worry, you can count on me. If I find out anything, you'll be the first to know. Now smile. You're cuter when you do."

"Well, you did bring food." Anthony sniffed the air.

"Mmm. Smells great. What did you buy?"

"Egg rolls, spare ribs, three kinds of dumplings, pork fried rice and sesame chicken. We can't have a bad movie night without munchies!"

Anthony headed into the kitchen for plates and forks while Colleen joined Max in the living room. When he came back, Colleen was kneeling in front of the coffee table, opening up white containers. The fragrant aroma of Chinese food filled the air, making Anthony's mouth water.

"Anthony always finds the best bad movies," Colleen said. "I don't know how he does it. It's like an instinct."

"It's an instinct most gay guys have," Anthony said, handing a plate to Colleen and then Max. "I think we're born with it."

There. He'd said it. Laid his cards out on the table. Until just a few moments ago, he hadn't come out and said to Max, "Hello, my name is Anthony DeMarco and I'm gay." But now Max knew. Without a doubt.

If Anthony's words had thrown Max, he didn't show it. He continued to fill his plate with Chinese food, while Anthony and Colleen did the same.

"What are some other bad movies that you guys have seen?" Max asked while dipping his egg roll into hot mustard sauce.

"How much time do you have?" Anthony asked. "Seriously. We live for these movies."

"We've seen *Mommie Dearest*," Colleen said.

"'No wire hangers . . . EVER!!!'" Anthony quoted.

"*Mahogany*."

"Oh, God, that one's my all-time favorite!!!" Anthony

turned to Max with an excited look on his face. "Diana Ross is a struggling fashion designer living in the ghetto in Chicago and she becomes an internationally famous model. The best known line of that movie is when she turns her back on love and her boyfriend tells her . . ."

Anthony turned to Colleen and together they screamed, "Success is NOTHING without someone you love to share it with!!!"

"And let's not forget *Showgirls*," Colleen said.

The doorbell rang again and Anthony went to answer it while Colleen started telling Max the plot of *Showgirls*. When he opened the front door, he did a double take and took a step back. Then he closed the front door behind him and stepped out into the hallway with Paige.

"Did you dress in the dark?" he hissed.

"What are you talking about?"

Anthony waved his hands in the air. "You look like a frump!"

Anthony couldn't believe what he was seeing. Paige was wearing an oversize NYU sweatshirt and a pair of sweatpants. And she hadn't done anything with her hair or makeup. She looked like she had rolled right out of bed.

"If we're trying to figure out if Max is gay or straight, this certainly isn't the way to do it."

"Is that what we're trying to do tonight? I thought we were getting together to watch some videos. You didn't tell me we had an agenda." Paige shoved a finger in Anthony's chest. "First of all, this is the way I *always* dress when we have bad movie night. Second, I didn't know there was a dress code. You didn't mention one when you called to invite me over. If I'm not passing inspection, I'll go home."

Anthony's mouth dropped open. What had gotten into Paige?

"I didn't mean to upset you. I'm sorry."

"You should be! There's nothing wrong with the way I look."

"What are you all worked up about?"

"Nothing. Now can we go inside and watch the movie?"

Anthony hadn't meant what he said. Okay, Paige didn't look her best, but she certainly was no frump. He'd only been kidding with her. But from the way she was walking to his front door, all rushed, it was almost as if she were trying to outrun him. Her cheeks were all red, and the only time her cheeks got red was when she was upset and about to cry.

Anthony touched Paige on the shoulder. "Hey, are you okay?"

Paige turned around and gave Anthony a smile. "Of course I'm okay!"

No, she wasn't. The smile on her lips was quivering. And her eyes looked moist. "You're not upset with me, are you?"

"Upset? About what?"

"What I just said. Paige, you know I think you're a knock-out. It's just that sometimes I feel like you don't want the rest of the world to know."

Paige gave Anthony a quick kiss on the cheek. "You're sweet. Now come on, let's go inside and watch a bad movie."

And with those final words, Paige went inside.

After Paige was gone, Anthony remained out in the hall-way, trying to figure out what had just happened. Something was up with his best friend and he was going to find out exactly what it was.

Paige had been lying to Anthony.

She *was* upset.

She knew his remarks hadn't been mean. Anthony loved her.

But there was no putting one past him. Anthony could always pick up on her moods and she was in a bad one.

She'd have to confess to him at some point. But not tonight. Tonight she just wanted to forget that this morning she'd turned on her TV and there in living color on *New York Live* was Camille.

Her mother was in New York and she hadn't called to let her know she'd be in town!

At first Paige had been excited. She figured that once Camille was through being interviewed she'd call her and they'd spend the day together.

But Camille never called.

She had stayed in the apartment all day, waiting for the phone to ring, and it never did.

Finally Paige couldn't stand it anymore. She picked up the phone and dialed Camille's cell phone. Naturally, her mother didn't pick up, so Paige left a message:

"So nice of you to make time in your busy schedule for me. I caught you this morning on *New York Live*. What was up with the lighting? You looked awful. All puffy and bloated. Unless it wasn't the lighting. You might want to call a plastic surgeon and see about some repair work. You looked at least ten years older than you actually are."

Paige had gotten some satisfaction with those final words. She knew Camille would freak out after hearing her message. Good. She cared more about her career and her appearance than her own daughter.

Was it too much to ask that her mother make *some* time in her life for her? She wasn't trying to be unreasonable. She knew Camille had a busy life, but how hard was it to find a way to squeeze her into it?

She'd spent all day feeling sorry for herself, and when Anthony had called to invite her over, she'd dressed without thinking. True, knowing that Max would also be there, she should have dressed to impress, but it was too late now. Now it was time to get over it all. She wasn't going to worry about the way she looked and she wasn't going to think about Camille anymore. Tonight she was hanging out with friends.

"Hey, Paige, come sit next to me," Max said, patting the spot next to him on the couch.

Paige couldn't help but notice the surprised look on Anthony's face. She'd bet anything that he'd been hoping to sit next to Max. Well, there was nothing she could do about that.

"You like nice and comfortable," he said as she settled down next to him.

"You don't think I look like a frump?" she asked, reaching for a plate and filling it with pork fried rice. Paige didn't know why she had said that; the words had just slipped out. Sometimes Anthony was such a know-it-all that it was nice to occasionally put him in his place. "Some guys would say I do."

"It's the perfect outfit for watching videos. Why get all glammed up when we're just staying in on a Saturday night?"

Paige looked directly at Anthony and tried not to smirk.

"I'm with you, Max," Colleen agreed, who was wearing a neon pink T-shirt and overalls.

"There's nothing wrong with looking nice," Anthony huffed, sitting down on the floor and aiming the remote at the TV.

The others wouldn't be aware of it, but Paige was sure Anthony had spent hours deciding what to wear. Even though he looked casual in his dark brown cords and light brown suede shirt, she was sure he'd agonized over his outfit.

"I'm sure you're still in the running for the best dressed award from *GQ*," Paige teased.

Anthony glared at Paige. "Thanks. Now everyone be quiet! It's time to watch the movie."

At first, Anthony was engrossed in watching the movie. But then he noticed that Max and Paige weren't paying much attention to the TV. They were paying attention to each other.

"How come you're using a fork?" Max asked Paige.

"What's wrong with a fork?"

"You can't eat Chinese food with a fork. You have to use chopsticks! Don't you know how?"

"Not really. I can pick the food up, but by the time it reaches my mouth, it falls back onto my plate."

Anthony gasped. Why, that little liar! She knew how to use chopsticks! She was just playing dumb. Something that he would have done!

"They're easy to use. Here, I'll show you."

Anthony's eyes nearly bugged out of his head as Max slid behind Paige and wrapped his arms around hers. Then he placed her chopsticks in her hand and scooped up a piece of chicken, lifting it toward her mouth.

"See? Easy. Nothing to it."

"Let me try myself."

Paige tried to use the chopsticks, but she couldn't seem to get the hang of it. Or so she pretended, Anthony noted. She kept picking up rice and vegetables, and just as they reached her mouth, they fell back onto the plate until Max wrapped his arms back around her and guided the chopsticks again.

"Why don't you just feed her?" Colleen suggested, her eyes glued to the TV screen. "It'll take less time."

Anthony pinched Colleen's leg.

"Ouch!"

He smiled pleasantly. "Sorry. But you know how much I hate talking during a movie."

And I don't need you giving Max romantic tips!

"Uh-huh," Colleen said, glaring at Anthony while rubbing her leg.

"Anyone want a fortune cookie?" Max asked.

"I'll take one," Anthony said.

"Me too," Paige said.

"Me three," Colleen chimed in.

"What's your fortune say?" Paige asked after Anthony had cracked open his cookie.

"Mine says I'll find fame and fortune where I least expect it," Colleen said.

Anthony popped a piece of cookie in his mouth and stared directly at Paige before reading off the slip of paper from his cookie. "Mine says I'll be stabbed in the back by my best friend."

Two hours later, the movie was over.

"So what did you think, Max?" Anthony asked.

Max rubbed his eyes. "I'm still in shock."

"What was your favorite scene?"

"I only get to choose one? Let's see." Max thought for a minute. "I guess it would have to be the scene where Neely and Tony have their singing duet in the mental hospital."

"Let's not forget the scene where Neely rips off Helen's wig and flushes it down the toilet," Colleen added.

"Is anyone up for another movie?" Anthony asked. "We could keep with the Hollywood theme and watch *Beyond the Valley of the Dolls*. It's an unofficial sequel and it's sooo bad it makes the original look like a classic!"

Colleen stretched and yawned. "I'm kind of tired and I've got a dance class early tomorrow morning. I'm going to call it a night."

"Me too," Max said, getting to his feet.

"I guess that just leaves you and me, Paige," Anthony said.

"How about if I walk you home?" Max said to Paige. "That is, if you're not staying."

"You don't have to do that," she said.

"I know I don't have to, but I want to. Let me go get my jacket."

Colleen raced over to Paige and squeezed her arm. "I'm going to leave now so you and Maxie can have some *alone* time. Call me in the morning!"

Anthony tried to fight against the jealousy rippling through him, but it was hard. His mind was racing with images—all of them romantic and all of them starring Max and Paige.

He got off the floor and headed into the kitchen with a stack of dishes, slamming them on the counter. Paige followed after him with the empty takeout containers.

"Is anything wrong?" she asked, tossing the containers into the trash.

"No."

"Are you sure?"

"Yes, I'm sure," he said as he began loading the dishwasher.

"Then why are you giving me the big chill?"

"I don't know what you're talking about."

Paige looked up from the white plastic trash bag she was tying shut. "Yes, you do. You've been ignoring me all night and I want to know why. We always talk back to the screen during *Valley of the Dolls* and you didn't do it once tonight, even when I did. And whenever I made some sort of comment to you, you shushed me. And let's not forget your so-called fortune. *You will be stabbed in the back by your best friend.* What was *that* supposed to mean? Are you mad because I snapped at you before?"

Anthony filled the dishwasher with Cascade and then turned it on. "You mean when you bit my head off for no reason?"

"Tell me what's wrong."

"The way you did when I asked you what was wrong?"

"Anthony! Stop answering my questions with questions!"

"Fine! I'm jealous, alright?" Anthony admitted. "You got to sit next to Max on the couch and now he's walking you home. Satisfied?"

"Is that my fault?" Paige asked, going to the sink so she could wash her hands.

"No, but—"

"I didn't ask him to walk me home."

"I know that!"

"Then why are you being so horrible to me?"

"You were horrible to me, too! Needling me with those comments I made out in the hallway and then saying I'd win the *GQ* award for being best dressed. You still haven't told me why you were so upset and I know something is up, so don't try to lie to me."

"I don't want to talk about it," Paige said, squirting her hands with SoftSoap and lathering up.

"Well I don't want to talk about this."

"That's really mature. I thought we had a pact. That we were going to help each other land Max. Is our friendship breaking up? Are we actually going to let a guy come between us?"

Paige's words were like a slap in the face and Anthony snapped out of his jealousy. "We better not!" He sighed. "Look, I'm sorry. When I saw all the attention Max was giving you, I lost it. I like this guy. I really like him. He's cute and sweet and adorable. I love spending time with him. I have these feelings for him and I can't tell him because it'll probably freak him out. We hardly even know each other! God. Listen to me. I sound like some dippy heroine from a Harlequin romance."

Anthony leaned against the humming dishwasher. "It's just that sometimes you meet a person and they blow you away. It's like they have this magical aura and they draw you in and you're helpless."

"Okay, this is getting a little heavy," Paige said, turning off the faucet and shaking the excess water off her hands. "We've only known Max a couple of weeks."

"I'm not doing a good job explaining myself. I like Max. I like him a lot. But if I tell him what I'm feeling and he's not gay, well, then I've blown our friendship because like all straight guys, he's probably going to be grossed out."

"Not necessarily."

"Paige."

"Well, you're not going to know until it happens. It's not like you have a crystal ball and you can look into it and see what the future is going to bring."

"I wish I did."

Paige wiped her hands dry on a dish towel. "Hey, no matter what happens, you know you still have me."

"I know that. And you have me. So, are you going to tell me what happened today?"

Paige sighed. "It was more of the same. Camille's in town and she didn't bother to let me know." Paige held up a hand so Anthony wouldn't speak. She knew he would find some way of defending her mother's actions and she wasn't in the mood to hear it. Maybe there was a reason why Camille hadn't called, but she doubted it. And if there wasn't, she didn't want to know. Feeling unwanted by your own mother hurt too much. "I'm over it. I should be used to it by now, right? She's been doing this to me my entire life."

"Paige?" Max called from the living room. "Are you ready to go?"

"Almost," she called.

"I'll meet you downstairs, okay?"

"Okay."

"One word of advice before you go," Anthony said.

"What?"

"If he's leaning more toward Straightsville, then the next move is yours!"

chapter nine

Was Max leaning more toward Straightsville? That was the question bouncing around Paige's head as she waited by herself for the elevator. From his behavior tonight, the answer seemed like yes. Maybe the walk home would reveal some definite answers.

The ping of the elevator's bell announced its arrival. Paige had just stepped into it when the brass doors were closing and a voice called out, "Hold that elevator!"

Paige stuck her hand out and the elevator doors sprang back open, allowing Paolo to step inside. As usual, he was wearing jeans and a sports sweatshirt.

"Don't you have *any* button-down shirts in your closet?" Paige asked.

"Hello to you, too," Paolo said, pressing the button for the lobby.

"What do you have against buttons? Do you not know how to use them?"

"What I wear is comfortable and I like being comfortable."

"You could at least shake up your colors. You're always wearing gray and black and blue."

"And the problem with that is?"

"Girls notice what guys wear."

"And you've been noticing?"

"How could I not? You *always* wear the *same* thing," Paige groaned. "I bet if you dressed up a little bit more you'd be spending less time glued to your TV. For instance, if you wore an aquamarine shirt, it would really bring out the color of your eyes."

"Now you're starting to sound like my brother."

"What's wrong with looking nice?"

"Nothing. But this is who I am. This is how I like to dress." Paolo waved at Paige's outfit. "Just like you. Relaxed and casual."

Paige self-consciously tugged on her ponytail. "I look a mess."

"You do not."

"I do too!"

"Says who?"

"Says—"

Paolo held up a hand and cut her off. "Wait. Let me guess. Anthony."

"Well he's right."

"He's wrong. You look very cute. Very girl next door."

Paige rolled her eyes. "Thanks. I think."

"What's wrong with that?"

"The girl next door never gets the guy! It's always the slutty cheerleader or sorority sister."

"True," Paolo agreed. "Then again, they're always the first ones to be killed in a horror movie."

"I'll remember that the next time I'm being stalked by a homicidal maniac."

"And if the phone rings, don't answer it. It means the killer's in the house."

"Where are you headed?" Paige asked. "Off to see some female boxing?"

"Cute. Very cute. Actually, I'm going to a jazz club in the Village. I'm meeting some friends." Paolo glanced around the empty elevator and whispered in Paige's ear. "Female ones, too!"

"You mean like a date?"

"No, just a group of friends hanging out together. Only we know who's gay and who's straight. So much for your theory about my being glued to my TV set because of my clothes. And you?"

"Home."

"Want to share a taxi?"

"Max is waiting for me downstairs. He's going to walk me home."

"*Maaaaxxxxx* is waiting. I see." Paolo nodded his head knowingly. "So he likes girls rather than boys."

"We still don't know."

Paolo's mouth dropped open. "How can you still not know?"

Paige shrugged. "I don't know. We just don't!"

"This is crazy! Just ask the guy and get it over with!"

"We don't want to."

"Why?" Paolo pointed a finger up in the air. "Because Brains upstairs says so? Do you do everything my brother tells you to do?"

"We made a pact."

"Pacts were made to be broken."

"Says who?"

"Says me!"

Paige was just about to respond when the elevator jerked to a stop. A second later the lights inside started blinking.

"What's going on?" she asked nervously, inching closer to Paolo. "Why isn't the elevator moving?"

Paolo hit the down button a few times, but the elevator remained motionless. "I guess we're stuck."

"Stuck? Stuck?!"

"Calm down. This sometimes happens. Usually it takes a few minutes to start up again. This building is ancient."

I will not panic, Paige vowed. *I will not panic!*

"Are you okay?" Paolo asked, concern in his voice.

"I don't like being in enclosed spaces for very long," Paige admitted. "It freaks me out."

Paolo wrapped his arms around Paige, holding her close. "Don't worry. Everything's going to be okay."

Paige didn't know why, but having Paolo's arms around her made her feel safe. Secure. She snuggled into his embrace, pressing her face against the front of his sweatshirt. It smelled like fabric softener. Paige's heart was beating pretty fast. Was she having a panic attack? How embarrassing! Maybe she was just anxious because she knew Max was waiting for her.

She gazed up into Paolo's eyes. "Promise?"

Paolo's blue-green eyes looked deep into hers and she could see he was telling the truth. "I promise."

A few seconds later there was the hum of an engine and the elevator began moving again.

"See, what did I tell you?" Paolo removed his arms from around Paige. "We're back in business."

"Sorry I freaked out up there," Paige said.

"Your secret's safe with me."

The elevator arrived in the lobby and Paolo held the doors open for Paige. As they walked to the entrance of the building, they could see Max waiting outside.

"You better get going," Paolo urged. "Your date is waiting."

"He's not my date!"

"New gay best friend?"

"Anthony would kill you if he heard you say that. You know that part's taken by him."

"Possible boyfriend?"

Paige mulled over the words. "Possible boyfriend sounds right."

"Have a nice walk home."

"Paolo?"

"Yeah?"

Paige gave him a smile. "Thanks."

Paolo gave her a wink back. "Anytime."

"What took you so long?" Max asked when Paige joined him. "And what were you doing with Paolo?"

Was it her imagination or did Max sound jealous? But of what? Paolo? That was a laugh! They could barely have a civil conversation. Besides, he was only interested in college girls.

"We got stuck in the elevator."

Max started walking down the street and Paige hurried after him. She kept waiting for him to take her hand in his, but he didn't. He just walked next to her in silence as they went from block to block.

Okay, this is weird. Why isn't Max talking to me? Is he mad because I took so long coming down?

They were waiting for a light to change at the corner of West 88th Street when a woman with a Yorkshire terrier stopped next to them. The dog started jumping up on Paige's leg and she couldn't resist the urge to pet it. "Aren't you adorable!" Paige said in a baby voice.

"Why do all girls do that?" Max asked.

"Do what?"

"Talk in a baby voice when they're petting an animal."

"I don't know. We just do."

Max knelt down and started petting the dog himself.

"Her name is Fifi," the woman said.

"Hello, Fifi," Max said as the Yorkie put her paw on Max's knee and began licking his hand.

"She likes you!" Paige exclaimed.

Max scratched Fifi behind her ears. "Do you have any pets?"

"I wish I did, but I can't. I'm allergic. My eyes get all red and I can't stop sneezing. How about you?"

"We had a Saint Bernard in California, but we had to leave him with my grandparents. Dad said that a New York

City apartment was too small for a dog that big."

"I'll bet you miss him."

The light turned green and Fifi and her owner crossed the street.

"Bye, Fifi," Paige called.

Fifi turned around and barked at Paige and Max.

"I do," Max said. "That's why I volunteer every weekend at the ASPCA."

"I didn't know you did that!"

Max shrugged. "There are so many dogs and cats waiting to be adopted. I clean cages. Give baths. Play with them. I love animals. It breaks my heart that so many of them aren't going to find homes. Sometimes I even think about becoming a vet."

Paige's heart melted as she listened to Max. There was so much to like about this guy! She couldn't wait to tell Anthony.

"I bet you'd be great at it. Fifi certainly loved you. It's like she knew you were an animal lover."

"Yeah . . . but becoming a vet takes a lot of hard work. And I also really want to pursue my acting."

"I'm sure if it's something you want, it'll happen. And who says you can't do both?" Paige stopped in front of a building with a green awning. "Well, this is where I live. Thanks for walking me home."

"Sure."

"Would you like to come upstairs?" Paige asked.

Max glanced at his watch. "Um, I should probably get home . . . another time?"

"Okay."

Max gave Paige a hug. "See you on Monday."

"See you," Paige said, watching Max walk away. Okay, he hadn't kissed her, but he had hugged her. And it wasn't like they'd been on a date, so the absence of a kiss didn't really mean anything. She still didn't know if he was gay or straight, but she felt like she knew the real Max a little bit better.

Once Max and Paige were gone, Anthony finished cleaning up the living room and kitchen. He tried not to think about Paige and Max walking home together. Or kissing each other good night. But it was hard.

If Max was straight, then he should be happy for Paige because it looked like Max was interested in her.

But what about me? Anthony asked himself. *When do I get to find someone?*

Once everything was cleaned up, Anthony decided to go to bed. He could have watched *Beyond the Valley of the Dolls*, but it was no fun watching a bad movie by yourself. And he didn't feel like watching *MAD TV* or *Saturday Night Live*.

After getting into bed, Anthony had a hard time falling asleep. He twisted and turned against the sheets, checking the time on his clock radio, wondering what was going on with Paige and Max. He should have told Paige to call him once she'd gotten home. He could call her now, but she'd probably think it was Camille and he didn't want to disappoint her.

chapter ten

Paige was awakened by the sound of a ringing phone.

Opening her eyes, she groaned when she saw it was nine o'clock. Who could be calling so early on a Sunday morning?

"Hello?"

"I held off on calling for as long as I could, but I'm climbing the walls! I've been up since six. I need to know what happened last night!"

Anthony. She should have known.

Paige plumped her pillows behind her back and sat up in bed. "You can give a sigh of relief. The big question still remains unanswered."

"What do you mean?"

"He didn't hold my hand when we were walking home and he didn't kiss me good night. All I got was a hug."

"What kind of a hug? A tight-hold-you-close hug or a quick squeeze?"

"A quick squeeze."

"Woo-hoo!" Anthony cheered. "That means I still have a chance! If he were straight and too shy to kiss you or hold your hand, he would at least try to cop a feel with a tight-hold-you-close hug because hugs are a gray area where extended body contact is socially acceptable."

"You don't have to sound so gleeful," Paige grumbled.

"Sorry."

"I'll bet you are."

"Hey, I get to live in my fantasy world for a little bit longer." Paige yawned. "At least for another week."

"What do you mean?"

"I know what my next move is going to be."

"Care to share?"

"In time. For now you'll just have to be patient. Talk to you later."

Paige had never before felt competitive with Anthony, but now she did. It was as if they were in a race to see who could win Max. Obviously, it didn't matter what either one of them did because in the end it was all going to come down to whether or not Max was gay or straight.

Of course, there was also going to be a deciding factor. If Max *were* gay, would he like Anthony as much as Anthony liked him?

And if Max were *straight*, well, would he like her as much as she liked him?

Last night's walk hadn't given her any clues.

It was time to get some answers.

Paige picked up the phone again, trying to work up her courage for the call she was going to make.

You can do this, she told herself. *You can do this.*

Just dial his number. You're inviting a friend for the weekend. That's all.

But was it? Paige was inviting Max to her father's house in the Hamptons because she wanted to get closer to him and get to know him better.

Because she liked him. A lot.

At first it was because he was so cute. Then she had found out how generous he was with his donations to the school. And now she knew about his love of animals and volunteer work. The more she learned about Max, the more she liked him.

Paige dialed Max's home number, but before the line could ring she hung up the phone.

Why was she so nervous? She'd called guys before and invited them to dances and parties. What was so different this time?

It wasn't like she had spent a whole lot of time with Max. Then again, he didn't spend a lot of time with anyone. He was kind of a loner. Whenever you saw him in the halls or cafeteria, he was always with a different group of people. It didn't look like he had made friends with anyone in particular, but was just coasting from clique to clique. He'd also joined a bunch of after-school clubs: Debate, Track, Yearbook, Tennis, the school paper, Spanish Club and Drama Club. And he'd had his father buy new uniforms for the basketball and football teams, too. Everyone at Peppington Prep knew who Max was, but Paige really didn't think anyone *knew* him.

Paige did feel like she and Max were becoming friends, though. He sat in front of her in A.P. History and they often talked before class started. He was definitely homesick for his friends in California and adjusting to a life without surf and sun. Sometimes he even shared his class notes with her—Mr. Owling talked a mile a minute and Paige couldn't keep up with his motormouth.

Paige picked up the phone again and dialed Max's number, forcing herself not to hang up.

"Hello?"

"Max! Hi! It's Paige!"

"Hey, Paige. What's up?"

"I was wondering if you had any plans for next weekend. I was going to head out to my dad's house in the Hamptons. Since the weather is still nice, I thought you might like going to the beach since you miss it so much."

"It's Felix's eighteenth birthday party next Saturday. I was planning to go. Who else are you inviting for the weekend?"

Okay, curve ball. Why was he asking her who else was going? Was it because he didn't want to be alone with her?

She couldn't tell him she hadn't invited anyone else. She didn't want him to think she was planning anything romantic.

"Hello? Paige? Are you there?"

Think, Paige. Think! Who else is going? Who else is going that would make Max want to come?

"I invited Colleen," she said in a rush. "And Bianca and Rachel. You met them at Anthony's party, remember?"

"Oh yeah, I remember them. Cute girls."

Bianca and Rachel would freak out if they heard they'd

been described as cute. Sultry was their new favorite word when it came to describing themselves.

"Is Anthony coming?"

Paige almost dropped the phone. Why was he asking about Anthony? Was it because he liked him and was hoping he could get closer to him? If that was the case, then why hadn't he already made a move?

"Anthony can't make it," Paige said, making a mental note to herself. She'd have to make sure Anthony told Max he had plans for that weekend. And she'd have to make sure Colleen, Bianca and Rachel canceled their plans for next weekend because they were going to be spending the weekend with her.

There was silence on the other end of the line. Why was he hesitating? She was inviting him for a weekend in the Hamptons with four girls! Any straight guy would be drooling. What more did he want?

Then the light bulb went on over Paige's head and she uttered the words she knew no guy—straight or gay—could resist. "There's a hot tub."

"I'm there!"

After getting off the phone with Max, Paige called Anthony and filled him in on Operation Hamptons.

"I'm impressed, Miss Paige. Very impressed, especially since he's skipping Felix's birthday bash. Very clever of you to mention the hot tub."

"Thank you," Paige said, feeling quite proud of herself. "You realize, though, why this has to be girls only, right?"

"Yes," Anthony sighed. "I would have loved to have seen

Max in just a bathing suit, but I understand. Promise to take pictures?"

"Promise."

"So let me ask you a question."

"Shoot."

"What happens once you get Maxie out to the Hamptons?"

"What do you mean?"

"How are you going to seduce him?"

"Seduce him?! I'm not going to seduce him!"

"Wrong word. Sorry. How are you going to tempt him? Or should I say *test* him?"

"Test him? I don't know. I haven't thought that far ahead."

"Well start thinking. You need to come up with a game plan, otherwise you're going to stuck with one bored guy who'll be looking at his watch, wondering when the next jitney is heading back to Manhattan."

"We're going to be in the hot tub."

"The *entire* weekend? Trust me Paige, you're not going to look good at your most wrinkled."

"What do you suggest then?"

"I know you're not going to like hearing this, but you're going to have to step up your game."

"Huh?"

"Show the goods, Paige! Show the goods! You're going have to plan out every outfit you're going to wear this weekend. From hair to shoes to makeup. I know you don't like putting a lot of thought into this kind of stuff, but you're going to have to if you want to keep Max's interest."

"You're wrong. Max isn't that kind of guy."

"You mean he's not straight?" Anthony sighed. "Paige, for

most straight guys it all comes down to how hot a girl is. Maybe Max is the exception to the rule, but if we *really* want to find out if he's gay or straight, then you're going to have to pull out all the stops. At least for this one weekend."

Paige sighed. "You really think I need to glam myself up? Show some skin?"

"Paige, gay guys have been advising women about fashion and makeup for hundreds of years. I think we're doing something right. But if you want the female point of view, why don't you invite Colleen, Bianca and Rachel over and have them go through your closets. They'll tell you the truth. And they won't sugarcoat it!"

"Fine, fine!" Paige huffed. "I'll have them come over this afternoon, but only to prove that you're wrong."

"No, I'm right," Anthony stated smugly. "You'll see."

Paige hated it when Anthony was right.

Colleen, Bianca and Rachel were staring at Paige's walk-in closet with horror.

"I knew it was going to be bad," Bianca whispered, "but not this bad. I think I need to sit down." She put a hand to her forehead, as if she were dizzy. "Where's the color? Have I gone color blind? Everything in this closet is muted. It's like somebody turned down the color on a television set!"

"It's worse than I thought," Rachel said, fingering through a rack of pleated skirts as if they were contaminated. "Much worse."

"Obviously we have a fashion emergency," Colleen said.

"I thought you said you bought a whole new fall wardrobe when you were out in California visiting your mother," Rachel said.

"I did!"

"Then why is everything in this closet nearly identical to what you wore last season?" Rachel asked.

"Maybe because I bought a lot of pieces from last year's collections?"

"Why?" Rachel wailed.

Paige shrugged. "They were marked down. You know how I can't resist a bargain."

"What happened to that cute low-cut red shirt I know you have?" Bianca asked. "You wore it that time Rob Kalinsky was flirting with you. You looked totally hot that night."

"That was last Valentine's Day," Paige said. "The night we went to that kegger party and you got sick, remember? After spending an hour with you in the bathroom Rob barfed all over me."

"I told you I had some bad mayo!"

"Whatever. Anyway, I threw that shirt away."

"Well, we'll have to replace it. Along with everything else!" Bianca declared. "There's nothing in this closet that's going to trap a man. Nothing!"

"Max is only seventeen years old!" Paige exclaimed. "He's hardly a man."

"That was just a figure of speech." Bianca stood up and twirled in front of Paige. "Take a look at what I'm wearing. Do I look like I'm seventeen years old?"

Bianca was wearing a form fitting brown suede miniskirt with a leopard print top that was low-cut.

"No, you look more like you're twenty-five. But then, you always have. Ever since we were freshmen and you stole

Victor Manning away from his girlfriend."

"Victor was the first senior I ever went out with."

"Until he found out you were a freshman," Colleen reminded. "And dropped you like a hot potato."

"But not until his ex-girlfriend spilled the beans," Bianca shot back. "And even she was unsure of how old I was. Don't you see, Paige? We have the advantage over boys our age. We can look older if we want. If we look twenty-five and catch the attention of a guy who's twenty-five, well, obviously we're doing something right! And that means guys our age will be all over us!" Bianca took another look at Paige's hanging clothes and threw herself dramatically onto Paige's bed. "This all says safe. Secure. Boring!"

"There's nothing surprising in here," Rachel said, sitting down next to her twin.

"Surprising?" Paige asked. "What do you mean?"

Rachel's eyes lit up. "Haven't you ever seen something in a store that you normally wouldn't buy for yourself? There's something so naughty about it, so forbidden, that you have to have it? Then you buy it and hide it away at the back of your closet, hoping you'll have the courage to someday wear it?"

"Mine's a red leather dress that laces up the sides," Bianca confessed.

"Mine's a pair of thigh-high white boots," Rachel said.

"Mine's a thong bikini," Colleen admitted as Paige's jaw dropped on that one.

"Everything in this closet is blah with a capital B," Bianca said.

"I like my clothes," Paige said, staring at the racks of expensive clothing. They were all designer names like Ralph

Lauren and Calvin Klein. "There's nothing wrong with them."

Bianca sighed. "Are you not listening to me?! We're young! We're beautiful! We're sexy! Why shouldn't we show it off? It's not going to last forever."

Paige squirmed. She liked her body; really, she did. She wasn't one of those girls who thought she was too fat or too thin. She just didn't like putting herself on display for the entire world to see. What was wrong with that?

She sighed. "Do I really need to do this?"

"Do you want to land Max?" Colleen shot back.

"Yes! But it shouldn't matter what I look like. Or what I'm wearing."

"Paige, he's a teenage boy. They think with their hormones. Or rather, they're led by their hormones and all those hormones collect in one place." Bianca and Rachel started giggling and Colleen joined in.

"You're going to need to turn up the heat," Rachel said. "And sizzzzle!"

"Are you up to the challenge?" Bianca asked, arching an eyebrow.

Paige bit her lower lip. Like Anthony had said, it was only for one weekend. She would think of it as acting. Yes, acting! And she would be playing a part. After all, she'd had small parts in some of Anthony's other films. She could do this. She'd just pretend it was another role.

"I guess so," she finally said.

Bianca rolled her eyes in exasperation. "*Such* enthusiasm! Stop! Please!"

"Paige!!!!" Rachel wailed. "Come on! This is going to be fun!"

"I'm nervous, all right?" Paige admitted. "I've never done something like this before. You know, aggressively gone after a guy."

"Well it's about time you did!" Bianca exclaimed. "Your problem is you worry too much, Paige. You're always afraid of what other people are going to say or think. Forget them! We're not going to steer you wrong. And we're going to be with you the entire weekend."

"All we have to do is shake things up a bit," Colleen said.

"How?" Paige asked, trying not to sound nervous.

Colleen's grin grew. "Three magic words that every girl knows: Daddy's credit card!"

Luckily, Paige's father was home that weekend. He'd gotten back to New York on Friday night after spending a week in Paris, but would be heading off to Amsterdam the following Wednesday for two weeks. He was working in his study when Paige knocked on the door and asked if she could borrow his credit card for some shopping. He'd given her the card without question, said hello to her friends, and told her to have a good time.

"Your father is a fox," Rachel said, after he'd given them his American Express gold card.

"Ew, gross!"

"No, seriously," Bianca said. "How come he never got remarried?"

"One word: Camille. She traumatized him for life. If he even hears wedding bells, he goes into hiding. Why are you two always asking about him?"

Bianca shrugged. "No reason. Just seems like a waste."

"I keep telling you he's like thirty years older than you. And he doesn't go for brunettes. Oh, and need I mention again that he's my dad?! The last thing I want is a stepmother who's the same age as me!"

"Don't worry, Paige," Rachel said. "Even though we like older guys, we don't like them *that* old!"

"Speaking of Camille, how is America's favorite daytime diva?" Colleen asked.

"I saw her yesterday on one of the Saturday morning talk shows," Rachel said. "Were you at the studio with her?"

"Camille's still Camille," Paige said, not wanting to discuss her mother. "We can talk about her later. Right now we've got something more important to focus on." She waved the American Express gold card in the air. "Shopping!"

They started at Victoria's Secret.

"Think of it as building a house," Colleen said as she and Paige walked through the store. "You need to have a strong foundation. You need to feel sexy in the underwear you're wearing. Nothing makes you feel sexy like something from Victoria's Secret."

"But Max isn't going to be seeing what's under my clothes," Paige pointed out.

Colleen smirked. "Are you sure?"

"Yes! I'm not that type of girl."

"Well, anyway, the underwear isn't for him. It's for you. It will make you feel confident."

"Try these on," Bianca urged, handing a stack of bras to Paige. "They're push-up bras, but without any padding! They make the most of what you have!"

"And Max is from the land of California blondes," Rachel chimed in. "That means one word: boobs!"

Paige resisted the lurid colors that Bianca and Rachel kept pushing on her. Instead, she settled for peaches and pinks and slipped into a dressing room. She had to admit, starting at herself in a full-length mirror, she did look good in the undergarments. And they felt fabulous! Silk was so much nicer than cotton!

And as much as she hated to admit it, Bianca and Rachel were right. They *did* make the most of what she had!

After they finished at Victoria's Secret, they decided to tackle shoes.

"Enough with the flats," Rachel exclaimed. "I don't think I saw one pair of heels in your closet. We need to get you a couple of pairs."

"And some boots!" Bianca added. "There's nothing hotter than a pair of boots!"

"Oooh! Let's go buy some Jimmy Choos or Manolo Blahniks! Please?" Rachel begged. "Pretty please?"

"Why not both?" Bianca suggested.

"Excellent idea!" Colleen exclaimed. "A girl can never have too many pairs of shoes."

"Or boyfriends," Bianca quipped.

Their first shoe stop was Jimmy Choo where the sales clerk brought out box after box of gorgeous shoes. Naturally, Bianca and Rachel had to try on a few pairs as well.

"These pinch my feet," Paige complained as she walked around the store in a five-inch crocodile sandal.

"Beauty is pain," Colleen said.

"Besides, look how long they make your legs look," Rachel said as she tried on a pair of pink python pumps. "Absolutely gorgeous!"

Paige admired her legs in a full length mirror. She hated to admit it, but Rachel had a point. The shoes did make her legs look good.

But the price!

"These are way too expensive," Paige said.

"When was the last time you splurged on yourself?" Bianca asked, trying to make up her mind between a pair of crystal jeweled sandals with a four-inch heel and a pair of beaded slides. In the end, she decided to take both.

Paige took another look at herself in the shoes. They *were* growing on her.

"Okay, I'll take them," Paige said quickly, before she changed her mind.

After Jimmy Choo, Paige resisted the urge to go to Manolo Blahnik. Instead, she and the girls went to the more reasonably priced Nine West where they found a pair of black boots, a sexy high-heeled sandal that laced up the leg and a pair of platforms. After that, they headed down to SoHo and went from one designer boutique to another, loading Paige down with skirts, blouses, tops and jackets in a wild array of colors and fabrics.

"I can't wear these clothes!" Paige wailed, inspecting herself as she tried on one outfit after another. Each outfit had the same thing in common. It was short and tight. "Anthony would call this designer white trash."

"No, he wouldn't," Colleen said. "Trust me."

"He wouldn't?" Paige asked skeptically.

"He'd call it *Eurotrash!*" Colleen exclaimed.

"That's just as bad!" Paige wailed.

"Are you crazy? What are you talking about?" Bianca asked. "You look hot! Hot, hot, hot!!! We'd wear something like that, wouldn't we, Rachel?"

"Absolutely," Rachel agreed. "You're just not used to showing off so much of yourself."

Paige took another look at herself in the mirror. "Colleen? You'd tell me the truth, right?"

"You're the daughter of daytime TV's number-one maneater. Some of that has gotta be in your genes! But if you don't trust me, here." Colleen held out a cell phone with a video screen. "Ask Anthony."

"Paige!" Anthony scolded from the video phone. "Our love lives are in your hands. Buy whatever the girls tell you to buy."

"But this isn't *me!*" Paige whispered.

"Why are you being so difficult?" Anthony moaned. "Bianca and Rachel have dated half the guys at Peppington Prep. From seniors to freshmen! They know their stuff."

Paige took another look at herself in the mirror. "You really think this outfit looks good on me?"

"The truth?"

"Yes!"

"Personally, as a gay guy, it does absolutely *nothing* for me. However—"

"So you *do* think it looks bad!"

"You didn't let me finish! A straight guy is going to feel differently. This outfit is gonna rock his world!"

"Is Anthony still trying to talk you into this outfit?"

Colleen moaned. "Come on, Paige! Make up your mind. Either you're going to take it or you're not. We've still got other stores to go to."

Paige turned back to the cell phone and stuck her tongue out at Anthony. "All right. All right! I'll buy it!"

"Bye!" Anthony said before disconnecting.

In the end, as they went from store to store, Paige allowed herself to be talked into the outfits the girls kept recommending. After all, when it came to acquiring boyfriends, Bianca and Rachel were the undisputed queens. Every other month, they had a hunky new guy. There was no arguing with success.

But Paige wanted more than a piece of arm candy. She wanted someone she could fall in love with. Even though Bianca and Rachel were always going out on dates, she really didn't think they cared about the guys they were dating. Otherwise why would they be going through boyfriends so fast? Why not take things slow? Try to get to know the person or at least work things out if there were problems? It was almost like they were flaunting their dates in their father's face. As a way of proving that they mattered to someone else.

After clothes shopping, the girls headed to the nearest Sephora and MAC shops, where they scooped up the latest lipsticks, mascaras, blushes, eye shadows, powders, lotions and perfumes.

"Now that I'm loaded down with everything I need for battle, I need to figure out a game plan," Paige said while they tried to hail a taxi.

"That's easy," Bianca said.

"It is?"

"Sure," Rachel said, looking away from her compact as she was applying a fresh coat of lipstick. "After all this shopping, you're ready to make your move. All you have to do is slip into one of these outfits and biology will take care of things! Max doesn't stand a chance!"

chapter eleven

The following morning Paige was at her locker when she felt a tap on her shoulder. She turned around and found Max standing behind her, his arms hidden behind his back.

"Hi!"

"Hi."

"How was the rest of your weekend?" she asked.

"Okay. How was yours?"

"The girls and I went shopping yesterday. We bought a couple of things for this weekend."

"Like?"

"You'll just have to wait and see."

"I did a little shopping, too."

"You did?"

Max gave her a mysterious smile. "Uh-huh."

Okay, something was up. "What'd you buy?"

"This."

Max held out the tiny pink shopping bag he'd been hiding behind his back.

"For me?" Paige was touched. "Max, you didn't have to do that."

"I know I didn't, but I wanted to."

"What is it?" Paige asked, rustling through the white tissue paper inside the bag.

"You'll see."

"Oh, he's adorable!" Paige cried, pulling out a small stuffed beagle.

"You seemed kind of bummed that you couldn't have a dog of your own because of your allergies. I figured this might be the next best thing."

"I love him." Paige gave Max a hug. A tight-hold-you-close hug and not a quick squeeze. Anthony would be proud of her. Then again, when he found out that Max had given her a gift . . . "Thank you."

"He even has a name. It's on his collar."

"Quincy," Paige said, reading his dog tag. "Thanks, Max. That was really thoughtful of you."

The bell for first period rang.

"I'm not going to leave him in my locker," Paige said, popping Quincy into her shoulder bag. "I'm going to take him to class with me. That way when I look at him, I'll think of you."

"Thanks again for inviting me this weekend. I'm really looking forward to it."

"Me, too," Paige said, remembering Rachel's comment about biology as she decided which sexy new outfit she was going to wear on Friday night. "Me, too."

"Where'd you get the pooch?" Anthony asked as he took his seat next to Paige in homeroom that afternoon.

Shoot! She'd forgotten to close her bag. She hadn't wanted Anthony to know about Quincy because she knew he'd get upset. She'd been trying to find the right time to tell him.

"It was a gift." She paused. "From Max."

Anthony stared at Paige in shock. "Max? *Our* Max gave you a gift?" His voice started to rise. "And you're telling me *now*? How many classes have we had together today?"

"Anthony, calm down."

"Calm down? Calm down? How can I calm down when he gave you a gift? For a teenage guy, that's like getting down on one knee and proposing."

"It is not."

"It is too and you know it. Guys only give gifts when they're serious."

"Well," Paige said, shrugging, "I guess Max is serious."

Anthony shot daggers at Paige. "I guess so."

"Please don't be mad at me!" Paige begged.

At that moment there was a hissing sound outside the window Anthony was sitting next to. "Ssss! Psst! Ants!"

Anthony left his seat and stuck his head out the second floor window. Standing outside the building was Max.

"Catch!" Max called, tossing a wrapped package up to Anthony.

Much to his surprise, Anthony caught the square wrapped box. "What is it?"

"Something I thought you might like. I came across it yesterday. I'll talk to you later. My mom's picking me up in five minutes. Dentist appointment."

Anthony slid back into his seat and started unwrapping the present from Max.

"What is it?" Paige asked.

Anthony gasped in delight. "A copy of *Bad Movies We Love*! I've been trying to get a copy of this book for years, but it's out of print." Anthony eagerly flipped through the pages. "There are hundreds of good-bad movies in here that we've never even seen and now we can hunt them down!"

Anthony gave Paige a smug smile. "Like you said. Guys only give gifts when they're serious."

"I wouldn't be too smug if I were you," Paige shot back, giving Anthony a smug smile of her own. "There's still this weekend."

Biology didn't take care of things that weekend.

Mother Nature did.

The Friday they left for the Hamptons, it rained. And not just a light spritz, but buckets and buckets of cold gray rain. Max and Paige didn't get to talk much on the drive up because he was driving and she was too busy giving him directions so they wouldn't get lost. In the backseat, Bianca and Rachel were loudly complaining about being booted from the reality show "Working Girls" earlier that week.

"What happened?" Colleen asked.

"We refused to wash dishes," Bianca said, holding up her hands. "Do these hands look like they should be soaking in greasy, sudsy water?"

"Ever hear of rubber gloves?" Colleen asked.

Bianca stuck her tongue out at Colleen. "We asked and they wouldn't give us a pair."

"Then what did you do?"

"We threw the dishes out and bought a new set at Saks," Rachel said. "Limoges. *Très* expensive! They were trimmed in gold."

"And the problem with that was . . . ?"

Bianca waved a hand dismissively. "Apparently the dishes we threw out were family heirlooms. They'd been in the family for like, I don't know, fifty years?"

"Sixty," Rachel corrected.

"But you should have seen them!" Bianca wrinkled her nose. "All chipped and faded. They came on a boat with the grandparents when they immigrated from Ireland."

"The dishes we bought were *much* nicer," Rachel said. "I don't know what the family was getting so upset about. They acted like we'd murdered their firstborn or something the way they were crying."

"I think it's called family history," Colleen said. "Memories. Tradition. Those are things that are irreplaceable."

"Whatever," Rachel said. "Our thougtfulness got us cut from the show."

"Don't you mean thought*less*ness?" Colleen asked.

"If those dishes meant so much to the family, they wouldn't have taken a check for $25,000 from the producers for the so-called mental anguish and distress that we caused," Rachel said.

"So much for family history!" Max laughed from the front seat.

For the rest of the car ride, they listened to CDs, as well as Bianca and Rachel strategizing their next career move.

"I think we should get invited to a movie premiere and have a wardrobe malfunction," Bianca said. "That would get us some attention."

"Great idea!" Rachel shrieked. "But it's got to be an event that's televised live, or what's the point?"

After a while, Paige tuned out the twins. As he was driving, she had the urge to place her hand on Max's shoulder—just as a way of letting him know she was there for him—but she didn't. It seemed like something a girlfriend would do.

Paige studied Max's profile. He seemed unaware that she was watching him, so intent was he on making sure they arrived safely. He really was a handsome guy. What would it be like to kiss him? Would he be a gentle kisser, or would his kisses be hard and demanding? Some guys liked to go slow when they kissed while others seemed insatiable. It usually depended on the guy's personality. In her experience, jocks were impatient. They wanted to get the kisses over with so they could move on to other activities (not that she allowed the other activities that they often wanted to pursue). Guys who were more into arts and culture took their time with kissing. They enjoyed it, savored it and made sure the girl they were kissing was as into it as they were.

Paige suspected that Max would be a very slow kisser. She could see kissing him for hours and hours. He'd probably even set the mood. If it was indoors, there'd probably be candles. Flowers. Or maybe an afternoon on a park bench. Red and gold autumn leaves falling from the trees. Small children running around with dogs barking and nipping at their feet. Couples walking hand in hand. And then the rest of the world would fade away as Max leaned closer, taking her face in his hands before leaning forward and . . .

"What are you thinking?"

Paige blushed. She'd been so preoccupied with thoughts of kissing Max that she hadn't been aware that they were in line to pay a bridge toll. Thank God it was dark inside the car!

"Nothing," she answered.

"You sure?" Max asked with a naughty grin, as if he could read her mind.

"Just daydreaming."

Max pulled up to the toll booth and paid the attendant. "Must have been a nice daydream. You were miles away."

Paige blushed again. "It was."

From the backseat, she could feel Colleen pressing her foot into the back of her seat, signaling her to make some sort of move. But what? They were in a car! With three people in the backseat! She ignored the nudge and turned the volume up on the CD player.

Three hours later—the bad weather had made the ride longer—they finally arrived in East Hampton.

"Where can I park?" Max asked.

The driveway leading up to the house was being repaved so Max had to park at the bottom of the driveway and they had to carry their suitcases up to the house in the rain. By the time they got inside, they were all soaking wet. It didn't help that the house was as cold as a freezer. The first thing Paige did was turn on the heat while asking Max if he would start a fire in the fireplace.

"We're going to go upstairs and slip into some dry clothes," Paige told Max. "Your room is at the end of the hall

146

to the right. My room is on the left. If you can't find it, just call out."

"Will do."

"This is the perfect opportunity to wear one of your new outfits!" Bianca whispered excitedly as they walked upstairs.

"Are you insane?" Paige said, her teeth chattering. "I'm freezing! All I want is a pair of thermal underwear, some thick socks and a sweater!"

Rachel pouted. "That's not going to get Max's attention."

"Look, Rachel, there's no way I'm going to be parading myself around in short little skirts and skimpy blouses in this weather. You think I want to get pneumonia?"

"We should have thought to put together a backup wardrobe," Colleen said. "But the weatherman didn't say anything about rain this weekend."

"Maybe it'll be sunny tomorrow," Paige said.

"Well, if you're going to insist on wearing a sweater tonight, then go braless!" Bianca said. "Boys like girls who bounce."

"I will not!"

Bianca threw her hands up in the air as she and Rachel headed for their room. "Hopeless. Absolutely hopeless!"

"It's only one night," Paige called after them as she followed Colleen into their bedroom. "I'm sure the weather will be better tomorrow. When it is, I'll be able to show a little more skin. But tonight I'm covering it all up!"

"Can I give you some advice?" Colleen asked as they started unpacking.

"What?"

"Listen to the twins. They know their stuff!"

"You're saying I should go braless?"

"No! But you must have a low-cut fluffy sweater in one of your drawers."

"Actually, I do," Paige admitted, opening a drawer and taking out a violet sweater made of angora.

"Nice! Fabulous color! You're going to look *so* cute in it."

"But the sleeves are short! And it's cold!"

"Hey, we all have to suffer for beauty. Now put it on!"

"Okay, okay," Paige grumbled, pulling her head through the sweater's opening.

After changing, the girls headed back downstairs to the living room, where Max had a roaring fire going. He'd also changed out of his wet clothes into a green turtleneck, brown pullover sweater and brown corduroys. His wet hair was slicked back and his cheeks were red from the heat of the fireplace. He looked like he'd stepped right out of an ad for Ralph Lauren. At that moment, all Paige wanted to do was snuggle up to him.

"You know what we need to set the mood?" Colleen said. "Some hot buttered popcorn and cocoa!" She grabbed Bianca and Rachel by the arms and headed in the direction of the kitchen. "We'll be back once it's ready."

Paige wanted to kill Colleen. Could she be any more obvious that she was leaving them alone on purpose?

"Nice house," Max said.

The décor of the summer house was very relaxed and laid-back. Lots of sheer draperies, pine and blond wood furniture, light green rag rugs scattered on hardwood floors, walls that were painted cream and yellow and eggshell white. It was like having a little bit of the beach indoors.

"Thanks. My dad does a lot of entertaining out here during the summer." Paige sat down on the couch, hoping Max would join her. Instead, he remained sitting on the floor next to the fireplace. Should she join him? But then she'd be invading his personal space. And she'd already sat down. It would look strange if she got up and joined him, wouldn't it? Why hadn't she thought to sit next to him on the floor?

"Are you hungry?" Paige asked. "We can order in. I can call Nick & Toni's or Della Femina. And Citarella has takeout. I'm going to call them to deliver some groceries in the morning."

"I'm not really hungry."

Even though Max had started a fire, the room was still cold. Paige walked over to the fireplace and threw some more wood on top of the fire. She shivered while watching the flames grow. Why had she listened to Colleen and worn this stupid sweater?

"Hey, are you cold?"

Before Paige could answer, Max was by her side, taking off his pullover. "Here, put this on."

"Thanks," Paige said, slipping into the sweater. *And thank you, girls! I'll never turn down your advice again!* The sweater smelled like Max. Citrusy and soapy. They were standing so close together, their noses were almost touching.

Kiss him! Come on! Kiss him! For once in your life, be daring. Spontaneous. Take him by surprise! Make the first move. Think how shocked Anthony would be!

Paige was just about to press her lips to Max's when he pulled away and said, "You know what? I'm pretty tired. That drive took a lot out of me. I think I'm going to turn in for the night, if that's okay with you."

What?! He wanted to go to bed? But it was only ten o'clock! The night was still young!

Say something, Paige. Anything! Don't let him get away! If you do, you'll only have one night left to figure things out.

Max smiled at her, and she smiled back as the silence between them grew.

Why wasn't he saying anything???

"Are you sure you want to turn in?" she finally asked, unable to come up with a compelling reason for him to not want to go to bed. So much for being a femme fatale! If Bianca had been here, she would have used her cleavage in some sort of tantalizing way to hypnotize Max and get him to do her bidding. It was definitely doable. She'd seen it happen more than once at Peppington Prep. "The girls will be back any second with the cocoa and popcorn."

"I'm going to skip it. Save my energy for tomorrow. Tell them I said good night."

"Okay." What else could she say? No?

Max got off the floor and brushed off the bottom of his cords. Paige couldn't help but notice how they hugged him nicely in all the right places.

"I'll see you in the morning. 'Night."

"'Night," she said, trying to keep the disappointment she felt out of her voice.

Paige watched Max disappear up the stairs. Ten minutes later, Colleen and the twins emerged from the kitchen with a bowl of buttered popcorn and a tray of cocoa-filled mugs.

"Where's Max?" Colleen asked, looking around the living room.

Paige walked over to Rachel and reached for a mug. She needed a chocolate fix. Desperately.

"He went to bed," she said, blowing on the steaming hot cocoa and taking a sip.

Bianca reached for a handful of popcorn and gave Paige a knowing look. "I hate to say I told you so," she said, munching on the popcorn, "but I told you so. You should have listened to me and gone braless!"

Going to see a horror movie by himself on a dark and stormy night had *not* been a good idea.

Anthony hurried down the deserted streets of Manhattan, looking for a taxi but unable to find one. Why would he? When the weather was this bad, they were practically nonexistent. And the subway line he needed to take was nowhere near here. Anthony struggled to keep his umbrella upright as the wind blew through it. He was walking past the Frosted Cupcake when he saw a light on inside. That was strange. Usually the bakery was closed by eleven. Anthony pressed his face against the bakery's dark window. He jumped back and screamed when a face loomed out of the darkness toward him. It took him a second to realize it was Roger. He was wearing black jeans and a black turtleneck, which was why he'd blended into the darkness.

"What are you doing out so late on a Friday night?" Roger asked as he unlocked the front door and let Anthony inside.

Anthony clutched his rapidly beating heart. "I could ask you the same question. You scared me!"

"Sorry," Roger apologized. "I was doing inventory in the stock room and then I was going to give the place a fast sweep before going home. I wanted to see if it was still raining outside. That's why I pressed my face against the window. I certainly didn't expect you to be on the other side of it!"

Anthony shook the excess water off his umbrella before closing it and walking inside. "I went down to Film Forum," he said. "You know, the revival house? They're showing horror movies from the '60s and '70s."

"I've been meaning to check that out."

Anthony was surprised. "You have?"

"I love those movies. They're so creepy. So much better than the horror movies made today with those indestructible killers. What are they up to now? *Friday the 13th Part 13? Halloween Part 9?* Gimme a break! What's the point of seeing them? You know the killer is going to survive to come back in another sequel."

"You're so right!"

"What did they show tonight?"

"*Rosemary's Baby.*"

Roger's face lit up. "That's one of my favorites."

"Mine, too! I don't know about you, but whenever I'm watching that movie, I feel like I can't breathe. There's such a great sense of paranoia. Is she really pregnant with the devil's baby, or is she just nuts?"

"Did you know they actually filmed it on the Upper West Side at the Dakota?"

"Of course I do! Hello! You're talking to a future film-maker."

"Oh. Cool! Well, what was the deal with those horror movies in the '70s?" Roger asked, walking back to the stockroom and picking up the pad he'd been making notes on.

Anthony followed after him. "Did you ever notice how they all had to do with the devil?"

"Yes!" Anthony exclaimed, getting excited. He *loved* talking about movies. "There was *The Exorcist, The Omen* and *Beyond the Door.* What I like about them is that everything is left to your imagination. You *imagine* the horror instead of seeing tons of blood and guts on the screen like what's done today. What your imagination can come up with is way scarier than anything a director can shoot."

"And then there are those TV horror movies from the '70s," Roger said.

"'Satan's School for Girls!'" Anthony shouted.

"'Let's Scare Jessica to Death!'" Roger shouted back.

"'Trilogy of Terror!'" Anthony and Roger exclaimed at the same time.

"I didn't know you were such a film buff," Anthony said.

"There's a lot of stuff you don't know about me," Roger said, scribbling on his pad before shutting off the light in the stockroom.

That was true. Anthony really didn't know much about Roger other than that he worked at the Frosted Cupcake and was a babe magnet.

"You're right," Anthony said. "We should rent some scary DVDs and watch them one night."

"That sounds cool."

"I should let you finish cleaning up."

"You can hang out if you want," Roger said. "It makes the time go faster when you have someone to talk to."

"I could help out."

"You wouldn't mind?"

"I wouldn't offer if I did."

"Okay. Thanks. You can just flip the chairs upside down on the tables. Then I'll run around with a broom and we'll be out of here."

While Anthony turned over the chairs, he and Roger talked. He found out that Roger had three younger sisters and lived only a few blocks away from the Frosted Cupcake. He hadn't decided where he wanted to go to college, but he was hoping he might win a scholarship to NYU.

"It would be nice to stay in the neighborhood, you know? And my parents can't really afford to send me away to school."

"My brother's a sophomore at NYU and he loves it."

"Are you thinking of going there?"

Anthony shook his head. "I want to go to UCLA. They have a great film program."

Roger slapped himself on the forehead. "Duh. That's right. You're the next Spielberg."

"Let's hope so! And you? Do you want to be a designer?"

"I don't know. I do like clothes and working with different kinds of fabrics, and I've made myself a few things, like shirts, but I don't know if I have the talent to become a designer that everyone would want to wear."

"You'll never know unless you try."

"True, true."

Fifteen minutes later, Roger had finished sweeping up the bakery. "That's it. We're all set. Ready to go?"

As they walked back outside, Anthony realized something. He never really hung out with straight guys. He didn't have anything against them and he had lots of straight male friends at school, but most of his close friends were female.

Paige. Colleen. Bianca and Rachel. He just found it easier hanging out with them.

But hanging out with Roger had been fun.

"I was serious about the DVDs," Anthony said as he opened up his umbrella and caught sight of an available taxi headed his way. "Taxi!" he called out.

"Just let me know when and where," Roger said. "You know where to find me."

The next morning the weather wasn't any better than the night before. Paige woke up to the sound of heavy raindrops hitting the roof.

"Am I hearing what I think I'm hearing?" Paige asked.

"You are," Colleen groaned from her bed across the room. Bianca and Rachel were in the guest room overlooking the garden at the front of the house while Max was staying in Paige's father's room across the hall.

"So much for Operation Hamptons," Paige said, knowing she wouldn't be wearing the skimpy outfits she'd brought. It was going to be another day of oversized sweaters and jeans.

"How about we console ourselves with a big country breakfast?" Colleen suggested. "I'll do the cooking."

Thirty minutes later, the kitchen was filled with the fragrant scents of hash browns, bacon, sausage, eggs, waffles, coffee and freshly squeezed orange juice. Bianca and Rachel were still sleeping, as was Max, but Paige and Colleen fixed themselves heaping plates and sat down at a table in the sun room, gazing out at a wet, sunless day.

"What should we do today?" Colleen asked.

"Unless the weather improves, we're stuck inside. We've

got DVDs that we can watch and there's a bunch of board games."

"Oooh! Monopoly! I get to be the little doggie! And when we play Clue, I want to be Mrs. Peacock. She was a full-figured gal."

"We can also make cookies and brownies."

"There's also the hot tub," Colleen reminded Paige. "That could take up a couple of hours. Why don't you go turn it on so it's all bubbling by the time Max comes down for breakfast."

"Great idea!"

"And maybe while you and Max are soaking, the twins and I will go on a shopping spree, leaving you and Maxie with a little alone time."

"Don't you dare!" Paige warned.

"Anthony would be so disappointed."

"Not if he doesn't know!"

Paige headed out onto the deck where she pulled the tarp off the top of the tub and then reached for the switch that would begin heating the water.

But when she flipped the switch, nothing happened.

The motor for the hot tub didn't come on.

The water remained still.

Paige tried the switch again and again, waiting for the bubbles to start appearing.

"What's taking so long?" Colleen called out.

"It's not working."

"What?"

"You heard me," Paige said, trying not to panic. "The hot tub isn't working!"

chapter twelve

Anthony woke up to the sound of buzzing.

At first the sound was so low and soft, he really didn't pay any attention to it. He just turned his head on his pillow and nestled deeper under the sheets.

But then the buzzing got louder.

And louder.

Anthony swatted at the air with a hand, his eyes still closed. How had a fly gotten into his bedroom? But this really didn't sound like a fly. It sounded more like . . .

Anthony's eyes popped open in horror as he realized what the sound was.

"Morning, Ants!"

Sitting on the side of his bed, holding his electric hair clipper in one hand, was Paolo.

"What are you doing in here?" Anthony gasped, scurrying

against the headboard of his bed. "And why do you have that *thing*? I thought we were over our fight."

"Oh we are, we are," Paolo said, waving the vibrating clipper. "I just wanted to have a little chat."

Anthony kept his eyes glued on the hair clipper. "A chat?"

Paolo nodded. "Uh-huh. See, a couple of the guys are coming over tonight. We're going to have a poker game."

"What does that have to do with me?"

"I want you to make yourself scarce tonight. Disappear. Vanish. I want the place to myself. Go hang out at Paige's place."

"I can't."

Paolo gave his brother a look of disbelief, lunging with the clipper. "*What* did you say?!"

Anthony screamed and threw his hands over his head. "Don't cut my hair! Paige is out of town. She went to her house in the Hamptons. But don't worry, I won't hang around tonight. I swear!"

"How come you didn't go with her? Are you guys fighting?"

"She's having a romantic weekend."

"A *romantic* weekend?" Paolo asked, switching off the clipper. "With who?"

"Max."

Paolo's eyes widened in shock. "Max?! What is she, crazy? She hardly knows anything about this guy and she goes off alone with him?" Paolo jabbed a finger in Anthony's chest. "And you let her! I bet this was your idea, wasn't it? All part of your stupid, 'Is he or isn't he?' scheme."

"No! It wasn't my idea! It was Paige's," Anthony explained, rubbing his chest.

"Stop being such a baby. I barely tapped you."

"And she didn't go alone with Max. Colleen, Rachel and Bianca went with her."

"That's a relief."

Anthony looked at his brother suspiciously. "Why do you care who Paige spends the weekend with?"

"I don't."

"Then why did you flip out when you heard she'd gone away with Max?"

"I didn't flip out."

"Yes, you did," Anthony stubbornly insisted.

"Unlike you, baby bro, I was once a straight high school boy and—"

"We still don't know if he's gay or straight!" Anthony interrupted.

"And I know how they think," Paolo continued. "Especially when they're around pretty girls like Paige."

"You think Paige is pretty?"

"Am I blind?"

"I've just never heard you mention it."

"Why would I?"

Anthony shrugged. "I don't know."

Paolo got up from the bed. "So, are we clear about tonight? I get the penthouse to myself and you get to keep your bouncing and behaving hair."

"I'll be gone by six. Is that early enough?"

"Perfect."

Anthony watched as Paolo left his bedroom. A thought had popped into his mind, but it was so outrageous, so over the top, that he ignored it. For just a second, he had thought Paolo was jealous of Max being alone with Paige, but why would he feel that way? Paolo barely got along with Paige and was always bickering with her. It had to be his overactive imagination. Yes, that's what it was. His overactive imagination. He wouldn't even mention it to Paige. She'd just laugh at him.

"What do you mean it's not working?" Colleen asked, joining Paige out on the deck where the hot tub was.

"Just what I said. When I turn it on, nothing happens."

"Maybe you should call your father."

"Good idea."

Paige went to her room to get her cell phone. Ten minutes later, she was back in the kitchen, a frown on her face.

"Uh-oh," Colleen said, looking up from the maple syrup she was pouring over her waffles. "You don't look happy."

"The hot tub isn't working. It needs to be fixed."

"Fixed? You mean it's broken?"

"Yep."

"Why didn't your father tell you?"

"Why would he? He didn't think I'd be using it. I'd also like to mention that he didn't seem too thrilled that I wanted to use it."

"No!"

"Yes." Paige sat back down at the table and began nibbling on a sausage link.

"After all, I'm still his little girl. Soaking in the hot tub with my girlfriends is fine. But with a guy? I think he was remembering his bachelor days and the wild times he used to have. At least that was the vibe I was getting."

"Maybe you should call Camille. She'd be thrilled."

Paige took a sip of her orange juice. "You know who's not going to be thrilled? Max. I promised him a weekend with a hot tub. Now the hot tub's not working. He's going to think I lured him out here under false pretenses."

"I'm sure he'll understand. Max doesn't seem like the type to hold a grudge."

"You think?"

Colleen shrugged. "We'll have to wait and see."

Max arrived in the sun room ten minutes later. After he had fixed himself a plate, Paige told him about the hot tub.

"It's broken?" he said. "There's no chance of fixing it?"

Paige couldn't help but notice that he looked like a disappointed little boy on Christmas morning who didn't find any presents under his tree.

"I'm really sorry. My dad didn't think I'd be using it. That's why he didn't mention it wasn't working."

"Oh."

And that was all Max said. He didn't say anything else.

"I feel awful about this," Paige apologized.

Max shrugged, pushing away his plate. "So what are we supposed to do with the rest of our time?"

He was mad. She could tell, but he was trying not to let it show. Paige didn't understand people like that. If there was a problem, she liked getting things out in the open and discussing it.

"Once the twins are up, we'll make a game plan," Colleen said. "We're going to have a blast this weekend!"

"I guess," Max sighed, taking a sip of his orange juice.

Paige studied Max across the table. What was going on with him? Last night he'd shown zero interest in her. Yes, it had been a long drive, but had Max *really* been so tired that he needed to go to bed at ten o'clock?

Or had he not wanted to be alone with her?

Maybe he didn't have romance on his mind the way she did. Maybe he had just been looking forward to a weekend in the Hamptons with four girls.

Hanging out with them in a hot tub, of course.

She could just imagine that story making the rounds in the boys' locker room at Peppington Prep. If Max was straight, he'd instantly bond with the other guys. If he was gay—and pretending to be straight—well, telling all the other guys about his weekend would make them think he was one of them.

Max came out ahead either way.

But the hot tub was broken and the bottom line was that Max was disappointed.

How could she fix things?

She needed some outside assistance. When the twins finally arrived in the sun room, Paige slipped into the bathroom and called Anthony on her cell phone.

"How's the weekend going?" Anthony asked.

"It's not. If you look out your window, you can see it's raining. It's freezing up here and I'm wearing nothing but shapeless sweaters and jeans. So much for the teeny skirts and halter tops and bikinis that I had planned to wear. Oh, and the hot tub is broken."

"Hmmm. This does present a challenge," Anthony said. "How to show off the goods when the goods are heavily under wraps? What's on the agenda for today?"

"Board games. DVDs. Maybe some baking."

"Any card games?"

"Probably. Why?"

"You could always play strip poker."

"I don't know how to play poker. And even if I did, I wouldn't!"

"Okay, what if you come out of the bathroom wrapped only in a towel and then *accidentally* drop it."

"So he can see me *naked*?! Absolutely not!"

"You're not making this easy for me, Paige."

"Come on, Anthony. Think! I know you can come up with something."

"We need to get the two of you alone in a situation that appears innocent but has an undercurrent of sexual tension. But what?" There was silence at the other end of the line. "I've got it! It's a little bit obvious but it could work, especially if he *is* straight. I can't think of a straight guy not being flattered by this."

"What? What?"

"You should *accidentally* walk into his bedroom in the middle of the night. Pretend you woke up for a glass of water and on the way back to your room, still half-asleep, you went through the wrong door."

"And then?"

"Do I have to spell everything out for you?" Anthony huffed. "Isn't it obvious? Fall into his bed! What else?"

Paige laughed. "I suppose it could work. But what's it going to prove?"

"Paige, honey, trust in biology. If Max is straight and you fall into his bed, you'll know if he's interested or not. Especially if you extend the encounter. You know, act dazed and confused. Touch him. Press yourself against him. Don't be so quick to jump out of his bed."

"I guess it could work," Paige reluctantly admitted.

"Trust me, it will. But one more piece of advice."

"What?"

"This is very important, so listen carefully. Are you listening?"

"I'm listening!" Paige exclaimed, starting to get impatient. Anthony never got directly to the point. He always loved to drag things out, caught up in the drama of the moment.

"When you dress for this mission, make sure you're wearing a baby doll nightie and not one of those oversized T-shirts that you love so much! And make sure you're wearing some makeup. And—"

"Good-bye, Anthony!" Even though Anthony had given her a good idea, Paige now knew that he was being a wiseguy and yanking her chain. "I'll call you tomorrow with the results."

And with those final words, Paige disconnected a laughing Anthony.

When Paige returned to the sun room, she discovered that everyone had decided to play Monopoly. The breakfast dishes had been cleared away and the game board was open on the table. Max, who seemed to have gotten over his bad mood because he was laughing at something Bianca had said, was playing banker, dealing out money to everyone.

"How good are you at Monopoly, Paige?" Max asked.

"Pretty good," Paige said, taking the seat across from him. "And you?"

"Oh, I'm lethal! Watch out, because by the end of the game you're all going to be flat broke!"

"We'll see about that," Colleen said as she shuffled the Chance and Community Chest cards.

Four hours later the game was still going on and Max was winning.

"Eight, eight, eight," Max chanted as Paige got ready to roll the dice.

"Stop that!" Paige scolded. "I don't want to get an eight! If I do I'll land on Park Place and you have two hotels on it."

Max gave an evil Bart Simpson chuckle. "That's right. And if you land on Park Place, you're wiped out and I win the game!"

Bianca and Rachel, who had already gone broke, were in the living room listening to the latest Gwen Stefani CD and flipping through *Vogue* while Colleen, who was the third player to be eliminated, was in the kitchen making chocolate chip cookies. The scent of brown sugar and vanilla wafted into sun room.

"Mmmm. Don't those smell good?" Paige said.

"Forget about the cookies and focus on the game," Max snapped.

Whoa! Paige couldn't believe Max's abrupt tone. It was only a game! Yet Max played to win. Who would have thought he'd be so competitive? He'd been ruthless with everyone, buying up every piece of property he could get his hands on, putting up houses and hotels as soon as he could and refusing to make any sort of side deals.

Paige closed her eyes and threw the dice, hoping for a seven or less.

She opened her eyes.

She'd rolled two fours.

"Yes!" Max exclaimed, jumping out from his seat, hands thrown over his head in victory. "I win! I win! I win!"

Paige pushed away from the table. "You win."

"Hey! Wait a minute! You have to move your shoe around the board. And then you have to give me your remaining cash."

"Why? You won."

"The game's not over until you hand everything over to me."

The way he said that was kind of sexy. Was he flirting? Or just reveling in his triumph?

Part of Paige wanted to refuse. She hated being told what to do. She'd been that way ever since she was a little girl. And Max was so smug! There was nothing she hated more than a sore winner.

Paige started counting out loud. When she landed on Park Place, Max rubbed his hands together like a greedy miser and then held out an open palm.

"Cold hard cash, please."

Paige counted out the money she had left and placed it in Max's hand. "Now is the game over?"

"Game over!" Max exclaimed, distributing Paige's cash into his piles. "How about we play something else? Do you have Trivial Pursuit?"

The last thing Paige wanted to do was play another board game with Max. She took a quick peek out the window and saw it was still raining, even harder than it had the day before. Trapped! She smothered a sigh. The job of a good hostess was to keep her guests entertained. "I'll go get it."

chapter thirteen

After getting off the phone with Paige, Anthony tried to figure out what he was going to do that night. Paolo wanted him gone and he had to comply with orders. Otherwise . . .

Anthony shuddered, not wanting to imagine the consequences. Not that he was afraid of his brother or anything. But Paolo was a guy who stood by his word. He'd always been like that. Anthony even admired him for it sometimes. But he also knew when to stay out of his way.

He could go to Felix Fennimore's 18th birthday party that night, but did he really want to?

Whenever Felix threw a party, he invited the entire world—friends and enemies (which was the category Anthony fell into)—so he could show off to everyone. His parties were always major events. Great food, great music and usually a handful of celebrities. The party was being held in Chelsea at a private club and Anthony was sure there'd be lots of good-looking guys there. It wouldn't be a Felix party if there weren't.

Anthony turned over the invitation in his hand, trying to make up his mind. He hated going solo to parties and he really didn't hang out much with Felix's crowd. All of Felix's friends were superficial, caring only about the latest gossip. The latest clothes. The latest parties.

The exception was Max.

Max!

No matter how hard Anthony tried, he couldn't get Max out of his mind. What was the deal with him? Was he gay or straight, and would Paige be able to find out this weekend?

Anthony pushed thoughts of Max out of his mind. No, no, no! He was going to drive himself crazy if he kept thinking about him. Maybe he should go to Felix's party. It would be a good way to forget about Max and whatever was going on out in the Hamptons. And it would be better than feeling sorry for himself.

Saturday night could be the loneliest night of the week.

Anthony sighed, thinking about Ian. On Saturday nights, he and Ian used to go to the movies. Afterwards, they'd grab something to eat and then spend the rest of the night talking.

And kissing.

Anthony tossed the party invitation on his dresser and opened the top drawer, moving around a pile of socks until he found what he was looking for, hidden away in the back.

It was a framed photo of himself and Ian.

The photo had been taken last June in Central Park after they'd gone to the Gay Pride Parade. It had been a sunny day and they were sitting on the Great Lawn, leaning into each other, arms wrapped around the other's shoulders, heads touching, smiling into the camera. They'd been so happy back then. Why had everything gone so wrong?

Anthony traced Ian's features with a finger. The hazel eyes that he'd loved looking into. The shoulder-length brown hair that was soft to the touch and always smelled like lemons. The lips that he could spend hours kissing.

Anthony sighed. He hadn't thought of Ian in a couple of weeks, but every so often he would pop into his mind. He supposed that was to be expected. After all, Ian had been his first serious boyfriend. He'd had deep feelings for Ian, and when you have feelings for someone you can't just turn them off the way you could turn off a running faucet.

In the early days of his breakup with Ian, he'd walked around with a dull ache in his heart. At night he couldn't sleep and when he was awake, all he could think about was Ian. He'd want to pick up the phone and call him, just to hear his voice, to ask if they could start over, but he didn't.

Instead he remembered the reasons why he and Ian had broken up and his anger returned, giving him the strength to move on.

Anthony picked up the party invitation, turning it over in his hands, trying to make up his mind. Maybe he should go to Felix's party. Maybe it was time to move on.

But then he wondered if Ian was going to be at Felix's party. He knew they were still friends. Would he come all the way down from Boston for it?

Anthony's stomach began to flutter as he remembered the way Ian made him feel when they kissed.

It had been so great between them in the beginning. Anthony remembered how he and Ian had first met. They'd been at the Barnes & Noble in Chelsea (where else would you go to find a possible boyfriend?) and Anthony had been in the fiction section, looking for something to read.

"This book is really good. I couldn't put it down."

Anthony turned around to see a dark-haired guy around his age standing behind him, holding out a copy of *The World of Normal Boys*, by K. M. Soehnlein. Anthony took the book from his hand, turning it over to read the back cover copy.

"It's a gay coming-of-age story set in New Jersey in the '70s. I could really relate to the main character."

"Is he the one who's gay?" Anthony asked, holding his breath for the answer. He was no dummy. Unless he was wrong, this guy was interested in him and had just given him a big clue.

"Yes."

Anthony lowered the book and took a closer look at the guy standing next to him. He was cute, no doubt about it. Anthony gave him a smile. "Hi, I'm Anthony."

"Ian."

Anthony held up the book. "This looks good. I'm going to buy it."

"Maybe we could get together and talk about it after you've read it?"

"Sure," Anthony said, trying to sound calm while his insides were quivering with excitement. *He likes me! This cute guy likes me!!!* He gave Ian his cell phone number, taking his. "I'll call you once I finish reading it."

Ian smiled. "I hope you're a fast reader."

After buying the book, Anthony raced home and spent the rest of the day reading so that he could call Ian the next day. (It didn't hurt that Anthony loved the book and the pages flew by.) They met for coffee at the Frosted Cupcake and instantly clicked, discovering that they had many of the same interests.

And it was at the Frosted Cupcake, on their second date, that they kissed for the first time.

Roger was on the way to their table with another order of cupcakes when Ian said, "There's something I've been wanting to do since I met you the other afternoon."

"What?" Anthony asked distractedly, busy scraping a blob of vanilla frosting off a cupcake wrapper.

"This," Ian said, as he leaned across the sofa, pulled Anthony into his arms and kissed him.

For Anthony, the kiss had been totally unexpected. He was enjoying his time with Ian, trying to figure out a way that he could make the first move, when Ian beat him to it.

For a first kiss, it had been the kiss of a lifetime. All Anthony had been aware of was the kiss. Ian was kissing him! In public! The entire bakery disappeared. The only person who existed was Ian and his magical lips. When Anthony finally landed back on earth, his head was spinning and he was tingling from head to toe.

Roger, to his credit, was unfazed. He might have looked startled for a second, but he quickly maintained his cool, putting their order down in front of them and leaving the check.

The second round of cupcakes was ignored. Instead, Anthony and Ian spent the rest of the afternoon in each other's arms, just kissing at the Frosted Cupcake. After that, they were officially a couple, calling each other all the time, going out together after classes, on the weekends and whenever else they could.

The more time Anthony spent with Ian, the deeper he fell in love with him.

He only wished that Ian felt the same.

It wasn't that Ian didn't have feelings for him. He did. He knew Ian cared about him. He showed him in countless little ways. Sending him e-mails. Leaving messages on his cell phone. Telling him he loved him.

That was in the beginning. But then as their relationship progressed, there were little arguments and spats. It seemed like Anthony could never do anything right. If he was even five minutes late for a movie, Ian would lose his temper. And then there was Ian's favorite catch phrase. Whenever Anthony did anything that annoyed him—like wanting to go down to Times Square and stand outside the windows of MTV's *T. R. L.* to catch a glimpse of his favorite pop princess or stay home to watch the season finale of his favorite show on the WB—he'd say, "You're such a high schooler!" The comment hurt. And it made Anthony feel inferior to Ian. Because he *was* a high schooler and Ian was the one going off to college in the fall. Ian was one step ahead of him, leaving high school behind, and probably looking to date someone more mature.

Anthony sighed. He was going to drive himself crazy if he tried to rework the past. What had happened with Ian was over and done with. It was time to move on.

And Felix's party was the perfect place to do it.

So he didn't have a boyfriend, big deal. He was never going to find another one if he didn't go out and meet new people.

And maybe Max *was* his next boyfriend.

Maybe if he went to Felix's party, he'd be able to find out the truth. After all, Felix was pretty close to Max.

If anyone knew whether Max was gay or straight, it would be Felix. But would Felix tell him what he knew?

Anthony's eyes fell back on his invitation and he snatched it up.

There was only one way to find out.

There were good-looking guys everywhere.

Blonds. Brunettes. Redheads. Tall. Short. Thin. Muscular. It was like that disco song from the early '80s, "It's Raining Men." And all of them had that unmistakable air of the rich and wealthy. From head to toe, everything about them was perfect.

Anthony felt like he'd stepped into the pages of a fashion magazine. Wherever he turned, there was another designer label. Prada. Hugo Boss. Calvin Klein. Michael Kors. Versace.

The girls were dressed just as well as the guys and were standing around in little clumps, posing as if waiting for the paparazzi to arrive. Knowing Felix and his hunger for fame, they probably would.

Anthony had dressed in a John Varvatos peach shirt that he wore untucked with a pair of caramel-colored pants and brown boots, but compared to everyone else, he felt underdressed.

Music was playing loudly, with a DJ taking requests, and a silver disco ball was spinning in the air, scattering the dark room with bursts of light.

Anthony hated feeling so inadequate. What was wrong with a little individuality? Of being yourself?

"Anthony!" Felix exclaimed. "What are you doing here? I

didn't think you were coming."

Anthony turned around with a smile. "Surprise!"

Felix was wearing a pair of hip-hugging jeans that looked like they were spray-painted on, along with a muscle shirt that said, KISS ME! IT'S MY BIRTHDAY! The T-shirt did a nice job of showing off Felix's arms and chest, which were quite buff, much to Anthony's surprise. Gone was the string bean. When had Felix started hitting the gym?

"I see you've been admiring the muscle boys."

"It's hard to take your eyes off them."

"I'm sure if you spent half your life in the gym, you could look like that."

Anthony shook his head. "I doubt it."

Felix pointed to the front of his shirt. "No more talking. Do what the shirt says!"

Anthony really didn't have much of a choice. After all, it was Felix's birthday. He leaned forward to give Felix a kiss on the cheek and was nearly pulled off his feet as Felix's arms wrapped around him like the tentacles of an octopus. Before Anthony could even get ready to give Felix a kiss, Felix's lips descended upon his.

Ugh! Anthony tried not to gag. It was a wet, open mouth kiss. *Much* more kiss than he was expecting. It was like taking a spoonful of bad medicine. Blech!!!

Finally, the kiss ended and Anthony was released from Felix's iron embrace. "You're not a bad kisser, DeMarco."

"Thanks." Anthony resisted the urge to wipe his mouth across his shirt sleeve. Instead, he handed Felix a sealed envelope. "I didn't know what to buy you, so it's a gift certificate to Versace."

"Thanks." Felix tossed the card on a table filled with wrapped presents and other envelopes. He then looped his arm through Anthony's and led him out onto the dance floor. "You have to dance with the birthday boy. I won't take no for an answer!"

The song that was playing ended and was replaced by a Donna Summer disco classic.

"I love this song!" Felix screamed, tossing his arms in the air while dancing wildly.

Anthony started dancing with Felix. It appeared as if the birthday boy had a birthday buzz going. He knew there was an open bar in the back, although it was supposed to only be serving juice and soda to the underage crowd. Yet when Felix had kissed him, he'd tasted something slightly medicinal. And it hadn't been mouthwash. Maybe vodka?

"Tell me what you're doing here," Felix yelled above the music. "I would have thought you'd be out in the Hamptons with Max and the girls. You know, having a pajama party."

"Would Max want to have a pajama party with me?"

Felix shrugged. "I don't know. Would he?"

"You're the only one who can answer that question, Felix."

"You think?" Felix shook his head. "Sorry to disappoint you, Anthony, but Max doesn't tell me everything."

"I find that hard to believe."

Felix shrugged. "What can I tell you? Max is a man of mystery. He only tells you what he wants you to know. I haven't even set foot in his apartment, if you can believe it!"

"Really? What's up with that?"

"His father guards his privacy and doesn't like having strangers around. Plus, I think Max wonders if people are interested in being his friend only because he's the son of a famous chef. He keeps his guard up."

"I never thought of that. It must be tough for him. But we're all in the same boat because of our parents."

"True," Felix agreed. "But we've all known each other since kindergarten, when none of that stuff mattered."

"I guess you're right."

"You like him, don't you?"

"What?"

"You heard me," Felix yelled over the loud music. "You like him."

"Sure," Anthony answered cautiously, not knowing where Felix was going with his line of questioning. "He's a great guy."

Felix shook his head. "Don't try to con me, DeMarco. You *like* him. A lot." Felix wrapped his arms around Anthony's waist and danced against him. "But is he or isn't he? That's what you want to know. I don't have a clue. And neither do you. But you know I am. So why not get closer to me?"

And with that Felix threw his arms around Anthony in a hug, giving him another wet, sloppy kiss.

Okay, this was *not* a birthday kiss. This was something more. Anthony knew he should be flattered, but this was Felix. Felix! His sworn enemy. If Anthony didn't know any better, he would think Felix was trying to make him his date for the evening.

Suddenly, he remembered what Paige had told him at his back-to-school party. About Felix maybe liking him. Could she have been right? Did Felix have feelings for him? But he didn't have feelings for Felix!

He'd have to be careful about what he did or said next. He

didn't want to piss Felix off. That could be social suicide.

And then, he saw him. Coming through the front doors. Ian.

At first Anthony became excited. All the old feelings he'd once had for Ian came back in a rush. All he wanted to do was break free of Felix and run to Ian's side. He was powerless over the excitement that was being stirred up inside him.

He was wearing a three-quarter black leather jacket over a BU sweatshirt and distressed jeans with motorcycle boots. His hair was a little longer, kind of unwashed, and he hadn't shaved in days. But the grunge look worked for him. It made him look rugged. More masculine. Less like a high school boy.

Anthony loved it.

He was just about to step away from Felix when he saw Ian hold out his hand to a guy standing beside him.

A guy who he pulled close and kissed.

Anthony felt like he'd been punched in the stomach. Suddenly he couldn't breathe.

All he could do was watch the scene that was unfolding.

The other guy laughed and then grabbed Ian by the chin, pulling him close for another kiss. He was a blond with glasses and was also wearing a BU sweatshirt, jeans and motorcycle boots.

They were definitely a couple. Aside from the kissing, it was obvious from the way they were dressed. Anthony didn't know why, but some gay couples loved dressing like identical twins.

Anthony took a deep breath. Okay, Ian had moved on. There was no going back. But that didn't mean they couldn't be friends, right?

Anthony broke away from Felix and moved himself to the

side so he'd be directly in Ian's line of vision as he walked farther into the club.

As he drew closer, Anthony caught his eye and smiled.

But Ian didn't smile back.

He didn't nod or wave.

Instead, he turned the other way, grabbing his boyfriend's arm, pretending he hadn't seen Anthony.

Anthony felt like a knife had been stabbed into his heart. The pain was searing. Why did Ian have to go and do that? Why couldn't he come over, say hello and ask him how he was doing? Why treat him like the Invisible Man?

Anthony's Italian temper started bubbling and he was tempted to make a scene. A big one. Who did Ian think he was? *He* was the cheater! *He* was the one who had done Anthony wrong. From the way he was acting, you'd think *Anthony* had betrayed *him*!

No, he wasn't going to make a scene. Ian would love a scene. Then he'd get to play the injured party with his new boyfriend and trash Anthony. If he hadn't already. Anthony could hear him now, "*He never got over me. You know how immature high school boys can be. You go out on a few dates with them and they think it's forever.*"

"What's the matter, Anthony?" Felix asked, coming up to his side, watching as Ian disappeared into the back of the club. "Blast from the past? I guess I should have told you Ian was coming with his new boyfriend. It must have slipped my mind."

Anthony turned to face Felix. He wasn't buying the innocent expression on his face. He knew Felix was hoping for some drama. "Did it?"

"Are you going to go over to them? I think you should," he urged. "Just to clear the air."

You'd like that, wouldn't you? Anthony thought, noticing the hungry gleam in Felix's eye. *Some angry words. A tossed drink. Maybe even a slap and some rolling around on the floor. Plenty of dirt for next week's column.*

Suddenly Anthony was tired. All he wanted to do was go home and crawl into bed, pulling the sheets up over his head, shutting out the entire world. Who said being a gay teenager was easy? "You know what, Felix? I'm going to cut out."

"So soon? But you just got here! We haven't even cut the birthday cake."

"Suddenly I don't feel so well." *And if I stick around for your cake cutting, I might be tempted to shove your smug face right into it.*

"Heartsick?"

"Something like that."

"He's not worth it. Listen, why don't you give Ian a dose of his own medicine? There are lots of good-looking guys here. Ask one of them to dance. Show Ian that you're over him."

Anthony had never been into playing games. It took too much energy to hold a grudge and plot ways to get even. "I'm just going to go home."

"A bunch of us are going to go to the Clubhouse later. Why don't you come?"

The Clubhouse was a gay dance club on West 17th Street where there was a dance party every Saturday night. Anthony had never been, although he'd wondered about it for years.

"Would we be able to get in?" he asked.

"Do you have a fake ID?"

"Yes. Don't you remember when we all went to that dance club last March in the East Village to see that British band? You had to be twenty-one to get in."

"Oh yeah! That photo of you is soooo dorky!" Felix laughed.

"Hey, it got me into the club, didn't it?"

"Then you should be fine tonight. But if anyone at the door gives you a problem, just mention my name. We're going to get there around eleven."

"I'll see how I'm feeling."

"Come! If you're still feeling down, I guarantee you'll feel much better."

"I'll bet." Anthony knew that a lot of illegal drugs were easily available at the Clubhouse.

Suddenly, Anthony was afraid for his friend. Until tonight, it never occurred to him that Felix might be grappling with the same problems that he was. Or that Felix might go down a different path than him to deal with those problems. Could that be a reason why Felix was so nasty? Could his behavior be a defense mechanism? A way of coping with being gay? He gave Felix a quick hug. "Enjoy the rest of your party. Have a good time tonight, but be careful, okay?"

"Don't worry. I'm a big boy. I know how to take care of myself."

Did he? Anthony wondered.

Outside the club, it had stopped raining, but a cold wind was blowing. Anthony pulled up the collar of his peacoat as he walked down 8th Avenue. Everywhere he turned, there were couples—gay and straight—walking arm in arm or friends out for fun on a Saturday night, laughing and talking.

And here I am, all alone. Feeling like an outsider. What have I done wrong?

Anthony sighed. Maybe the best thing for him to do was to grab something to eat and go home. He'd hide out in his room. Paolo shouldn't have a problem with that. He'd already been gone for a couple of hours.

Walking down the next block, he could see the bright lights of a supermarket. He'd buy some veggies and hummus and a container of Ben & Jerry's and then head home.

Inside the supermarket, Anthony grabbed a basket and started loading it up. He grabbed a bag of baby carrots, a package of sliced celery, some pita bread and a container of hummus. The yellow apples looked good, so he threw one into his basket, as well as a box of raspberries. That should tide him over. Now for the ice cream.

As he walked down the aisles, Anthony noticed that there were some gay couples who were grocery shopping for the upcoming week. And they didn't look like they lived at the gym twenty-four/seven. Instead, they were regular-looking guys, debating which laundry detergent made their clothes smell fresher or which brand of pasta tasted better.

Watching these couples, Anthony suddenly felt hopeful. Here was proof that you didn't have to be a part of the gay party scene in order to be happy. You could be a regular person who washed clothes, cooked pasta, clipped coupons, did weekly grocery shopping and happened to be gay.

As he was making his way down the frozen food aisle, he

heard someone call out his name. The voice was familiar but he couldn't place it. When he turned around, he saw Roger headed his way, along with his latest glamazon.

"Hey, Anthony! I thought that was you. What are you doing down here? Don't you live on the Upper East Side?"

"I was heading home from a party and got the urge for munchies. How about you?"

Roger jerked a finger at his sidekick. "Amber and I have been studying and we decided to take a break. We're picking up some frozen pizzas."

Amber turned around a box of microwave pizza with her French-manicured fingers, squinting at the directions. "Do we have to defrost this first?" she asked, oblivious to the READY IN FIVE MINUTES! banner on the front of the box. "Because I don't want to wait. I'm really hungry."

Anthony wanted to roll his eyes. Great. Another airhead. What did Roger see in them?

Amber, who was wearing a low-cut pink sweater, leaned over the frozen food case for another pizza and Anthony got his answer. Duh. Stupid question. He could see what Roger saw in Amber.

"You want to have some pizza with us?" Roger asked as Amber joined his side, snuggling up next to him.

And watch the two of you make kissy-face at each other? I don't think so. I already got my daily dose of kissy-face at Felix's party.

"Thanks for the invite, but I'm kind of beat. I'm going to go home, eat my snacks and then go to bed."

Roger shrugged. "Okay. Guess I'll see ya around the bakery."

"Yeah, see ya."

"Bye," Amber said, waving her fabulous fingers.

Anthony watched as Roger and Amber headed for the cash registers at the front of the store, her arm wrapped around his waist.

I am not going to get depressed. I am not going to get depressed. I am NOT going to get depressed. So what if Roger's always got a new girlfriend? He's a straight high school boy. They're allowed.

Anthony turned back to the ice cream case and threw in a container of Ben & Jerry's Chocolate Fudge Brownie. And Mint Chocolate Cookie. And Vanilla Caramel Fudge.

It was official.

He was depressed.

Anthony took a bite of his apple as he headed to the front of the supermarket. The crunchy sweetness of the apple didn't make him feel instantly better, but it helped.

As he started unloading his basket for the cashier, Anthony checked the time on his watch, wondering what was going on out in the Hamptons. Hopefully, Paige was having a better Saturday night than he was.

chapter fourteen

$\mathcal{I}$t was showtime in the Hamptons.

The grandfather clock in the living room had just chimed twelve and everyone was asleep. Everyone, that is, except for Paige, who was in her bathroom, staring at herself in a mirror.

You can do this, she told herself. *You can do this.*

What was she so nervous about? All she was going to do was walk into Max's bedroom and fall into his bed.

It's not like they were going to *do* anything.

Of course, the whole purpose of this test was to see if Max *did* want to do *something* . . .

But they wouldn't.

This was nothing more than an experiment. An experiment in Biology 101.

She just had to remember Anthony's advice. Act dazed and confused. Initiate accidental body contact. Stay in his bed as long as possible.

Paige took another look at herself in the mirror. She was wearing a lace-trimmed peach nightie that showed just a tad of cleavage (thank you, Victoria's Secret!), she'd run her fingers through her hair so it looked like a wild, messy mane (for once she was following Anthony's advice) and at the insistence of Colleen and the twins, she was wearing a touch of makeup. Just some blush on her cheeks and a bit of mascara to give herself an enhanced "natural" look. She had to admit, even though she felt a little uncomfortable with her appearance, she did look pretty good. What straight guy would be able to resist this?

She was inspecting her image one last time when there was a soft knock on the bathroom door.

"Who is it?"

"Colleen."

Paige opened the door and let her into the bathroom. "What are you still doing up? I thought you were asleep."

"I figured you might need some support. Not getting cold feet, are you?"

"Of course not!"

"Then why are you hiding in here?"

"I'm not hiding!"

"Yes, you are. This is like the time in eighth grade when we went to Bianca and Rachel's birthday party and you heard that Michael Paxton was planning to kiss you during Spin the Bottle."

"Wouldn't you have done the same thing? Michael was the hottest guy in our class!"

"You tried to hide in the bathroom during the entire

game. Until I pulled you out. And wasn't it worth it?"

"Michael did know how to kiss," Paige said.

"You've been in here for at least a half hour. I've been timing you. If you can't go through with it, I'll do it."

"I can go through with it."

"Afraid that I'll squash him?" Colleen joked.

"Ha ha. Very funny. I'm going to do this. I *want* to do this. Besides, if I don't, Anthony will never let me live it down."

"Then what are you so nervous about? Come on, Paige. Fess up."

Paige chewed on her lower lip. "Do you really think he's going to buy my story?"

"If he's straight, what does it matter? He'll be flattered that you fell into his bed. And he'll get the message that you're interested in him!"

"Unless I'm not his type."

"If he's straight, any girl is his type. Let's go over your story again, alright? You woke up in the middle of the night. You were thirsty. You went to get a drink of water and on your way back to your room, you went the wrong way. Easy enough mistake to make because the hallway was dark, you were half asleep and you couldn't see where you were going."

"He's really going to believe this?"

Colleen pushed Paige out of the bathroom. "There only one way to find out."

Colleen headed back to bed while Paige, her heart pounding, took a deep breath, walked down the hall and slowly opened the door to Max's bedroom. It was pitch black inside the room but she could see him lying in bed, his back toward her, covered from head to toe in a down comforter.

When Paige closed the door behind her, she could barely see. She listened for the sound of Max's breathing and as she did, she realized something.

This is actually going to be the first time that I'm alone in the same bed with a guy!

Putting her hands in front of her like a blind woman, she shuffled toward the bed, still listening for Max's breathing, hoping it would guide her.

But she must have miscalculated her steps because as she got closer to the bed, she rammed her left foot into the nightstand next to it, stubbing her pinky toe. A jolt of pain shot through her body.

"Ow!"

The words were out of Paige's mouth before she could stop them. She couldn't help it. It hurt!

She bent over to massage her sore toe, pressing one hand on the bed's mattress for support.

As she did so, Max bolted out of bed in surprise.

Before Paige could pull away from the bed, his head slammed into her face, sending her falling to the floor.

The pain was nothing compared to what she'd experienced seconds earlier. It was ten times worse!

"EEEOUCHHHHHHH!!!" she screamed, making her earlier "ow" sound like a whisper.

"Paige? Is that you?" Max asked, his voice groggy with sleep. "What happened? What's going on?"

Nothing is going on, Paige thought, grasping her nose. *Absolutely nothing. Except I'm in excruciating pain!*

After scrambling out of bed and turning on a light, Max quickly took control of the situation. He carried Paige back to his bed, arranging the pillows and blankets around her while she explained how she wound up in his room. Thankfully, he didn't question her story. Then he raced down to the kitchen and came back with a small plastic bag of ice, pressing it gently against her nose, asking her if she was in pain and if she wanted him to take her to the nearest emergency room.

While Max had been running around, Paige couldn't help but notice that he was only wearing a pair of Joe Boxer shorts. They were black with yellow smiley faces on them.

Max had a body to die for!

"Paige, I'm really sorry about your nose."

For the last half hour, Max had been apologizing nonstop.

Paige removed the icebag she was holding over her nose, tearing her eyes away from the sculpted perfection of Max's chest. Did it feel as hard as it looked? She wished she could touch it. Why hadn't she thought to rest her head against it when he'd carried her to bed? Oh, that's right. She'd been preoccupied. With pain. "That's okay, Max. It wasn't your fault. Really."

It was my fault for thinking Anthony's stupid plan would work! The next time she saw him, he was a dead man!

So much for glamour. So much for testing Max's straightness. She looked like Marcia Brady from the infamous "Oh, My Nose!" episode of "The Brady Bunch." It was like she had a big fat potato smack in the middle of her face. And her "natural" look was all smeary from the ice bag she'd been pressing against her face.

"You're so gorgeous, I'd feel awful if I did anything to mess up your looks."

Had Paige heard Max correctly? He thought she was gorgeous? No, he did *not* just say that. But she had to know!

"You think I'm gorgeous?" she asked, hating herself for wanting to hear the compliment again.

"All the guys at school think so."

Hmmm. He'd avoided a direct answer to the question. Why? Not interested or did he not want to mislead her if he was gay? Then again, Max was engaging in conversation with guys who found her gorgeous. That might mean something. Obviously, they were straight. Which means they were talking about other girls as well. Unless Max was pretending to be straight while talking with these guys? Just going with the flow?

"You're lying," Paige said. "They do not."

But if they did, where were they?!

"Why would I say something that wasn't true?"

I don't know. Maybe to flatter me? To get me to like you? But you don't have to do that because I already do!

Max placed both his hands at the sides of Paige's face, gently lifting her head up toward the light next to the bed. "It doesn't look like it's broken, but you really should make sure."

Paige smothered a tiny sigh. Max's hands were so gentle. It was like he was afraid of bruising her. "I will. Once we're back in Manhattan." Paige slid out of the bed. "It's getting late. I better get back to my room. You're probably exhausted."

Max slid back under the sheets. "I'll see you in the morning. Hopefully by then the swelling will have gone down and you'll be your usual gorgeous self."

He'd used the word gorgeous again!

"Oh, and Paige?"

She paused in the bedroom doorway and turned around, her heart fluttering. Part of her was hoping he would ask her

189

to stay. To slip under the sheets and snuggle up against him. Outside she could hear the wind howling. She was sure there was no place in the world cozier than being next to Max.

"Yes?" she asked hopefully.

Max reached out to turn off the light next to his bed. "Maybe you should leave a pitcher of water next to your bed from now on. That way the next time you're thirsty, you won't have to get out of bed." He clicked off the light. "Good night."

"Good night," Paige said, thankful for the darkness so Max couldn't see the way her cheeks had turned burning red.

"Why didn't you return any of my calls last night?" Anthony asked. "I must have called at least five times. And then you weren't in school today. I'm *dying* to find out what happened on Saturday night!"

"This is what happened," Paige said, stepping out from behind the front door of her apartment on Monday afternoon.

Anthony gasped. "What happened to your nose?"

"*You* happened to my nose."

"Huh?"

"This is all your fault!"

"My fault? *My* fault? How can that be? I was in New York City the entire weekend."

"It was your bright idea that I walk into Max's bedroom after getting 'lost' on my way back from the bathroom."

Anthony cringed. "The plan backfired?"

"The plan backfired."

"How?"

Paige pointed to her swollen nose. "What do you mean *how*? Isn't it obvious? His head slammed into my face."

"Ouch!"

"It was more than ouch. More like double ouch!"

"Did you have to go to the hospital?"

"No. Luckily there was no bleeding and I could still breathe through it. I went to my doctor for an x-ray this morning. That's why I wasn't in school. He says it's just swollen."

"Can I call you Marcia from now on?"

"Very funny."

Anthony walked into the living room, tossing his book bag on the hardwood floor and plopping himself down on the couch. "Okay, so I guess we're back to square one."

"*You're* back to square one. I'm throwing in the towel."

Anthony jumped off the couch. "What?!"

"You heard me."

Paige had done a lot of thinking over the past two nights. As much as she liked Max, she wasn't getting any sort of sense that he was interested in her romantically. Even with a swollen nose, the rest of her body had been on display in his bed and she hadn't caught him peeking at anything he shouldn't have. Yes, he was sweet and nice, but she wasn't feeling a romantic spark coming from him. Maybe there wasn't one there.

"But you can't give up!"

"Why not? We've been at this for what? A couple of weeks? And we haven't made any progress."

"So it's going to take some more time. Isn't the end result worth it?"

"For one of us, maybe."

"Maybe?"

"Don't you think by now that if Max were interested in either one of us, we'd know it? He would have done or said *something* to show us his interest."

"Not necessarily. Maybe he's just shy."

"Maybe."

"Nothing at all happened this weekend to give you a clue whether he plays for your team or mine?"

"He did say something interesting," Paige admitted.

"What?"

"I'm gorgeous."

"He said that? He said, 'Paige, I think you're gorgeous.'"

"His exact words were 'You're so gorgeous, I'd feel awful if I did anything to mess up your looks.' This was after he'd slammed my nose with his head, so he had to say something. And then when I asked him if he thought I was gorgeous, he said all the guys at school think so."

"I could have told you that."

Paige's temper flared. "Then why haven't you? Maybe if I knew someone else was interested in me, I'd be spending less time obsessing over Max."

"You don't like hearing stuff like that."

"Excuse me?"

Anthony sighed. "Paige, you run away from compliments. You hate hearing nice things about yourself. As for the guys at school, the ones who think you're gorgeous?"

"Yes?"

"They think you're unapproachable."

"Unapproachable? That's crazy! Why would they think that?"

"You give off an ice princess vibe."

Paige could not believe what she was hearing. "Ice princess vibe?! I do not!"

"You do too."

"How can you say something so horrible to me?"

"It's not horrible. It's the truth. Paige, you're my closest friend. You know how much I love you. I'm not saying this to hurt you. I'm trying to help."

"*Help* me?"

"Paige, you're really beautiful and sometimes I feel like you don't want the rest of the world to know it. You've always been this way. It's like you're ashamed of your looks and so you downplay them. And you act cold and aloof to keep people at a distance because you're not sure if they like you for who you are or because of the way you look. I think it has something to do with your mother."

"Why does everything always have to come back to Camille?" Paige demanded.

"Because it's true, isn't it?"

"Yes!" Paige shouted. "Yes, it's true that I don't want to be anything like my mother, alright? All her life my mother has used her looks to get ahead. It's all she's ever had. It's how she got off that potato farm in Idaho where she grew up and her real name was Irma Sue Baxter."

Anthony gasped in delight. "Camille's real name is Irma Sue? How very *Yields of Passion!*"

"When she was young my mother used her looks to get work as a model in New York. Then she used her looks to become an actress and then she used her looks to marry rich men. Her looks have gotten her to where she is today, but what's going to happen once her looks are gone?"

"Paige, that's Camille's problem, not yours. And I think you're underestimating your mother. Camille will always land on her feet. She's a survivor. My God, she escaped life on a potato farm and the name Irma Sue! But you're not your mother. Give yourself a little credit. Yes, you're beautiful, but you're also smart. Smart enough to know that it takes more than a pretty face to get to where you want to go. So I want you to make me a promise."

"What kind of promise?"

"I want you to promise that you're going to start letting the world see how beautiful you really are."

Paige pointed to her nose. "I think that may take awhile."

"I'm willing to wait."

Paige sighed. Why was it that Anthony was always the one to make her do what she didn't want to do? Even though she *knew* without a doubt that he was right? She *had* been hiding her looks for a very long time. But maybe it was time to stop hiding.

"I may have to take baby steps."

"I'll be right by your side."

"And I'm not used to being the center of attention."

"You're planning to become the center of attention?"

"Of course! But I'm not going to do any of this until you tell me which guys at school think I'm gorgeous."

"I'll tell you *after* you give Max one more chance. Deal?"

Paige hesitated before answering. Did she want to get her hopes up again only to have them dashed? Despite telling Anthony she wanted to give up, she still had feelings for Max. And they were only going to get stronger as more time passed. She liked him so much! He was smart, kind and thoughtful. Well, except when it came to Monopoly. And she really didn't want to throw in the towel. Not yet. Not if it meant she still had a chance with him.

Wasn't love worth fighting for? Sometimes you had to go after what you wanted. And she wanted Max.

"Deal," she said. "One more chance. But then that's it! I can't spend the rest of my life chasing after Max!"

"Great!" Anthony exclaimed happily, clapping his hands. "Now turn on the TV. It's time for *The Yields of Passion!*"

An hour later the doorbell rang.

Paige aimed the remote control at the TV, turning it off. "I wonder who that can be."

"Is it Justine coming back from the supermarket?"

Justine was the Cranes' live-in housekeeper from Jamaica. She'd been working for Paige's father since before he had married Camille and was considered part of the family. Paige adored her.

"She went home to visit her family last week," Paige said, walking out into the hallway. "She won't be back until the end of next month."

Paige opened the front door, surprised to see who was there. "Max! What are you doing here?"

Max held up a shopping bag. "I come bearing gifts."

Paige accepted the bag. "Mmmm. Something smells chocolatey."

"I just wanted to check up on you. See how you were doing. I still feel bad about what happened."

"Don't feel bad. It was all my fault. And I'm doing okay. It was sweet of you to come by."

"How's the nose?"

"It looks bad but it feels fine. The doctor says the swelling should be gone by the end of the week." Paige peeked into the bag. "What did you bring me that smells so yummy?"

"Desserts. My dad was trying out some new recipes in our kitchen."

"I never say no to sweets! Why don't you come with me into the kitchen and we'll sample them? Anthony's in the living room."

"I wish I could, but I can't."

Paige tried not to feel disappointed. After all, Max had surprised her with his visit.

"Maybe another time?" he asked.

Paige's spirits instantly lifted. "Sure."

"How about Friday night?"

"Huh?" She couldn't have heard him correctly.

"Friday night," Max repeated. "Are you doing anything on Friday night?"

Paige's breath caught in her throat.

Friday night. Friday night was date night. Was Max getting ready to ask her out on a date?

"No plans. Why?"

"My dad's network is throwing a party and he gave me some extra invites. You're more than welcome to come. It's not going to be people just from the Cooking Channel. There are supposed to be a ton of celebrities."

So much for being alone with Max. Still, he had invited her. That had to count for something.

"It sounds like fun. I'd love to go."

"Great. Mention it to Anthony as well."

"Anthony?" Paige felt like a storm cloud had just descended on her sunny day.

Max nodded. "And Colleen. And Bianca and Rachel. I already invited Felix."

The storm clouds kept gathering, but Paige kept a smile pasted on her face. *Great, the whole gang's going to be there!*

"I better get going," Max said. "See you at school tomorrow?"

"I'll be back."

"Okay." Max gave Paige a quick hug, catching her off guard. Before she could hug him back, he let her go. "Bye!"

"Bye."

A hug. Okay, a hug was nice, but why not a kiss?

Paige closed the door and headed back into the living room, where Anthony was lying on the couch, flipping through a magazine.

"Who was at the door?"

"Max."

Anthony jumped off the couch. "Max was at the door and you didn't tell me? How could you? If I didn't know you better, I'd think you were trying to keep him for yourself."

Paige rolled her eyes. "Calm down. This isn't an episode of *The Yields of Passion*. Don't have a meltdown. He wanted to see how I was doing and he brought me some desserts made by his father."

"A guy bearing gifts is always a good sign," Anthony grudgingly admitted as he snatched the bag from Paige and began pawing through it. "And this puts you one gift ahead of me, you know. Maybe I can get him to bop me with a basketball later this week in gym class. Or better yet! Maybe I can smash my face into his elbow while we're playing basketball. That might be easier to do."

"Anthony!"

"Sorry! Obviously I'm freaking out because you now have the competitive edge."

"Do I?"

"Don't you?"

"Well, he did ask me if I was doing anything on Friday night."

Anthony gasped. "You mean he asked you out on a date?"

"I guess you could call it that."

"No! He didn't!"

"He did, but he also invited you."

Paige told Anthony all the details.

"Don't you *ever* scare me that way again!" Anthony scolded Paige, clutching his heart. "What are you trying to do? Kill me? Shame on you! Making me think my Maxie could be straight."

"He could be," Paige reminded. "He did invite Colleen, Bianca and Rachel."

"But he also invited Felix."

"Which means we still don't know if he's gay or straight!"

"But we will. Eventually we will. And since we're going to have competition on Friday night, we're going to have to make sure we dress to kill!"

The doorbell rang again and Paige looked at Anthony in surprise. "Do you think that's Max again?"

"If it is, we're not letting him leave."

Paige went to the front door and was surprised to find Paolo waiting in the hallway.

"What happened to you?" Paolo exclaimed. "You look like you slammed your face into a wall."

"More like Max's head."

"What?!" Paolo held up a hand. "I don't want to hear it. I sense another one of my brother's crazy schemes." Paolo shook his head sadly. "I thought you were the sensible one, Paige."

"What's that supposed to mean?" She had a feeling she'd just been insulted.

"Who's at the door, Paige?" Anthony walked out in the hallway. "Pow? What are you doing here?"

Paolo pointed to his watch. "You were supposed to meet me downstairs fifteen minutes ago. We're picking up Mom and Dad at the airport. Come on! Move it! I'm double parked."

"Why didn't you just call me on my cell phone?"

"Because I don't have a cell phone."

"Why not?" Paige asked.

"I need to be walking around with a phone glued to my ear? Sometimes I like walking around listening to my own thoughts. I don't need to be talking to someone else."

"He's lying," Anthony whispered into Paige's ear. "He's just too cheap to spring for one."

"I'll meet you downstairs," Paolo said.

"Wait a minute," Paige said, grabbing Paolo's arm. "Not so fast. What did you mean when you said I was sensible? The way you said it, it didn't sound very nice."

"You should be smart enough to know that all this plotting and scheming when it comes to Max isn't going to lead to anything. You can't force someone to fall in love with you. Love just happens. Isn't that what you told me the first night you met him? But when it comes to Max, the two of you don't seem to realize that."

"Love doesn't *just* happen," Paige said. "Sometimes it

needs to be nurtured and grown."

Paolo laughed. "And the two of you are nurturing Max's love?"

"We're nurturing our friendship with him," Paige said. "A lot of people start out as friends first before falling in love."

Paolo shook his head in exasperation. "Why is it that high schoolers don't get it? There's more to life than just love and romance!"

"When did you become so socially aware?" Anthony asked, staring at Paolo like he was a crazy man.

"And why are you so down on love?" Paige asked. "Was your heart broken that much by your last girlfriend?"

"Paolo's usually the heartbreaker," Anthony informed Paige.

"What would life be without love?" she continued. "It's why we do the things we do. If you don't see that, if you don't understand that, then I feel sorry for you."

Paolo pointed a finger at Anthony. "If you're not downstairs in five minutes, I'm leaving." He then pointed a finger at Paige. "Ever think of writing an advice column for the lovelorn? All that crap you just told me? They'd eat it up."

With those final words, Paolo left.

"I think you pissed off my big brother," Anthony said, ducking into the hall closet and grabbing his denim jacket.

"Argh!" Paige screamed. "He makes me *so* angry! Sometimes I don't even know how the two of you can even be brothers!"

chapter fifteen

"*I*f I asked you to kiss me, would you?" Anthony asked Max.

Max shrugged. "I don't know. I've never kissed a guy before."

"Never?"

"Never."

"Have you ever wondered what it might be like?"

"No."

"Not even a little?"

"Not even a little."

Anthony laughed, a devilish glint in his eye. "I think you're lying. And I'm going to prove it."

"How?"

"Like this."

But before Anthony could close the distance between

himself and Max, giving him the kiss he'd been waiting weeks for, Max held up the script he was holding.

"And that's when Dominick kisses Michael for the first time, right?" Max asked.

Argh!!!

Foiled again!

Anthony bit back a sigh, keeping a smile on his face. Was he *ever* going to get a chance to lock lips with Max? They'd been rehearsing his screenplay for weeks and they still hadn't kissed. Either they rehearsed up to the kissing scene, or when they picked up where they left off, they ran lines after the kissing scene.

Patience, Anthony reminded himself. *Patience. All good things come to those who wait.*

"Right." Anthony tossed his copy of the screenplay on his bed. "I think we've done enough for today."

"We're making good progress," Max said. "We've almost got the whole script memorized."

Was it his imagination or did Max seem more relaxed now that the threat of a kiss was over?

But that didn't explain anything. Despite the lack of lip action, Max was sending out signals that indicated he *was* interested in Anthony. There was never a lack of body contact between the two of them. If they were walking down the school hallways or down the street, Max was always throwing an arm around Anthony's shoulders. If they were at the movies or watching TV together, Max would press his leg against Anthony's to get his attention. And Max was always willing to go over lines to his screenplay, even though they hadn't rehearsed the kissing scene yet.

What did it all mean?!

Was it all in his mind? Was Max just a friendly guy? Or was he trying to tell him something?

He didn't know!

Anthony didn't want to think about it anymore. It made his head hurt. Instead, he was going to think about something fun.

"Thanks again for the invite to your dad's party. I'm looking forward to it."

"Even though it's a black tie event, it should be a blast."

"Paige tells me you've been stopping by her apartment all week with yummy desserts. I wonder if she'll still be able to fit into the dress she bought for tonight."

"I feel bad about what happened out in the Hamptons. Guilty conscience."

"You didn't know she was going to be in your room."

"Neither did she."

"Do you really believe that?"

Max gave Anthony a puzzled look. "What do you mean?"

Anthony decided it was time to make things a little interesting. Toss out a little bait and see if Max nibbled on it.

"Maybe she didn't go into your room by accident." Anthony gave Max a pointed look. "Maybe she knew *exactly* where she was going."

"Why would she do that?"

"Because she likes you?"

"She likes me?"

Oookay, either we've underestimated Max's level of intelligence and he's just another pretty boy with nothing upstairs, or he really doesn't have a clue. . . .

Anthony knew he'd better do some backtracking. Paige would kill him if he told Max that she liked him. Plus, he really wasn't sure if he wanted to know if Max was straight. And that he might like his best friend as much as she liked him. Was it selfish of him to want Max to be gay and like *him* instead?

"Ants, does Paige like me?" Max asked, breaking into Anthony's thoughts.

"I think so, but I'm not a hundred percent sure. She hasn't come out and told me that she likes you. But if you want, I could try and find out."

"You could?"

"Uh-huh. Paige and I are best friends. We tell each other everything, although so far she hasn't told me anything about you. Paige is like that when it comes to guys; she's afraid if she shares her feelings, she'll jinx things. So, do you want me to find out?"

Max shook his head. "No."

"No?" That hadn't been the answer Anthony was expecting. "Why not?" He tried not to sound shocked. *What was wrong with Paige? Any guy would be lucky to have her as his girlfriend. Was she not good enough for Max? Was that it? Because if it was, Max was going to get an earful from him!*

"I like Paige. A lot. She's a good friend."

But not good enough to be a girlfriend? Is that it? Because you're really looking for a boyfriend? If that's the case, you don't have to look very far. The perfect boyfriend is standing right in front of you!

"I don't have time in my life right now for a relationship with anyone. There's too much other stuff going on." Max glanced at his watch. "I better get going. I still have to pick up my tux, shower and change. See you later."

"Later," Anthony said, watching Max leave his bedroom as the wheels in his head started churning.

Hmmm. He doesn't have time in his life for a relationship with anyone. Anyone could be a girl . . . or a guy . . .

When Paige arrived at Anthony's to pick him up for the party, she was expecting him to open his front door.

Instead, it was opened by Paolo.

Paige was taken by surprise. She hadn't seen him since their argument at her apartment earlier in the week and she didn't know what to say to him. Should she apologize? After all, he was entitled to his opinion. But that didn't mean he had to put down hers. Before she could decide what she was going to say, Paolo spoke first.

"Where are you going all dressed up? Wait. Don't tell me. Let me guess." Paolo closed his eyes and started rubbing the sides of his forehead. "My ESP powers say this has something to do with Marvelous Max."

"He invited us to a party that the Cooking Channel is throwing for his father," Paige said, walking past Paolo into the living room. As usual, the TV was on and tuned to a sports event. Where was the remote control? Just once she'd like to see something other than sports on this TV!

"And of course the two of you instantly accepted," Paolo said, following after her.

"Why wouldn't we?"

Paolo plopped himself down on the couch and picked up the remote control hidden between two cushions, switching to another sports channel. "Ever hear of playing hard to get? The two of you are making it so easy for this guy!"

"What do you know about playing hard to get?"

"Guys are intrigued by girls who they can't get right away. They like the chase."

"Did you chase after all your girlfriends?"

"Some of them. And some of them chased after me."

Paige stared at Paolo. "Did you just say what I think you said?"

"Huh?" Paolo asked, his eyes glued to the TV. Paige walked over to it and shut it off.

"Hey!" Paolo shouted. "What are you doing?"

"Answer my question. You're saying some of your girl-friends chased after you?"

"Yes."

"You are *such* a hypocrite!" Paige screamed. Oh, he was so infuriating! "How can you criticize Anthony and me for chasing after Max when you've been chased after?"

"Easy," Paolo said smugly, aiming the remote control at the TV and turning it back on. "I was aware that I was being chased. Mysterious Max is clueless!"

"Where are your parents?" Paige asked, deciding she wasn't going to discuss Max anymore with Paolo. For some bizarre reason, Max bugged him. "I want to say hello to them."

"They're in Rome. They were only here for two nights. They're going to be there until the spring."

"Rome is supposed to be one of the most romantic places in the world," Paige sighed. "I've always wanted to go there."

Paolo made the sign of the cross with two fingers, as if warding off a vampire, and hissed. "Let's avoid all talk of romance. You remember what happened last time."

"How could I forget?" Paige began hotly just as Anthony stuck his head in the living room.

"Ready to go?"

"Ready," she said, eager to leave Paolo behind.

"Hey, Paige," Paolo called out as she left the living room. She turned around. "Yes?" she asked coldly, expecting him to toss another zinger at her.

"The swelling in your nose went down. You look like your old self again. I'm glad."

Paige touched her nose self-consciously, surprised that Paolo had noticed. "Thanks," she said.

Once Paige and Anthony had stepped into the limousine they had rented for the night to take them to the Rainbow Room in Rockefeller Center where the party was taking place, Anthony dropped his bombshell. He told Paige what he'd told Max.

"You told Max you thought I might like him? You didn't!" Paige screamed.

"I did!"

"How could you?!"

"How could I not? Remember how you were ready to throw in the towel?"

"That was just a temporary lapse," Paige said. "A week's worth of Max's TLC has given me hope!"

"Well, now my hope is gone." Anthony gazed out his limousine window. "I'm starting to feel the exact same way you did. If he's straight, then I want you to have him."

"That's so noble of you."

Anthony turned away from the window and looked at

Paige. "It is, isn't it?"

"What's the problem? Tell me."

"We *still* haven't rehearsed the kissing scene in my screenplay."

"But you *will* get to kiss him. Eventually." Paige began rummaging through her Celine pink tote. "I don't see what you're complaining about."

"Do you think it's going to be as good as I'm expecting it to be?"

"Probably not," Paige said, taking a gold compact and tube of lipstick out of her purse.

"Thanks a lot."

"You want me to lie? Anticipation is always the best part of something you've been waiting for. The rest is all downhill."

"Not always. Someone as cute as Max can't be a bad kisser. Even if it's a fake kiss."

Paige, who was applying a fresh coat of ruby red lipstick, glanced away from her open compact. "A fake kiss is better than no kiss."

"Have I told you how nice you look?"

Paige was wearing a geranium silk dress with a plunging neckline that stopped at the waist with a sparkly brooch. She'd also used a flat iron on her hair so that it fell over one shoulder in a long sleek sheet.

"Thank you. You don't look so bad yourself."

"You can't go wrong with a basic black tuxedo."

"I wonder how many celebrities are going to be there."

"Whoever's on the Cooking Channel, at least."

"I wonder if there's going to be a red carpet for us to walk down," Paige said, as their limo pulled in front of the NBC building, where the Rainbow Room was located.

"I'm sure there will be. With our luck, Felix will be right on it, scribbling away like mad for his column."

When they arrived at the party, the first thing they saw was the food. Everywhere they turned, there were buffets manned by waiters and waitresses ready to serve.

"Where should we start?" Anthony asked, grabbing a plate and silverware wrapped in a linen napkin.

"Appetizers first. Then we'll move on to the main course."

After filling their plates with a variety of goodies, Anthony and Paige found themselves a corner table that would allow them to watch the entire ballroom.

"Do you see anyone we know?" Anthony asked.

"There are the twins," Paige said, pointing them out at the open bar where they were both sipping Cokes.

Rachel was wearing a black Empire waist dress designed by Chanel. Both the bodice and the skirt were embroidered with white daisies. Bianca, as usual, was wearing an eye-catching color. She had on a Zac Posen scarlet red chiffon dress pleated on the diagonal with a halter neckline.

"They both look like they're posing," Anthony said.

"Why wouldn't they? This is a golden opportunity for them. With all the network executives here, they're probably hoping someone will offer them a cooking show."

"What's the premise going to be?" Anthony snickered. "How to order takeout?"

"Be nice," Paige scolded. "You know how much being on TV means to them."

"I'm only teasing!" Anthony said. "Have you seen Colleen?"

Paige gazed around the ballroom. "There she is. Over by

the stuffed lobsters."

Anthony waved to Colleen, who saw him and headed in his direction.

"Don't we look nice," Paige said as Colleen put her plate down and pulled out a seat.

"This old thing?" Colleen said, referring to her bejeweled emerald green Dolce & Gabbana chiffon baby doll dress.

"It looks fabulous on you," Anthony said.

"Thanks. I wish Miranda had felt the same way."

Miranda was Colleen's mother, and from the way Colleen had uttered her name, Anthony sensed trouble. Miranda O'Brian was one of Manhattan's top socialites. Blond, super thin and constantly having plastic surgery to keep her face youthful and wrinkle free, her name was one that was always in the New York City gossip columns. Which she loved. The one thing she *didn't* love was her daughter's weight and was constantly nagging Colleen about it, trying to get her to slim down.

"She didn't like the dress?" Anthony asked.

"She *loved* the dress," Colleen said while digging into her pasta salad. "She just didn't love it on me. She felt it was too *revealing* for someone of my size."

"She's right, you know."

Bianca and Rachel approached the table with their barely touched Cokes.

"Excuse me?" Colleen said. "I don't remember asking for your opinion."

"You're going to get it anyway," Bianca said.

"We're your friends, Colleen," Rachel said, putting a hand on her shoulder. "Best friends. We care."

"And because we care, I'm not going to sugarcoat this,"

Bianca said, tossing her long hair over one shoulder. "Your dress shows too much. Way too much."

"And that's a problem because . . . ? *You* always show too much."

"But there's less of me to show! And what I *do* show, people want to see!"

"And they don't want to see me in this dress?" Colleen pushed away her plate. "Come on, Bianca. Spit it out. Is this a dress a fat girl shouldn't be wearing?"

Bianca shrugged. "I know this is going to make me sound like a bitch, but you said it, not me."

"And we're not making judgments," Rachel said hurriedly. "Honest. But a lot of people have been commenting."

Colleen picked up her fork and started eating again. "Let them. I don't care what other people have to say. I'll wear what I want, when I want. I'm supposed to wear a shapeless sack? Or better yet, a sweat suit?"

"Obviously there's no reasoning with you," Bianca sniffed. "So much for trying to help a friend. Come on, Rachel. Let's go mingle."

"Can you believe those two?" Colleen said after the twins had left.

"They didn't mean to sound malicious," Paige said, coming to the twins' defense. "They were only looking out for you. You know they'd never intentionally hurt your feelings."

"They're as bad as Miranda. And speaking of Mommie Dearest, listen to this! As if complaining about my dress wasn't bad enough, there's some fat farm she wants me to go to in Palm Springs. I told her no way. Why can't she be proud of my accomplishments? I'm a plus-sized teen model! People are paying me because I look like this and I don't have a problem with my size. I like myself. If I didn't, I'd do something about the weight. It's like she's competing with all her other socialite buddies because their daughters are the perfect debutantes."

Just then the sound of applause came from the table next to them. Anthony and Paige turned around to see a late-twentysomething woman dressed in a black leather miniskirt and blazer approach their table. Her short black hair was slicked back, her black glasses were cat-eyed, and around her neck and wrists she wore a triple strand of black pearls.

"Allow me to introduce myself," the woman said in a low, raspy voice. "I'm Devorah Schwartz."

"Doesn't she mean Devour?" Anthony whispered in Paige's ear.

Paige giggled. "Stop!"

"Why? She's fabulous! She doesn't look like she takes any crap from anyone! All she needs is a whip!"

"I didn't mean to eavesdrop," Devorah said, "but I couldn't help overhearing your conversation."

Colleen buttered a roll. "And?"

"I found it positively refreshing! You are who you are and you make no bones about it. I like that. I like it a lot."

"Thanks," Colleen said.

"What would you say if I were to offer you your own TV show?"

Colleen dropped her butter knife while Anthony and Paige's mouths dropped open.

"Excuse me?"

"You heard me. I'm head of development for TTV. That's Terrific Television. We're launching next September. We're another division of the corporation that owns the Cooking Channel. I'm seeing a reality series that follows you during your days as a plus-sized model."

"What would you call the show?" Anthony asked.

Devorah held up her hands in a square, as if creating a TV set. "*Fat Model.* It says exactly what the show is, don't you think? You don't have a problem with that, do you, Colleen? Let's face it, 'plus-sized' is just another word for 'fat.' And fat is a word that's going to grab people's attention."

"I love it!" Colleen exclaimed.

"Good!" Devorah handed Colleen her business card. "Have your modeling agent call my office in the morning. We'll set up a meeting."

After Devorah left, there was silence at the table. Then Anthony, Paige and Colleen began screaming excitedly.

"Oh my God! Oh my God! Oh my God! I'm getting my own TV show!" Colleen shrieked. "Miranda's going to die! I can just see her telling her friends the name of my show. Not!"

"Who needs *Hairspray*?" Anthony said. "Reality TV is creating new stars every day."

"But the show could also follow me around as I try to make it as an actress!" Colleen exclaimed. "It would be like a televised audition every week for producers and directors in Hollywood!"

"What's going on here?" Bianca asked, rejoining the table with Rachel. "We could hear you screaming all the way across the room."

Anthony leaned close to Paige and whispered in her ear. "Ever seen a human volcano?"

"No."

"Get ready. Because you're about to see one, possibly two, explode."

"What are you talking about?"

"Keep your eyes on the twins. As soon as they hear Colleen's news, they're going to erupt."

"Guess who's getting her own TV show?" Colleen asked.

Rachel shrugged. "I don't know. Who?"

"Me!"

"*You're* getting your own TV show?" Bianca gasped.

"Yes!" Anthony exclaimed. "Isn't it fabulous?"

"B-b-but that's impossible!" Rachel sputtered.

"Why is it impossible?" Paige asked. "Are only thin people allowed to have TV shows?"

"She doesn't want to be a TV star," Bianca said. "We do! We should be getting our own show, not her!"

"If you're nice, I'll let you guest star," Colleen said, "but I can't promise any special billing,"

"*Guest star?!*" Bianca shrieked in horror. "We'll never guest star on your show or anyone else's!"

"We're going to have our own show!" Rachel proclaimed.

"Speaking of guest stars," Anthony interrupted, "it looks like our guest of honor is here."

Everyone's eyes turned to the entrance of the ballroom, where a waving Steve Coulter was arriving with his wife on his arm. Max's mother was dark-haired, slim and pretty, wearing an elegant ivory-colored dress and gold earrings. Walking in behind them was Max.

There was no mistaking Steve Coulter. Even though he was wearing a tuxedo and bow tie, he gave off waves of testosterone. From the black cowboy hat on his head, the

214

black cowboy boots on his feet and the cigar he was chomping, he was macho with a capital M.

From the way Max was standing behind Steve, out of sight, trying not to draw attention to himself, it was obvious that he was overshadowed by his famous father.

At that moment, Anthony's heart went out to Max and all the pieces of the puzzle fell into place. Why hadn't he realized it sooner?

"I think we may have found the answer to our question," Anthony said to Paige.

"What question?"

"Max. Is he or isn't he?"

"I'm not following."

"His father."

"What about him?"

"Didn't you notice? Steve Coulter is a man's man. A frat boy all grown up. I wouldn't be surprised if in a couple of hours he's wearing his tie around his forehead like a bandana while chugalugging a bottle of beer. If that guy was your father, can you imagine telling him that you were gay? He'd freak out. Big time! Max might not be ready to face up to things because of his father."

"So he's staying closeted?"

"Wouldn't you?"

"If that's true, then you're never going to get him to admit he's gay."

"Never say never, Ms. Crane. You underestimate the power of my lips. If Max *is* gay, once he gets a taste of them, I guarantee he'll be coming back for more!"

chapter sixteen

$\mathcal{D}$ecisions, decisions. It was time for some dessert and Paige couldn't make up her mind between a slice of triple chocolate fudge cake and a slice of chocolate cream pie.

"Why not take both?"

Paige turned around with a smile. "Max!"

"Having a good time?"

"Yes. How about you?"

Max shrugged, tugging at the collar of his tuxedo shirt. "I've been to tons of these parties since Dad's show took off. They're always the same. Everyone kissing his ass, telling him how great he is."

Paige was shocked at the bitterness she heard in Max's voice. "Well, he is a big star."

"But he wasn't always." Max waved a hand around the crowded ballroom. "Before all this happened, my dad was

216

just a regular guy who owned his own restaurant and spent time with his family when he wasn't working. Now we're lucky if we see him once a month. He's always jetting off somewhere with plans to open up another restaurant, spending hours in the studio taping, working on his book or going out to parties."

"I know what it's like having a famous parent."

"How do you deal with it?"

"I've never dealt with it," Paige said as she reached for a slice of triple chocolate fudge cake. "I've just accepted Camille for who she is. She's selfish, immature, insecure and everything else in her life comes before me." Paige laughed at the shocked expression on Max's face. "What?"

"That's pretty harsh."

"It's the truth. I'm not going to lie and tell you how great my mother is. Over the years she's let me down more times than I can count."

"And that doesn't bother you?"

"Of course it bothers me, but what am I going to do?" Paige took a bite of her cake. "You would think that being a parent would be her number-one priority, but it isn't. Her career comes first."

"My dad is the same way. And because he's such a big celebrity, he thinks he can do whatever he wants. It doesn't matter who he hurts."

"Like you?"

Max looked around before answering. Then he grabbed Paige by the hand and walked with her to a secluded corner of the ballroom, far from the crowd.

"Like my mom," he said. "He's cheating on her. All those

nights that he's supposedly working late? It's a lie. He's got girlfriends and my mom knows it, but she doesn't say anything because she loves him. She thinks it's a phase he's going through, but it's not. My dad's selfish. He's only thinking about himself and what he wants. Do you know how hard it is hearing your mom cry herself to sleep at night?"

The sweet piece of cake that had been sliding down Paige's throat turned to a hard lump. She hadn't been expecting to hear the marital secrets of Max's parents. This was way too much information. But obviously Max needed to talk to someone and she was touched that he trusted her enough to confide in her.

"Your mom must love your dad a lot if she's willing to put up with other women," she said.

"I guess. If she were smart, she'd hire a good divorce attorney and take him for half of everything, but she won't. Like you said, she loves him, even though he's hurting her. That's never going to happen to me."

"What?"

"I'm never going to fall in love with anyone. There's too much risk."

"You shouldn't say that!"

"Why not?"

"Because everyone has to fall in love. At least once, anyway!"

"Why? Have you ever been in love?"

"No, I haven't," Paige said, not sure why she was so reluctant to admit it. After all, she was only seventeen years old! She had plenty of time to fall in love. "But Anthony has. I guess you could say he's loved and lost."

"Anthony's a cool guy."

"He's a great catch."

"I agree. Any guy would be lucky to have him as a boyfriend."

Is that guy you? Paige wanted to ask. The words were on the tip of her tongue, but she didn't want to say them. Max seemed so down. So vulnerable. It wasn't about whether or not he was gay or straight or who he liked better. It was about helping a friend.

"Your parents need to work things out for themselves. There isn't anything you can do to fix things."

"I know, but it's hard to see my mom hurting. Falling in love is too painful. Too messy. I don't ever want to go through what she's going through. You give your heart to someone and what do they do? They throw it on the floor and stomp all over it."

"Not always."

"More often than not, it seems."

"Boy, you're really cynical. But you're wrong and I'm going to prove it. I want you to make me a promise."

"What kind of promise?"

"Promise me you're going to fall in love someday."

"I can't promise that."

"Why not?"

"What if I don't meet someone?"

"You will. There isn't a doubt in my mind. Trust me. Now promise!" Paige peeked behind Max's back. "And no crossing your fingers!"

Max gave Paige a wide smile, showing off his adorable dimples and she knew, that just for a few seconds, she had helped him forget his problems.

"Okay, okay, I promise," Max said, holding his hands up in the air so Paige could see he wasn't crossing his fingers.

"Good! Now when the day comes that you fall in love, I want you to call me. Day or night."

"And then?"

"I want you to tell me how wonderful it is! And that I was right."

Max's smile grew wider. "You know something, Paige? You're a romantic. But that's okay. I still like you."

And with those words, the last thing that Paige expected to happen, happened.

Max kissed her.

She wasn't sure if he was planning to kiss her on the lips. He had leaned in close to her, probably planning to kiss her on the cheek but instead of standing still, she'd moved her head.

When she had, his lips had fallen on hers.

And then they'd locked.

For Paige, it was like two magnets connecting. Click! She'd wanted to kiss Max for weeks and now that she had the opportunity, well, she wasn't going to turn it down.

She resisted the urge to wrap her arms around his shoulders. That might scare him away and end the kiss and she didn't want that. No, no, no! She wanted the kiss to last and last and last.

As a kiss, it was pretty nice. Gentle. Sweet. She was expecting something a little bit extra, but she didn't know what. Maybe because it wasn't a planned kiss Max hadn't thrown everything he had into it.

Still, it was a kiss!

And he *was* still kissing her. He hadn't pulled away. Hmmm. What did that mean? Five seconds ago he was saying he was never going to fall in love.

"Wow," Max said. "That was unexpected."

"But nice, definitely nice," Paige said, hoping he'd pick up the hint and kiss her again.

"Yeah, right. Nice," Max said, smiling nervously.

Uh-oh. Something was wrong.

"Listen, I better go hook up with my parents. Thanks for listening. You're a really good friend, Paige."

"Anytime," Paige said, tracing her fingers over her lips as she watched Max walk away. "Anytime."

"He kissed you! Max kissed you!"

Anthony was practically bouncing off the sides of their limousine as their chauffeur drove through Central Park.

"I almost died when I looked across the ballroom and saw him pressing those lips against yours."

"It wasn't a real kiss, though," Paige clarified. "It's not like he planned to kiss me on the lips. It was an accidental kiss."

"His lips puckered. They pressed. They made contact with your lips. Whether planned or accidental, it was a kiss!"

"If you're going to be technical about it," Paige said, "then yes, it was a kiss. And . . . it was definitely nice."

"Oh, I am *so* jealous! If we weren't best friends, I'd want to tear your hair out!"

"But it didn't mean anything!"

"How can that be? It looked like you and Maxie were having a cozy little chat. Did you tell him how you feel? Is that why he kissed you?"

"Max did most of the talking. I just listened and after listening, I have my own theory about his love life."

"Which is?"

"I think Max is afraid to get close to anyone because of his father."

After swearing Anthony to secrecy, Paige told him everything that Max had told her about his parents' marriage.

"Wow. Poor guy," Anthony whispered. "You know, now that you mention it, at the party I noticed that Max's father spent most of his time with other women and not his wife."

"Can you blame Max for not wanting to get involved with anyone? He's probably afraid he's going to hook up with someone who'll treat him the way his father treats his mother. And I don't think he was too happy that we locked lips. He couldn't run away from me fast enough."

"Did you have bad breath?"

"Anthony!" Paige swatted him on the arm.

"Okay, so he's been distancing himself from others. And he didn't expect to kiss you. But he did and you've given him something to think about if he plays for your team. Hopefully your little chat fixed things, but we still have to find out if he's gay or straight. If we don't do something soon, we're going to wind up going to the Senior Prom with each other!"

"Any suggestions?"

"It's time for a new plan. How do you feel about a little breaking and entering?"

"What?!"

"Don't worry, we're not going to steal anything. We're just

going to do a little exploring and get a look into Max's secret world."

"Which is?"

"His bedroom."

"His bedroom?"

"We haven't set foot in Max's apartment since we've become friends with him. There has to be a reason."

"Felix told you the reason. Max's father guards his privacy. He doesn't like strangers in the apartment. That includes Max's friends."

"Come on, Paige! Get real! I'm sure if Max wanted to have a few friends over, he could. He's hiding something."

"Maybe he doesn't want anyone around because of the problems his parents are having. Maybe things are really tense at home."

"Maybe . . . but we've got to get a look inside his bedroom."

"And how are we going to do that? Max lives in a doorman building. The doorman isn't going to just let us go up."

"That's true," Anthony said. "But the doorman *will* let us up if we go visit Felix. Remember, they live in the same building."

"And then what?"

"We visit with Felix and then we leave. But instead of heading back downstairs, we go upstairs instead."

"How dumb do you think Felix is? He's going to know we're up to something."

"No, he isn't. Felix and I bonded at his birthday bash. We're tight."

"You're tight with Felix?" Paige asked skeptically.

"As tight as you can be with a back-stabbing snake," Anthony said. "Trust me, this plan will work!"

"And if it doesn't?"

"We'll worry about that when the time comes. But I've got a feeling this is finally going to get us some answers. So, are you in?"

"If doing this means I'll eventually get Max, then . . . yes, I'm in!"

chapter seventeen

*A*nthony met Paige at the corner of Max's apartment building the following Wednesday afternoon. At lunch, he'd found out from Max that his mother would be at her beauty salon all afternoon, getting ready for a party that his parents were throwing that night. His father was going to be at the studio taping an episode of his show and Max had a debate club meeting. Except for the hired help and caterers getting ready for the party, the apartment was going to be empty. It was the perfect time to strike!

Anthony checked the time on his watch. Where was Paige? Looking down the street, he was relieved to see her heading in his direction.

"You're late!" he scolded.

"Sorry. I had to meet with my guidance counselor this afternoon. She was telling me about more open houses this weekend. There's going to be one at NYU and one at Columbia. Can you come with me?"

Anthony made a face. "I'm sick of college open houses. Why do you keep dragging me along with you?"

"Because I'm hoping you'll change your mind and not want to go to UCLA. Why can't you go to film school in New York? NYU has got a great program at Tisch. Besides, you need to have some backup choices in case you don't get into UCLA."

"Bite your tongue!"

"Do you really want to go out to California and leave me behind?"

"Of course not! But you know that's where I've always wanted to go. Why don't you come out to UCLA with me?"

Now Paige made a face. "And be that much closer to Camille? I don't think so." Paige inspected Anthony from head to toe. "*What* are you wearing?"

"Do you like it?" Anthony asked, twirling around in his black leather trench coat, cap and wraparound sunglasses.

"You look like you stepped out of a sci-fi movie."

"I call it my spywear. It sets the mood for our mission. I was tempted to dye my hair like Sydney Bristow from *Alias*, but I think that would have been a bit too much, don't you think?"

"Yes, especially since yearbook pictures are next week. Your mother would have killed you if you'd had your picture taken with neon pink hair."

"This is going to be so much fun! It's even given me an idea for a new screenplay."

"It has?"

"A gay James Bond! I'm calling it *The Gay Spy Who Loved Me*. Everyone in the movie would be gay. Our hero, the villain, and of course, the love interest, who gets his heart broken in the end because our spy commits to no one man! And there'll be plenty of eye candy. The male kind!"

Paige laughed. "That sounds like a hoot!"

"So, are you ready?" Anthony asked as they neared Max's building.

"What's the plan again?"

"We tell the doorman we're here to see Felix. When we get up to Felix's place, we tell him we came to personally invite him to a party we're having. His ego will love it and it won't make him suspicious."

"We're having a party?"

"We are now."

"And then? How are we going to get into Max's apartment? We don't have a key, remember?"

"His parents are having a party tonight. I'm sure tons of hired help are coming and going from their apartment. All we have to do is bide our time and we'll be able to slip in and slip out, sight unseen."

"The only thing I'm seeing is trouble."

Anthony sighed. "Paige, must you always worry? This is going to work. Trust me."

When they got to the building they told the uniformed doorman that they were there to see Felix. He rang up and five seconds later they were allowed to take the elevator to the tenth floor.

"So far, so good," Anthony said, taking off his sunglasses.

"If I had a nickel for every time I'd heard you say that,"

Paige muttered under her breath.

"Very funny! Just leave everything to me, okay?"

Felix was waiting for them when they reached his apartment. He had a totally surprised look on his face.

"It is you," Felix said, his voice filled with disbelief.

Anthony threw out his arms. "Who else?"

"When the doorman told me you were here to see me, I wasn't sure if he'd gotten the name right. When was the last time you stopped by, Tony? Five? Ten years ago?"

"You're such a kidder," Anthony said as he and Paige followed Felix into a book-lined living room. Felix sat in a brown leather armchair while Anthony and Paige sat on the couch.

"To what do I owe this visit?" Felix asked, a suspicious look on his face. "What do you want?"

Anthony knew it was time for the next phase of his plan. Good thing he'd thought ahead.

"Mind if I take this off?" Anthony asked, unbelting his trench coat. "It's a little hot in here."

Felix shrugged. "Sure."

Anthony noticed Paige's mouth drop open as he took off his trenchcoat. He couldn't blame her. Instead of wearing a bulky sweater suitable to the blustery October weather outside and his usual loose fitting jeans, he was wearing a tight muscle shirt that showed off his arms and chest and jeans that were one size too small. (He'd had to lay down on his bed and take a deep breath to get them zipped up. Girls weren't the only ones who suffered to look good!) He'd purposely chosen the tight-fitting clothes because he knew they showed him off and he needed to use his body to distract

Felix. Kind of like what his gay James Bond would do when facing off against his nemesis.

From the glazed look in Felix's eyes, he could see he was focused on one thing: him.

Success!

"So, Felix, Paige and I are having a party later this month and we'd love it if you could come. You don't have to cover it for your column, but you can if you want."

"Do you have a date for this party?" Felix asked.

"It'll probably be on a Saturday night," Anthony said.

"Not that kind of date," Felix said. "Have you asked someone to be your date?"

Felix's question threw him and Anthony answered without thinking. "A date? No. Why?"

"Because I'd love to be your date that night."

"You would?" Anthony almost choked on the words.

"I hate going to parties alone and at the moment I'm between boyfriends. We had such a great time at my birthday party, but you left too early and then you never came to the Clubhouse." Felix pouted. "Don't you like me, Anthony?"

Awk! Awkward silence. Awkward silence! Anthony scrambled for an answer. *What do I say to this egomaniac to keep him happy?*

"Of course I like you, Felix. You're one of my oldest friends."

Did that sound as lame as I thought it did? Anthony wondered.

Felix got a miffed look on his face.

Uh-oh. It did. Wrong answer. Anthony gave a Paige a desperate look. *Help!*

"If you don't want me to come as your date, just say so," Felix said, a pissy tone creeping into his voice.

Save me from drama queens! Anthony silently cried.

"Of course Anthony wants you to come as his date!" Paige exclaimed in a rush. "After all these years of being friends, you caught him by surprise asking to be his date. Isn't that right, Anthony?"

Anthony didn't reply. Felix? His date? Ick! He'd probably be touchy-feely the entire night. He'd outfoxed himself with this outfit. Argh! Who knew it would produce such great results? On the wrong guy! What had he been thinking? And then there was Max! Yikes! Max was probably going to be at the party and if he saw Felix hanging all over him, he'd think they were boyfriends. And if he were gay, he'd think Anthony was off limits!

"Anthony!"

Paige's voice cut into his thoughts and Anthony felt her give him a not so gentle kick in the ankle.

"Felix, I really want you to come to our party." Anthony had to force out his next words. "And since I don't have a date, your idea sounds great."

"You can be co-hosts," Paige said.

"When I'm invited to a party, I don't do any hosting," Felix sniffed. "I'm there to be entertained."

I'd like to entertain you with a good swift kick in the butt! Anthony thought.

"So, ask me," Felix said.

Anthony was confused. "Ask you what?"

"To be your date."

"I just did."

Felix shook his head. "No, you didn't. You said my idea sounded great. But you didn't ask me."

Anthony could feel his Italian temper start to rise. They'd gotten into the building; they'd spent more than enough time with Felix so they could leave without it looking suspicious. Did he really need to put up with his demands?

He felt Paige's hand on his, giving a warning squeeze. Anthony smiled, trying not to grind his teeth.

"Felix, will you be my date the night of my party?"

"I'll think about it and let you know."

"What?!" Anthony almost jumped up off the couch, ready to wring Felix's neck.

"Anthony, you know how busy my social schedule is. I'm always being invited to parties. And you don't even know when your party is going to be. I'm sure my answer will be yes, but touch base with me in the next couple of days."

Anthony got to his feet. He'd had enough of Felix for one afternoon. "Come on, Paige." He grabbed her by the hand, yanking her off the couch. "Let's go."

"We really hope you can make it," Paige called out as Anthony dragged her out of the apartment.

"Can you believe that guy?" Anthony fumed once they were out in the hallway.

"Could you please let go of my arm before you tear it out of its socket?"

"Oops. Sorry," Anthony said as he pressed the up button for the elevator.

Paige rubbed her shoulder. "Why didn't you tell me what was under that trench coat?"

Anthony gave Paige a smug smile. "Didn't think I had a

body that buff, did you?"

"Have you been secretly working out?"

"I've been using my gym membership more than I have in the past," Anthony admitted.

"And that's because?"

"Because I need to look good, Paige! You know. For Max. Just in case he plays for my team."

The elevator arrived and they stepped into it, pressing the button for the twentieth floor.

"Well, it got results."

Anthony rolled his eyes. "More than what I was expecting."

"Felix likes Anthony! Felix likes Anthony!" Paige teased in a sing-song voice.

Anthony covered his ears. "Stop! Please! You're torturing me."

"I told you he likes you!" Paige said, a smug smile on her face. "But you wouldn't listen to me."

"He doesn't like me."

"He doesn't?"

"No. The only thing Felix likes is playing games with people. He likes calling the shots and pulling the strings. The fact that I *don't* want to date him makes him *want* to date me. I've known Felix a lot longer than you have. Trust me, that's all it is. Oh, and he wants to stop me from getting Max!"

The elevator bell dinged and the doors opened to the twentieth floor.

"Well, here we are," Paige said, stepping out of the elevator. "What's our next move?"

"Now we wait."

"For how long?"

"As long as it takes."

"In case you didn't notice when we came in, the building has video monitors. I'm sure the doorman will get suspicious if he sees us lurking in the hallway."

"We're not going to get caught lurking!" Anthony said as they approached apartment 20G. "Look, the front door is open! Come on!"

Anthony grabbed the door before it closed, listening for movement on the other side. After a minute, he slowly opened the door and peeked inside. "The coast is clear!"

"Wow! This place is huge!"

Max's apartment was a three-level duplex decorated very simply. There were shiny hardwood floors, Mission Oak–style furniture and lots of artwork on the walls.

"I feel like I'm in a museum," Paige whispered as she admired the paintings. "Look at this one! It's a Monet!"

"Paige, we don't have time for a tour," Anthony said, heading for the stairs. "We've got to find Max's room. It must be upstairs."

When they reached the third floor, they started opening doors. They found Max's bedroom when they opened the second door. Like the rest of the apartment, the décor of the room was very simple. There was a bed, a desk with a computer, a bookcase and a dresser. The walls were bare except for some framed landscapes.

"What are we looking for?" Paige asked.

"I don't know," Max said. "We'll know it when we find it."

"This room is as neat as a pin," Paige said.

"Maybe his father is a neat freak. You know, like Joan

Crawford in *Mommie Dearest*. Remember that line with the maid? 'I'm not mad at you, I'm mad at the dirt!' Or when she bopped Christina on the head with a can of cleanser?"

"Anthony, we don't have time to be discussing good-bad movies."

"Right. You start in the closet and I'll look in the dresser drawers."

"I feel so guilty doing this," Paige said. "It's an invasion of privacy."

"It's not like we're looking for something we can black-mail him with!" Anthony said. "We're just trying to figure him out."

"Maybe he doesn't want to be figured out," Paige said, as she began sorting through the hangers in Max's closet. "Maybe we should respect that."

"Too late now. We're here. Find anything?"

"Nope."

Anthony headed over to the bookcase. There were novels by Tom Clancy, Dean Koontz, Stephen King and Robert Ludlum. "Guy" books. Where were the novels by Edmund White? William J. Mann? Bart Yates? Alan Hollinghurst? He'd even settle for a Danielle Steel novel!

"I think we've struck out," Paige said.

"Check under his mattress. There's got to be a magazine under there."

"Is that where you hide yours?"

"I'm not admitting that I buy those types of magazines, but if I did, I'd be much more clever with my hiding space. I'd never stick a magazine under my mattress."

Paige lifted the mattress and took a peek. "Nothing."

"Nothing?" Anthony gasped. "Not even an Abercrombie and Fitch catalog?"

"Nada. Zip." Paige dropped the mattress and made sure the sheets were tucked back in and the bedspread was smooth. "It looks like this mission is a failure."

"We've got to get answers before our party!" Anthony insisted. "There's no way I'm locking lips with Felix again. No way! And you know he's going to want to."

"I think the two of you make a cute couple," Paige teased.

"That's not funny!"

"Where's your sense of humor?"

"I left it downstairs." Anthony checked the time on his watch. "We'd better get out of here."

"Should we check his computer before we go? Maybe we can see what websites he's visited."

"Good idea, but he probably has a password." Anthony sighed. "I guess we've struck out. So much for my bright idea."

Anthony and Paige were making their way back to the first floor when a voice called out to them.

"Hey! You two! What are you doing up there?"

Anthony and Paige froze in their tracks.

"Oh no! We're caught," Paige whispered. "What do we do? What do we do?"

"Don't panic." Anthony turned around with a smile, facing an older woman with a teased silver bouffant and wearing a black-and-white maid's uniform. "Hi. We're here to help with tonight's party. The agency sent us. The front door was open so we let ourselves in."

"Finally! Follow me."

"Lead the way," Anthony said.

"Anthony, what are you doing?" Paige hissed.

"You don't want to get arrested, do you?"

"No!"

"Then just do what I do and we should be fine."

They arrived in the laundry room where the maid pointed out a pile of wrinkled tablecloths and linen napkins on an ironing board. There had to be at least a hundred napkins.

"Those need to be ironed for tonight's party," the maid instructed.

Anthony nodded his head. "Right. Ironed."

"Call me when you're done."

Anthony saluted the maid. "Will do!"

The maid turned to Paige. "You come with me."

Paige widened her eyes at Anthony who indicated with his that she should do whatever the maid told her. After shooting Anthony a dark look, Paige left the laundry room.

After they left, Anthony inspected the tablecloths and pile of napkins. Okay, this shouldn't be too hard. Just turn on the iron and rub it back and forth over the fabric. Piece of cake.

Anthony turned on the iron and ran it over a tablecloth. He expected the wrinkles to disappear but they didn't. Hmm. Maybe the setting needed to be higher. Anthony turned the knob and tried again. Still nothing. He tried to remember what his family's maid, Wanda, did when she was ironing. Sometimes she had a bottle of water that she spritzed on the clothes she was ironing.

Anthony left the iron face down on the tablecloth and went to look for a spray bottle. When he got back to the ironing board, he could see wisps of black smoke wafting off the tablecloth. Uh-oh. Not a good sign.

Anthony removed the iron to find a scorched triangle in the middle of the tablecloth. Yikes!

He rolled the tablecloth up into a ball, trying to decide what he should do with it. Finally, he tossed it into the dryer. Beginner's mistake. He'd do better with the next one.

Six scorched tablecloths and twenty scorched napkins later, Anthony still hadn't figured out the art of ironing. Deciding it was better to quit while he was ahead, he turned off the iron and went in search of Paige. He found her in the kitchen where she was sitting in front of a chopping block.

"Paige! Psst!"

Paige looked up from the pile of onions she was chopping, her eyes all wet and teary.

"Anthony!" she sobbed.

He grabbed her by the hand. "Come on! Let's get out of here. We weren't raised for this kind of work. We've lived in the lap of luxury for far too long!"

Thirty minutes later they were at the Frosted Cupcake sipping hot chocolates. Anthony was gazing at a photo of Max that Paige had taken on their weekend in the Hamptons.

"We have to ask him," Paige said. "What else can we do? Every plan we've come up with has failed."

"But it's going to mess everything up."

"Wouldn't you rather know?"

"Yes. No. I don't know!"

"Who's that a picture of?" Roger asked while dropping off some extra marshmallows for their cocoa.

"Our crush," Anthony said.

"*Our* crush?"

"We don't know if he's gay or straight," Paige explained.

"And you both like him."

"Uh-huh," Anthony said.

Roger plucked the picture from Anthony's hand and stared at it. "Well, you both have good taste. He's cute."

"You think?" Anthony asked.

"Yep. Just make sure he's not a player like your last boyfriend."

"What do you mean?"

"I didn't know how to tell you at the time and then when you broke up with him, I figured, well, what was the point? But Ian used to drop in here a lot without you. And it wasn't just for the cupcakes."

"Spill it, Roger."

"A lot of gay guys come here. You know that. Ian knew it, too. He'd flirt with them. Exchange phone numbers. That sort of thing."

"I knew it!" Anthony exclaimed. "I knew it, I knew it, I knew it! He was cheating on me way before P-Town!"

"You were right about him all along," Paige said.

"How could I have such lousy taste in a boyfriend?" Anthony moaned.

Roger gave the picture of Max back to Anthony. "Not really. I mean, you broke things off with him. You went with your instincts."

"Don't worry, Anthony," Paige said. "You'll find your Mr. Right. Eventually."

"Eventually could be five years from now. I want eventually to be today!"

"Why do you want eventually to be today?" Colleen asked, walking up to the table.

"Boyfriend issues," Paige explained.

Colleen slipped into the armchair opposite Paige.

"What can I get for you?" Roger asked.

"I'll have a cup of peppermint tea. By the way, I love your vest. So colorful! Where did you buy it?"

"I made it," Roger said, looking down at the colorful vertical stripes of his vest.

After Roger left to get Colleen's order, she reached into her gold python Gucci clutch and pulled out a flyer.

"Who would have thought a straight boy could be so stylish?"

"Maybe you should make a play for Roger," Paige suggested.

Colleen rolled her eyes. "I come here a lot. I know the score. Roger likes them stick thin. That ain't me!" Colleen passed over the flyer. "If you two are still looking for boyfriends, this may be the answer to your problems."

Anthony picked up the flyer. "What is it?"

"Peppington is having a Bachelor Auction in two weeks. It's for charity. The girls are going to bid on the guys. There's a list of who's participating on the back of the flyer."

Anthony scrolled down the list. "Yes! Max is on it!" he exclaimed excitedly, his eyes lighting up.

"So?" Paige asked.

"This is it, Paige! Our final plan."

"Oh, no," Paige groaned, covering her ears. "I thought we were finished with plans."

"We are after this one. Just listen to me. Are you listening?"

Paige reluctantly dropped her hands from her ears. "I'm listening."

"We're going to go to this auction and you're going to bid on Max. Then after you win him and you're out on a romantic date with him, you're going to tell him how you feel."

"And then?"

"And then he'll give you an answer."

Paige snapped her fingers. "Just like that?"

"Just like that!"

"In case you've forgotten, we haven't gotten an answer out of him so far," Paige reminded Anthony.

"This time we will."

"And that will be because . . . ?"

"He's going to have to be honest with you. After all, you'll have won him!"

"It sounds like it could work," Colleen said.

"What do you say, Paige?" Anthony asked. "One last time?"

Paige sighed. "If it wasn't for charity, I'd say no, but since it is . . ."

"Excellent!" Anthony proclaimed, raising his mug of hot chocolate. "Let the bidding begin!"

chapter eighteen

*T*he moment Anthony had been waiting for had finally arrived.

It was time for the kiss.

He'd brushed his teeth, flossed, gargled with mouthwash twice and chewed half a pack of Dentyne so his breath would be minty-fresh.

He and Max were going to go through his screenplay from beginning to end, acting out every scene, and then they were going to start filming next week. The first scene Anthony planned to film was the kiss, which took place in Washington Square Park in Greenwich Village. When Max asked him why he was shooting the scenes out of order, Anthony explained he wanted to film as many exterior shots as possible while the weather was still good. He also told him that this was the way many directors shot their movies, which was true. He certainly didn't want Max to think he had any ulterior motives for wanting to shoot the kiss first!

The doorbell rang and Anthony hurried from his bedroom, only to stop in his tracks when he saw Paolo heading for the front door.

"What are you doing here?" he wailed.

"I live here, remember?"

"But only on weekends!"

"Check your calendar. Today's Friday. That's part of the weekend."

"But not until after five! It's only three thirty."

Paolo folded his arms over his chest. "Okay, what's going on? Why don't you want me around? What are you plotting that I shouldn't know about? Or do I not want to ask?"

"I'm not plotting anything!"

"Then why don't you want me here?"

The doorbell rang again.

"Max and I are rehearsing *Not All Italian Boys Are Straight* in the living room."

"And that affects me how?"

"I don't want an audience."

"That's a twist. You usually love having an audience."

"Not today."

"What's the big secret?"

"Paolo, *please*," Anthony begged, as the doorbell rang a third time.

"Tell me why you don't want me around," Paolo insisted. "Otherwise I'm not going anywhere."

Argh! Today of all days Paolo decides to be more annoying than usual!

"I don't want to make Max uncomfortable," Anthony admitted. "We're going to kiss for the first time and I don't want anyone watching."

"Oh . . ."

"Yes! *Oh* . . . It needs to just be me and Max. Now leave. Vanish. Vamoose!"

"Fine. I'll go where you always banish me. My bedroom. Satisfied?"

"Make sure you stay there," Anthony said as the doorbell rang again. Was it his imagination or did the ring sound impatient? Oh, no! Maybe Max thought no one was home and was getting ready to leave.

"I'll be right there!" Anthony called out, shooting daggers at his brother. "*Go!*" he insisted.

"I'm going. I'm going. But first I want you to answer a question for me."

"*Now?*"

"You've been rehearsing this screenplay for weeks and *today's* the first time you and Max are going to rehearse the kissing scene?" Paolo shook his head. "I know you don't want to hear this, but I think Max is telling you something, baby bro."

Anthony covered his ears with his hands. "That's right. I don't want to hear it and I don't have time to explain things to you. Why must you *always* be the voice of gloom and doom?"

"Because I'm your big brother and because I care?"

"Well I don't want you to care today!" Anthony snapped. "Just keep your theories to yourself and go to your room!"

Paolo held his hands up in surrender. "I'm gone."

Once Paolo was out of sight, Anthony took a deep breath,

trying to calm down before opening the front door. Sometimes his brother made him so angry! Did he think he was that stupid? That naïve? Of course he had been wondering why Max didn't want to do the kissing scene. But the wondering was over. Today was the day.

"Sorry it took me so long," he said, opening the front door.

Max smiled at him, his cheeks red from the brisk October air and his hair tousled from the wind. He looked *so* adorable! It was all Anthony could do to stop himself from running his fingers through Max's hair, smoothing it back into place.

"I thought maybe you'd forgotten we were supposed to rehearse."

Forget? How could I forget? I wasn't able to sleep a wink last night. I've been up since six o'clock this morning counting down the hours!

After taking Max's coat and hanging it in the front closet, Anthony led Max into the living room.

"So, are you ready to get started?" he asked, trying to ignore the butterflies in his stomach and keep his voice steady. He was so nervous! What if this turned out to be a disaster? What if when they finally reached the kissing scene and it was time to kiss, Max pushed him away and told him he couldn't do it. That the idea of kissing another guy was revolting to him and even though he thought he could do it, he really couldn't and he was dropping out of the project. The movie wouldn't get made! His admissions packet for UCLA would be incomplete because there wasn't time to get another actor to play Michael. He wouldn't get into the college of his choice!

He felt a hand shaking him. "Huh? What?"

"You spaced out," Max said.

Anthony blushed. "Sorry. I was thinking about the script."

"I'm ready to start whenever you are."

They started from the first page and the dialogue flowed smoothly as they remembered all their lines. They were no longer Anthony and Max, but Dominick and Michael. After forty-five minutes, they finally got to the kissing scene.

Lips, don't fail me now! Anthony prayed as he closed the distance between himself and Max. They were sitting on the couch, which, when they were filming in Washington Square Park, would be a park bench. The one thing that Ian had told him more than once when they were together was that he was a great kisser. Ian might have lied about everything else, but Anthony was pretty sure he'd been telling the truth about that. Ian had *loved* kissing him.

Anthony wrapped his arms around Max's shoulders, pulling him close. It felt so good having his arms around him! He wished he could press his head against Max's chest and just cuddle with him. But that wasn't in the script. Rats! Was there time for a rewrite? Maybe he could work it in. Until then, though, there was only the kiss.

Anthony gazed into Max's eyes, hoping he could see inside him. Hoping he could see that the feelings reflected in his eyes weren't Dominick's feelings for Michael, but his own feelings for Max.

And taking those feelings, using them to give him strength, to show Max that he cared about him, Anthony leaned in and pressed his lips to Max's.

It was a soft, gentle kiss. Tentative. Exploring. Then, as his lips pressed against Max's, deepening the kiss and giving him a taste of what he'd been denied for so many weeks, it became bolder. Hungrier. He wanted more. Much more. He moved his hands from Max's shoulders and cradled his head as his kiss turned into an open-mouthed one.

At first, Max stiffened when Anthony's lips locked with his. There was no mistaking the body language. The tension in his muscles. He wasn't enjoying the kiss. He didn't like it.

"I know you don't want to hear this, but I think Max is telling you something, baby bro."

Why was he hearing his brother's voice?

Get out of my head, Paolo. Now! Out!

This wasn't good. This wasn't good at all. If he was aware of Max's discomfort, then it was going to come across on camera. And that wasn't good because Max's character was gay and what gay guy didn't like kissing another guy? Max's character was supposed to be enjoying this.

But then something happened as Anthony's kiss changed and became bolder.

Max started to relax. The stiffness and tension left his arms. He sort of melted into Anthony's embrace, wrapping his own arms around Anthony's shoulders, pulling him close and deepening their kiss with an open-mouthed one of his own.

Anthony was stunned.

Max was kissing him back!!!

Calm down, Anthony. Calm down. This does NOT *mean anything. Max is not kissing you. It's Michael. Michael is kissing you back. And you're not Anthony, you're Dominick. This is a scene from your movie. It's not real. Keep reminding yourself of that. It's* **NOT** *real!!!*

But real stars fell in love every day from working together, he stubbornly reminded himself.

Why couldn't it happen to them?

Why couldn't this kiss be real?

The kiss had to be real.

Max wouldn't be kissing him this way if it wasn't.

Finally, he had the proof he'd been waiting for!

Max was gay!

And maybe this was the moment Max had been waiting for as well.

Maybe Max *did* feel something for him and this was his way of telling him!

Anthony could have gone on and on kissing Max, but they had to get through the rest of the screenplay. Now wasn't the time to find out if Max had feelings for him. Anthony broke their kiss and pulled away from Max, giving him a sly smile as he delivered his next line.

"For someone who's never kissed a guy," he said, "you sure knew what you were doing."

The rest of the rehearsal went well. They even went through the screenplay a *second* time, including the kissing scene. Anthony almost pinched himself to make sure he wasn't dreaming when Max suggested the second run-through.

"Just to make sure we've got it knocked. Are you game?"

What was he going to say? No? Of course not!

And when they kissed again, there was no hesitancy on Max's part. His lips met Anthony's when they were supposed to and melded with his in a kiss that was sweet, magical and perfect.

This can't be acting. It just can't. It's too good not to be real.

When they finished rehearsing, Max gave Anthony a high-five, telling him he couldn't wait to start filming the next week. As Anthony walked him to the front door, he wondered if the next time they kissed—in front of the camera—would be the last time they kissed. Or could it be the beginning of something else?

Ten minutes after Max left the apartment, Paige showed up to find out how the rehearsal had gone.

"Break it to me gently," she said, taking off her scarf and tossing it on the couch.

"We kissed," Anthony said. "*Twice.*"

"Twice?" She stopped unzipping her jacket. "But there's only one kiss in the screenplay."

"We went through it twice. The second time at *his* suggestion." Anthony shrugged. "What can I say? These lips are addictive!"

"I will not be jealous, I will not be jealous," Paige began chanting.

"You got a kiss from him," Anthony said as he went to hang Paige's jacket and scarf.

"But he meant to kiss me on the cheek!" Paige reminded. "That's almost brotherly."

"Speaking of brothers," Anthony scowled as Paolo entered the living room, "mine almost ruined things!"

"I kept my end of the bargain. I stayed in my bedroom when Lover Boy was here. Now he's gone." Paolo flopped down on the couch and aimed the remote control at the TV.

"Did you get to kiss him?"

Anthony stuck his tongue out at Paolo. "Yes, I did."

Paolo looked away from the TV. "But you know you were just acting, right? That the kiss wasn't real."

"I thought that at first," Anthony said and then turned to Paige. "But when he suggested we do it a second time, I don't know, Paige, I think he was trying to tell me something."

"Tell you what?" she asked.

"That he likes me."

"Then why wouldn't he say it?" Paolo asked.

"Because he's afraid."

"Of what?"

"I think he might be closeted."

"And I think you need a reality check," Paolo said.

"*What* are you doing here?!" Anthony screamed. "Last time I checked, this was a private conversation between Paige and me."

"Fine. I'll butt out. But here's a news flash, Ants. Max wasn't kissing you. He was kissing Dominick."

"Maybe the first time we kissed. But not the second," Anthony insisted. "He wanted to kiss me again. I know he did. Why else would he have suggested we do it again?"

"Practice makes perfect?"

"Oh, go back to your stupid TV show!"

Paolo sighed. "The two of you have wasted enough time on this joker. I'll bet he even knows what's going on and is getting his jollies by jerking you both around."

"Max wouldn't do that!" Anthony exclaimed.

"How do you know?"

"I just do!"

"You don't even know if he's gay or straight!" Paolo shouted. "Trust me, if he was gay and he was interested in you, he'd be finding a way to make the first move."

"He did. Today! When he kissed me a second time."

Paolo ignored Anthony's comment. "As for you, Paige, what I said to Ants also applies to you. If Max was interested, he'd have already made a move. And if Max *is* straight and he's not interested in you, then he's nuts."

"Thank you, Dear Abby," Anthony sneered.

Paolo shut off the TV and angrily tossed the remote onto the coffee table.

Anthony's eyes widened. "Temper, temper, Pow."

"I'm outta here. The two of you don't want to listen to a word I have to say? Fine. Keep making fools of yourself over this guy. I just don't want to see you both get hurt. That's all. Excuse me for caring."

After Paolo left the room, Anthony raised an eyebrow at Paige and smirked. He hadn't thought it was possible, but what he had just seen had confirmed his suspicions.

"What???" Paige demanded. "Why are you making that weird face at me?"

"Did you see how upset Paolo was getting?"

"Uh, yeah."

"Haven't you been noticing, Paige?"

"Noticing what?"

"Paolo's jealousy."

"His jealousy?"

Anthony sighed. "Come on! The clues have been there. Almost from the very beginning! I had started putting the pieces together myself but then told myself I was being crazy."

"Paolo's jealous of us?"

"No! He's jealous of *Max*!"

"Max?" Paige looked at Anthony in confusion. "Why would he be jealous of Max?"

"Oh, I don't know," Anthony said, looking at his nails before locking eyes with Paige. "Maybe it's because *he wants you for himself*!"

Paige's mouth dropped open in shock as Anthony started laughing hysterically. "You should see the look on your face," he howled, clutching his sides. "It's priceless!"

"You didn't just say what I think you said. Did you?"

"I did! Paolo *likes* you. You should have seen how jealous he was the weekend you were in the Hamptons with Max."

"Paolo was jealous? Why didn't you tell me?"

"Because I thought I was nuts! But I've been noticing that every time the two of you have a fight, Max comes up."

"You're jumping to conclusions. Paolo does *not* like me. And I don't like him! He's rude and arrogant and he's *obsessed* with sports."

"Why else would he be looking out for you?"

"Same reason that he's looking out for you. The big brother gene."

Anthony thought it over. "You think?"

"I know."

"Well, maybe you're right. But I'm going to keep a close eye on Pow and see if I can find anything out."

"You're wasting your time. Besides, I'm not interested in Paolo. I'm interested in Max!"

"Ah yes, Maxie! The reason we live and breathe! We've got to strategize for tomorrow's Bachelor Auction."

"How much do you think this is going to cost us?"

"Money is no object!" Anthony said. "Remember, it's for charity!"

"We're not going to have to spend everything we have, are we?"

"We want to win him, don't we?"

"Yes, but how much do you think he'll go for?"

Anthony shrugged. "A couple of hundred? No more than a thousand."

Paige sighed in relief. "That's doable. I was thinking the price might go higher."

"For Max? Paige, he may be a catch, but he's not the catch of the day! There are a lot more hunkier, handsomer guys at Peppington Prep with richer daddies than Steve Coulter. I have a feeling our Max is going to be an overlooked item at the auction and that'll give us the perfect opportunity to scoop him up."

"So what's the plan?"

"I don't think we should make the first bid. Let's wait and see what happens. I mean, I'm sure someone will make an offer for him, but let's see what the starting bid is, and then if he gets any other offers."

"Sounds good to me!"

Anthony looked at his watch. "By this time tomorrow, we'll have our answer!"

chapter nineteen

*P*aige was dressed to kill.

She stared at the image of herself in her full-length bed-room mirror and she had to admit, she looked *hot*.

No more beating around the bush.

Tonight was *the* night.

She was going to find out if Max was gay or straight and, if he was straight, then she wanted him to see what he had been missing out on.

And could have if he wanted!

She was wearing a strapless, blush-hued gown by Calvin Klein that plunged provocatively in the front—she still couldn't believe she'd had the courage to wear it! But when she'd tried it on at the store, she knew she had to buy it. It clung to her curves in all the right places and made her look older. More mature. She certainly didn't look like a teenage girl.

A new gown required new shoes, and the Jimmy Choos on her feet were a new pair in hot pink, wickedly pointed at the toe and sinfully high at the heel. Because she wasn't used to high heels, she'd had to practice walking around in them so she wouldn't fall. It had taken a few days, but she'd finally gotten the hang of it.

She'd set her hair with hot rollers and now her head was a wild, messy mane of waves and curls, exactly the way Anthony always suggested.

Jewelry was minimal. A chunky gold bracelet on one wrist and a thin gold chain around her neck.

Her makeup was flawless. She'd accentuated her eyes with a smoky shade of eyeshadow and plumped up her lashes with mascara. She'd highlighted her cheekbones with a slight touch of blush and painted her lips a yummy shade of raspberry with a finishing touch of lip gloss to make them shimmer.

Paige couldn't stop staring at her image. She couldn't ever remember looking this beautiful. Yes, that was the word. Beautiful. After telling Anthony how she felt like she'd been living in her mother's shadow, she'd decided it was time to do something about it. Just because she was her mother's daughter didn't mean she was going to turn out the same way as her mother. Camille was Camille, and she was herself.

And so today's transformation.

She felt like a different person.

Stronger.

More confident.

She knew she was going to turn heads at the auction.

And she couldn't wait!

She was sure everyone was expecting her to arrive in a demure, quiet gown. Something very Laura Ashley with her hair in its usual French braid or pushed back with a headband. Very ice princessy.

Boy, were they going to be surprised!

She almost wished Paolo could get a look at her. She could just imagine the stunned surprise on his face. She'd love to leave him speechless for once. Every so often, Anthony's comment about Paolo liking her popped into her head, but she chased it away. It was so crazy! Paolo did *not* like her.

Did he?

She chased away all thoughts of Paolo. Tonight wasn't about him.

It was about Max!

She turned back to the mirror, admiring herself one last time.

Why hadn't she done this sooner? It had been fun getting all dressed up. She wouldn't want to do this every day, but once in a while wouldn't be too bad.

Now, was she forgetting anything?

Scent!

She reached for a bottle of perfume and spritzed it in the air, then walked through it the way she'd seen her mother do on countless occasions when she was a little girl.

She wondered what was up with Camille. She hadn't heard from her in a few weeks. The scalding message she'd left had never been returned, although according to one of the tabloids, Camille, attempting to disguise herself with huge sunglasses and a head scarf, had been spotted using the

private entrance of an exclusive Beverly Hills plastic surgeon. Paige hoped she wasn't going to have anything too
drastic done. Her mother was a beautiful woman and she
certainly didn't look her age.

Her cell phone rang and she picked it up without checking the incoming number, expecting the caller to be Anthony.

"Calm down, I'm almost ready."

"Paige!" Camille wailed from three thousand miles away.

"Mother?"

"Darling, you've got to help me! You must!"

Paige held back a sigh. Of course, a crisis call. Why else
would Camille be on the line?

"What's wrong?"

"I'm trapped on the West Coast because of the weather.
Some sort of fog that's as thick as pea soup. No planes can
leave the airport."

"What do you want me to do about it?"

"Tonight is the *Soap Opera Magazine* Awards in New York
at the Waldorf Astoria. I've been voted Best Villainess. It's a
fan-voted award, but it looks like I'm not going to be there
because of this horrible fog. I can't let my fans down!
Darling, you have to help me!"

Camille was talking so fast, it was taking Paige a while to
process everything. But certain words jumped out at her.
New York. Waldorf Astoria. **Tonight.**

"Let me get this straight," Paige said, trying to stay calm
because if she was thinking what she was thinking . . . no, she
didn't want to go there. Camille wouldn't make the same mistake twice, would she? "There's an awards show tonight in
New York that you're supposed to be at, but you can't make it."

"Yes, yes, yes! That's why I'm calling."

"Oh?" Paige knew what coming next. Without a doubt. She'd stake her life on it.

"You have to take my place at the show and accept the award on my behalf."

Bingo!

"I do?" Paige tried not to sound snotty. "Really?"

"Yes! I have to show my fans how much I appreciate all their love and support. It would be a slap in the face to them if someone wasn't there to accept my award."

Paige almost dropped the phone. Camille's words were like scalding acid thrown in her face. *All **their** love and support? What about mine? Doesn't my love and support count?*

"I don't believe you," Paige whispered hoarsely, the words lodged in her throat and unable to come out. "I absolutely do not believe you!"

"Paige? Darling? What's wrong? Speak up. I can't hear you. Is the line breaking up?"

"What's wrong? What's *wrong*?!" Paige asked incredulously, her voice rising. "You have the gall to ask me what's wrong? Are you that clueless?"

"Paige, I have no idea what you're talking about."

"You were going to be in New York tonight and it slipped your mind that you have a daughter who lives here? A daughter who maybe might like to see you? This is just like when you appeared on *New York Live*. Why weren't you going to tell me you'd be here?"

"The thought never crossed my mind."

"Why not?" Paige demanded. "Do you think so little of me? Or do you not think of me at all except when you want something? Did you ever stop to think that maybe I'd like to spend some time with my mother?"

"But darling, you have your life and I have mine."

"So? What does that have to do with anything? That doesn't mean our lives can't overlap. I'm your daughter!"

"I don't know what to say," Camille said. "It never occurred to me that you'd want to spend time with me. Why didn't you say something sooner?"

"Why should I? You're my mother. I would think you'd have some interest in me. You always expect me to come through for you. To save you. Rescue you. Clean up your messes. What about me? What about all those times you've let me down? All those missed ballet recitals and plays and award ceremonies because they couldn't fit into your sched-ule. You're never there for me. Ever! Thank God for Daddy! At least he doesn't make me feel like an afterthought."

"I thought you didn't want me," Camille said. "That's why I never came."

"What?" Paige couldn't have heard her correctly.

"You have your father and your life in New York. When I moved back to California and you decided you wanted to stay in New York with your father, well, I thought . . . well . . . that you didn't need me. That you didn't want me in your life."

"That's not true!" Paige exclaimed. "Of course I want you. You're my mother. I love you!"

As soon as she said the words, Paige realized they were true. Why hadn't she said so for the last ten years? But was that the root of all their problems? Miscommunication? Could it be that, with this one phone call, they were going to work things out? It couldn't be that easy, could it?

"And I love you!" Camille cried. "When I think of all the time we've lost! All the time we could have spent together. It makes my heart ache. Ache! But that's all over now. The future is ours and we can do anything we want with it. Anything!"

Wait a minute. Camille's last couple of sentences sounded vaguely familiar. Where had she heard them before?

It came to Paige in a flash. Last year on *The Yields of Passion*. When Priscilla thought she was dying of a deadly blood disease and then learned she wasn't dying. She'd said these exact same words to her younger sister, Suzette, with whom she'd been feuding with over—what else?—a man.

"Mother, stop acting," Paige said.

"Acting? I'm not acting."

"Yes, you are. For a while there, you were genuine, but then you slipped into Priscilla."

"I didn't do it on purpose," Camille grumbled. "Our writers are so good, why shouldn't I recycle their dialogue? Especially if I'm trying to say the same thing!"

Paige knew Anthony was going to kill her, but she had no choice. She had to do this. "I'll go to the show for you."

"You will?"

"Yes, but on one condition."

"Anything, darling!"

"When I get off the phone, you go to the nearest airline counter and book yourself a flight to New York. We're going to start spending some time together. A lot of time. Otherwise the next time you call and I hear your voice, I'm pressing the disconnect button."

"I'll have to check my taping schedule, but I think I'm free the first weekend of next month. Oh, and we can spend Thanksgiving together. And Christmas! How does that all sound?"

"Perfect. And Mother?"

"Yes?"

"Even though you're more selfish, self-centered and self-absorbed than I'd like, and you worry about your career far too much, I'm glad you're my mom and I love you."

"Oh, Paige, those are the nicest words anyone has ever said to me. If I weren't wearing waterproof mascara, I'd be tearing up! But I am and I'm glad because some photographers are headed this way. Gotta go. Bye!"

Paige laughed. "Good-bye, Mother."

Paige shut off the phone. She knew it was going to take a while to make things right, but for the first time in a long time, the anger she felt toward her mother was gone.

"What do you mean we can't go to the Bachelor Auction?"

Anthony, bundled up in a white terry cloth robe, was pacing in front of Paige, a green mud pack on his face, his wet hair wrapped in a turban. He'd been getting ready for the auction when Paige arrived at his penthouse.

"I thought you would have jumped at the chance to go to a soap opera award dinner," Paige said. "Think of all the celebrities that are going to be there!"

"Any other time, yes. In a heartbeat. But not today! Paige, today's the day we've been waiting for!"

"Well it's too late now. I promised Camille I'd go for her. I can't back out. She'd be devastated."

"Okay, there's an easy solution to this. You go to the awards dinner. I'll go to the auction and bid on Max for you. I'll be your proxy."

"But I don't want to go to this soap dinner by myself!" Paige wailed. "I won't know anyone there."

Anthony inspected Paige from head to toe. "Paigey-poo, the way you're dressed, you're going to have every hunk in daytime lining up for your phone number. You're not going to be sitting all by your lonesome. Trust me. You look fabulous!"

"I still don't want to go by myself," Paige grumbled.

"Well, I can't be in two places at the same time," Anthony said.

Just then, the front door opened and a sweaty Paolo walked into the apartment, dropping his basketball and athletic bag on the marble floor. When he got a look at Paige, he did a double take.

"What's with the outfit?"

Paige gave Paolo a confused look. "What do mean?"

"Did you raid Camille's closet? That doesn't look like something you'd normally wear. Can you even breathe in that dress? And what's with all the makeup on your face? Are you going to a costume party or something?"

"Paige is going to a soap opera awards dinner tonight and she needs an escort," Anthony said. "I was just about to tell her that you were going to take her."

Paige gave Anthony a get-real look, but he ignored it.

"Are you outta your mind? No way! I've got tickets to the Knicks game tonight. I'm not missing that for anything. Sorry, Paige." Paolo kicked off his sneakers and headed in the direction of his bedroom.

"Thanks for trying," Paige said, trying not to feel dejected. So much for Anthony's theory that Paolo liked her. He hadn't even noticed what she was wearing. Well, he'd noticed, but not in a good way!

"I'll be right back," Anthony said. "Don't go away."

Anthony stormed down the hallway to his brother's bedroom. When he got there, he slammed the door shut behind him.

"Listen and listen good, because I'm only going to say this once," Anthony said, closing the distance between himself and his brother, who was at his desk, working on his laptop. "You're taking Paige to that awards dinner tonight."

"Oh, I am, am I?" Paolo said, eyes glued to his computer screen.

Anthony hit the off button on his brother's laptop. "Yes, you are! Because if you don't, I'm going to tell Mom and Dad every secret I have on you, I'm going to steal the batteries from every remote in this penthouse and I'm also going to cancel every sports channel that we have in our cable package."

"Hey!" Paolo cried, tearing his eyes away from his computer screen. "You just made me lose what I was working on!"

"How stupid are you?" Anthony raged. "Do you know how long it's taken me to build up Paige's confidence? To get her to look like that? She looks beautiful! Any guy in his right mind would be drooling over her. But not you! No, not you! What do *you* do when you see her? Do you compliment her? Do you tell her how great she looks? No! You tear her down! You take away her confidence. You make her feel ugly."

"I didn't mean—"

Anthony cut him off. "That's my best friend out there and *nobody* hurts her. Nobody! Not even you!"

"Ants, I was only kidding around with her."

"Well it wasn't very funny. And if you care for Paige the way I think you do . . ."

Anthony watched as his brother swallowed nervously.

"That's right, Pow, I'm on to you."

"On to what?"

"Don't try to deny it. I know what's going on. I've noticed the way you get jealous whenever Max's name is mentioned. You're interested in Paige. I don't know if she'd be interested in you—after all, you drive her *crazy*—but if you don't want Max to have her then you better do something about it.

"Now I'm going back out there and I'm going to tell Paige that you've agreed to take her to that awards dinner. When I get back in here, you'd better be showered and shaved and dressed like you could be shot for the cover of *GQ*. Otherwise I'm going to buy an ice pick and puncture every soccer ball, tennis ball, basketball and football in this penthouse!"

With those final words, Anthony left Paolo's bedroom and returned to Paige with a huge smile on his face.

"Guess what? Paolo made a mistake about his tickets. The game's tomorrow night so he can take you to the dinner."

"He can?" Paige asked suspiciously.

"Yep."

"Are you sure?"

"He's getting ready right this instant."

"What did you have to do to get him to agree to go?"

"Nothing. I swear. So here's the plan. You and Paolo are going to the dinner; I'm going to the auction. You don't have to stay for the whole dinner, do you?"

"No, just for Camille's award. I'm sure we can leave after I accept it."

"Once that happens, call me. I'll let you know what's going on at my end. Then we'll join up and lay our cards down on the table with Max. Just think, by the end of tonight, we're going to know if he's gay or straight."

"Are you ready to go, Paige?"

Paige turned around to see Paolo wearing an L & F tuxedo. His hair was slicked back and he had a trace of five o'clock shadow. Devilishly handsome was what sprang into her mind.

"You clean up pretty nice," she said. "Are you sure you want to come? I can go by myself. It's no big deal."

"Are you kidding? You look sensational. I should have told you that when I first came in, but you caught me by surprise. It's just that usually you don't dress up so much. I like it."

"That tuxedo fits you like a glove," Anthony raved. "Maybe you should skip Paige's dinner and come with me to Peppington Prep. I could make a bundle auctioning you off."

Paige threw herself across Paolo's chest, holding on tight. "Back off! He's mine!"

Hmmm. She'd never noticed it before, but Paolo had a nice chest. Firm. Muscular. And his biceps weren't too bad either. For a last-minute date, she hadn't done too badly.

Paolo held his arm out to Paige and gave her a smile. "Shall we?"

Paige hooked her arm through his. "Let's."

chapter twenty

nthony was in seventh heaven. Five guys had already been auctioned and each one was hunkier than the next. So far, the highest bid had been five hundred dollars for Jared Banderas. Brazilian boys were hot, and in Anthony's opinion, Jared had been worth every cent he'd gotten. Anthony glanced at the flyer in his hand. Two more bachelors were going to be auctioned off and then it was Max's turn.

Anthony began fidgeting in his chair as he gazed around the crowded auditorium. Both parents and students were here, all dressed in their very best. He recognized a handful of faces, but most of the room was filled with strangers. He was starting to get nervous and the palms of his hands were sweating. What was Max going to think when he heard one of his bids come from a guy? And what was everyone else going to think? He was out to his friends, but he wasn't out to everyone at Peppington Prep. Would they be shocked to see a guy bidding on another guy? Even though Anthony didn't want to, he knew he'd have to explain that he was bidding for a female friend. Otherwise his bidding on Max might stir things up and the auction could come to an end.

"What are you doing here? Didn't you get the memo saying this was a *straight* auction?"

Anthony looked up from his flyer. "Hello Felix."

"Where's your sidekick?"

"Paige couldn't make it tonight, so I'm going to bid for her."

"You're bidding for *Paige*? Yeah, right," Felix sneered. "Who do you think you're fooling? You're going to bid on Max for yourself. You've wanted him since the night I brought him to your party and now you think you've got the perfect way of landing him."

What was the deal with Felix? He was all over him at his birthday party and now he'd reverted back to his nasty self. Was he jealous that Anthony was interested in Max? "Believe what you want, Felix. You always do."

"I wouldn't be too confident of winning, Anthony. Anything can happen at an auction."

With those words, Felix disappeared and Anthony forgot all about him as the next two bachelors went for two hundred and three hundred dollars. Then Max was standing on stage, wearing a tuxedo and looking ultra handsome.

Suddenly, Anthony felt a pang in his heart. It wasn't a painful pang, but more of a wistful, longing pang. A pang of regret. Of sadness. Of hope. He really did have deep feelings for Max and even though he'd tried not to let those feelings grow, they had. Day after day, week after week, his feelings had gotten stronger and stronger until they were a part of him. He hadn't realized that until just now, staring at him up on the stage.

Until tonight, there was nothing he could do with those feelings. But in just a couple of hours, he was going to tell Max how he felt. And either his news was going to be joyfully received or he was going to have his heart broken.

Ms. de la Vega was the auctioneer and she opened the bidding for Max at one hundred dollars. A female voice called out one hundred, followed by another voice that offered two hundred.

Anthony raised his hand and offered five hundred dollars. "Before everyone gasps," he quickly explained, "I'm bidding for a friend. Paige Crane. She couldn't be here tonight, but she sent me in her place. She's had her eye on this bachelor for quite a while and hopes to win him tonight."

There. After hearing those words, there was no way Max could not know that Paige had feelings for him. If he didn't, he was pretty dumb.

"Five hundred dollars," Ms. de la Vega announced. "Do I hear six hundred? No? Then the bid is at five hundred dollars. Going once. Going twice . . ."

Yes! Max was going to be his! The plan had worked. This had gone so much easier than he thought he would. And cost less than what he'd expected.

"One thousand dollars!" a voice called out.

Anthony spun around in shock, his head whirling to where Bianca Torres, wearing a floral print evening gown in black and pink silk, was sitting, a smug smile on her face.

What?!

"Two thousand dollars."

Anthony's head whipped in the opposite direction, where Rachel Torres, looking fabulous in a shimmering silver lamé gown with a beaded neckline, had just topped her sister's bid, a determined look on her face as she glared at her twin.

"Three thousand dollars," Bianca called out.

"Four thousand dollars," Rachel said.

No, no, no! This wasn't supposed to be happening. Max was supposed to be his. The bidding was supposed to be over. What was going on?

Colleen, who was wearing an antique ivory silk gown, slid into the empty seat next to Anthony and he grabbed her arm. "Why are they bidding on Max?"

"Felix."

He should have known! "What about him?"

"I overheard him at the punch table. He's pitted the twins against each other."

"How?"

"He told Bianca that the only reason she hasn't made it as a star is because Rachel is holding her back. And he told Rachel that the only reason she hasn't made it as a star is because Bianca is holding her back."

"And they believed him?"

"You've always known they don't have much in the brains department."

"I always thought Rachel was a smidge smarter than Bianca."

"Felix told each one separately that she's the more talented twin, but that everyone thinks they're a package deal, so Bianca needs to step out of Rachel's shadow and Rachel needs to step out of Bianca's shadow . . . and what better way to do that than by dating Max since his father is *the* current hot celebrity chef in America and it's only a matter of time before Max starts getting his own coverage and TV show. That's why they're bidding on him."

"They're going to ruin everything!" Anthony wailed.

"How much money do you have?"

"Paige will kill me if I bid five thousand dollars and we win him. Originally we'd planned on only going to a thousand."

"Last time I was over at Casa Torres, Papa Torres told the twins that they had to cut back on their spending. There's no way they can offer more than five thousand dollars. Offer six thousand."

"But I don't have six thousand dollars!"

"I'll get my mom to give me a check. She needs a couple more tax write-offs this year."

Anthony gave Colleen a hug. "You're an angel!"

"You can thank me with an outfit from the L & F spring couture line."

"Done." Anthony jumped out of his seat. "Six thousand dollars."

"Six thousand dollars," Ms. de la Vega shouted out as the auditorium gasped and Max's mouth dropped open in shock. "Going once, going twice . . . sold to the gentleman in the fifth row!"

Anthony collapsed in his seat while the auditorium burst out in applause and the twins stormed out of their seats. Up on stage, Max tipped the side of his head with his hand and bowed in Anthony's direction.

Anthony smiled back at Max while at the same time wondering, *Now that I've won him, what do I do with him?*

chapter twenty-one

*P*aige felt like a princess.

From the moment she placed her arm through Paolo's, her evening became magical.

It was like being in a fairy tale.

She assumed they would take a taxi to the Waldorf Astoria, but when they left the penthouse and arrived downstairs, there was a horse and carriage waiting for them.

"I thought this might be more fun," Paolo said, helping her step into the carriage, where she found a bouquet of pink roses waiting.

"How did you arrange all of this on such short notice?" she asked in amazement, holding the flowers close to her nose as their carriage headed in the direction of Central Park.

"You'd be amazed at what you can get done when you call

someone and tell them you're Lorenzo and Francesca DeMarco's son."

"You're saying I should be thanking your parents?"

"Hey!" Paolo laughed. "Give me a little credit. It was my idea."

Paige was touched by his thoughtfulness. He must have called for the carriage and arranged for the flowers when he was in his bedroom.

The magic continued when they arrived at the Waldorf Astoria and walked down the red carpet. Paige, who wasn't used to the spotlight, found it a bit intimidating as cameras were thrust in their faces and flashbulbs snapped madly. Microphones were held out and questions shouted:

"Who are you?"

"What are you wearing?"

"What soap are you on?"

"Who's your date?"

Paige could hardly see, but Paolo kept a steady arm around her waist, leading her inside.

"They actually think I'm somebody," she whispered into Paolo's ear, "but I'm nobody."

"Don't say that."

"But it's true."

"No, it's not. To me and Anthony, you're someone special."

Paige was shocked. Could Paolo be any sweeter? Why was he doing this?

When they got into the hotel, they were whisked to the dining room and brought to their table, which was at the front of the room. As they sat down, Paige caught sight of the waiting awards and panicked.

"I haven't even prepared a speech! What am I going to say?"

"Keep it short and sweet."

"Short and sweet don't apply to Camille. The last time she accepted one of these things, she went on for twenty minutes."

"Ouch! What caused that punishment?"

Paige laughed and instantly felt better.

"You're not your mother. You're you. Say whatever pops into your head, accept the award and leave the stage. Simple enough?" Paolo handed Paige a fluted glass. "Since we're not legal and can't indulge in a glass of champagne, I got us the next best thing."

Paige stared at the golden liquid. "Ginger ale?"

"How'd you guess?"

"It was a no-brainer."

Paolo clinked his glass against Paige's. "To the next diva of daytime."

Paige laughed while taking a sip from her glass. "Yeah, right."

"You've never thought of becoming an actress? You seem like a natural."

"I hate looking at pictures of myself, so I can't even imagine seeing myself on a TV screen."

"How come?"

Paige shrugged. "I don't know. I just do."

"I've seen you in some of Anthony's short films. You're really good."

"Those were just for fun. Acting silly and goofing around."

"You're underestimating your talent."

Paige laughed. "Are you thinking of becoming a director? Is that what this is all about? I thought Anthony was the one in the family with the Hollywood ambition."

"Me? A director? Nah. I haven't even declared a major yet. Anthony's lucky that he knows what he wants to do with his life. I'm still trying to figure it out."

"You will. One day it'll pop into your head and you'll know."

"We'll see. In the meantime, you shouldn't be so quick to say no to being an actress. Like I said, you have talent. And you're certainly beautiful enough."

Paige almost choked on the ginger ale she was sipping and started coughing.

"Are you okay?" Paolo asked, patting her on the back.

Paige nodded while trying to catch her breath.

He thought she was beautiful?

If Paige had to compare herself to the other girls in the room, she'd say they were prettier. Sexier. Bolder. They knew what they wanted and how to go after it. Case in point: Paolo. He had definitely caught their attention and a number of them were walking by the table, slowing down to get a closer look at him and trying to gain his attention.

But Paolo was unaware of them.

His eyes remained focused solely on her.

It was nice having one of the handsomest dates in the room. Paige turned around in her seat, pretending to look around at the room full of soap stars when what she was really doing was taking another peek at Paolo. When had he turned into such a hunk? For years, he'd been Anthony's older brother, the jock, who was always dripping sweat and guzzling out of a bottle of Gatorade. But when you took him out of his sweats and popped him into a tuxedo, he cleaned up nicely. *Very* nicely.

His table manners were impeccable—he knew which fork and which spoon had to be used for each course, unlike some of the other guests at their table. And when one of the female guests left to the use the ladies' room, he always rose from his seat and when she returned, he was always ready to pull out her chair.

Where had this Paolo been hiding himself? When she and Anthony hung out with him, he usually had manners like Homer Simpson!

And she had to admit, she did like arguing with him. She usually didn't agree with what he had to say, but he made her think. There was never a dull moment when the two of them were together. If he was mad, he let her know it. He didn't sulk like a spoiled brat the way Max did.

Now where had *that* thought come from?!

Paige watched Paolo check his watch. Was he trying to figure out how long they'd have to stay here? He was probably bored out of his mind.

"What time does this thing start?" he asked.

"Five."

"And the bachelor auction started an hour ago. How long do you think this is going to go on for? Two hours? Three?

"At least three."

"We should be able to get to Peppington Prep just as

things are winding down. Sooner if we cut out after you accept Camille's award."

He wasn't looking to leave! He just wanted her to make part of the auction!!

"How come you decided to ditch the auction?" he asked.

"My mother needed me. I couldn't say no to her."

"But what about Max?"

Paige shrugged. "What about him?"

"I thought tonight was *the* night."

"It was. It *is*. But I had to make a choice and I chose my mother. She means a lot to me."

"It's nice that you could help her out. I've heard you complain to Anthony about her."

"Do you actually watch TV when you're on that couch or are you constantly eavesdropping on our lives?"

"I think that it's cool that you made a sacrifice for your mom."

"This dinner was only happening once. I've got the rest of the school year to make my move on Max." Paige crossed her fingers. "I hope Anthony makes the winning bid for him."

"If I know my baby brother, he will. You know, it's going to be tough turning you over to Max."

If she didn't know any better, Paige would think Paolo was jealous. Could Anthony be right? Did Paolo have feelings for her? Nah, it couldn't be. He'd been a perfect gentleman the entire evening. He hadn't acted like most of her dates usually did, with grabby hands and suggestive comments.

"I'm all yours until then," she teased.

"Good!" Paolo whispered in her ear. "That's just how I want it."

Before Paige could say anything, the lights in the room dimmed and the awards show began, which was a relief because she was definitely blushing.

chapter twenty-two

"*L*ooks like you're stuck with me until your date arrives," Anthony said to Max when the auction was over. "I called Paige and left a message on her cell. I'm sure she'll call back once she's able to."

"Not a problem." Max handed Anthony a wicker picnic basket. "My dad made these up for all the bachelors. I don't know about you, but I'm starving. I was so nervous about not getting a bid that I didn't eat anything at all today. Why don't we have a picnic in Central Park and Paige can join us once her awards show is over."

It was an unseasonably warm day, and it was still light out, so the idea of a picnic in the park sounded fun.

"Don't go getting a swelled head because you went for so much money," Anthony said as they walked to the park.

"What was the deal with that?"

Anthony filled Max in on the twins' career plans and how they thought he could be of use to them.

"Really?" Max laughed. "Where'd they ever get a stupid idea like that?"

Anthony bit his tongue. Max and Felix were friends, and so far, Max was unaware of Felix's slimier side. Anthony didn't want to be the one to expose it to him. He shrugged. "Who knows? At least Paige had a good reason for wanting to win you."

"She did?"

"Remember when we were talking about her a couple of weeks ago? How I said I thought she might like you? Well, I asked her and she does. A lot. If you were to ask her out on date, she'd probably say yes."

Max pointed to an oak tree whose branches were filled with yellow, orange, gold and red leaves. "This looks like a good spot." He reached into the picnic basket and pulled out a red-and-white-checked blanket, spreading it on the ground. Then he started unpacking sandwiches, salads and drinks.

"Do you want turkey or ham?" he asked.

"Turkey." Anthony accepted a sandwich as he sat down on the blanket across from Max. "Did you hear what I said? Paige likes you. She wants to go out with you. Aren't you going to say something?"

Max removed the tie of his tuxedo and loosened the buttons of his collar. Then he bit into his ham sandwich and started chewing. "What do you want me to say?" he asked after swallowing. "That I like her, too?"

"Do you?" Anthony asked, holding his breath as he waited to hear Max's answer.

This was it. The moment he and Paige had been waiting for . . .

Max sighed. "Paige is great, Ants. Don't get me wrong. But I'm just not that into her."

"You don't have *any* romantic interest in her?"

"None."

"Not even a little?"

"She's a friend. A good friend. But that's it. Nothing more."

"And what about me?" Anthony asked, forcing himself to ask the question, not looking at Max and playing with the crust of his sandwich, pulling off bits and tossing them to the pigeons in the park. "Am I a friend?"

Max gave Anthony a smile as he put a hand on his arm. "You're more than just a friend. Don't you know that?"

Hearing those words, Anthony's heart began beating furiously. *I did not just hear those words. No, it couldn't be. It was too much to hope for.*

Max took another bite of his sandwich. As he did, a dab of mustard fell on his chin.

"You've got some mustard on your chin," Anthony said.

Max grabbed a napkin and wiped his chin. "Gone?"

"Nope."

Max wiped again. "Gone?"

"Still there." Anthony reached for a napkin. "Here, I'll do it." He leaned over to wipe Max's chin and as he did, started to fall into Max's lap. As he lost his balance, Max's arms wrapped around him, breaking the fall. When Max caught him in his arms, Anthony couldn't help himself. His own arms wrapped around Max, at first just to steady himself.

But as he tightened his grip and found himself drawn closer to Max, he was unable to resist the pull of attraction. The desire to do what he'd been wanting to do from the day he first met Max.

He kissed him.

For real.

It wasn't a rehearsed kiss from out of a script.

It was a kiss meant to show Max how much he meant to him. How much he wanted him.

Pressing his lips to Max's, Anthony poured all the feelings he had been keeping locked up inside himself into the kiss, wanting Max to know how much he cared for him.

But instead of Max kissing him back, he pulled away from Anthony's embrace, staring at him with wide, shocked eyes.

"What's wrong?" Anthony asked, starting to get a bad feeling in the pit of his stomach. Uh-oh. This wasn't good. Not good *at all*. Max wasn't supposed to be looking at him this way. Like he was some psycho killer in a horror movie. He was supposed to be smiling at him with joy in his eyes and then he was supposed to take him into his arms and kiss him back.

"What are you doing?" Max asked.

"Kissing you."

"I know that, but why?"

"Because . . . I wanted to. Paige isn't the only one who likes you, Max. In case you haven't figured it out, I like you, too. A lot." Anthony looked away and then back at Max. If there was ever a time when he was going to tell Max his feelings, this was it.

"What?" Max asked.

"I like you a lot," Anthony whispered. "I have feelings for you. Strong feelings."

At first Max didn't say anything. Then he ran a hand through his hair. Once, twice, before taking a deep breath and letting it out slowly. Anthony thought he looked even more gorgeous than usual. Then Max looked into Anthony's face and in that moment, Anthony *knew*. Max was straight.

"Anthony, I'm not like you. I'm into girls, not guys."

Anthony knew what he'd heard, but he didn't want to believe it. He wasn't ready to believe it. Not yet. "You're telling me you're straight?"

"Why do you sound so surprised?"

Anthony's head was spinning. Where did he begin?!

"You can't be straight. You just can't! It's impossible."

"Huh?"

"What about that kiss at my apartment?"

"What about it?"

"You were into it."

"Sure I was. So?"

"So? So? So?! How can you say 'So?' when you just admitted you were into it?"

"I was acting. My character, Michael, was into the kiss, but I wasn't."

"You were acting?"

"Yes, acting. I was pretending that I was kissing a girl."

He was pretending he was kissing a girl. Not you. NOT YOU!!! He hadn't been kissing me because he wanted to, or because he was attracted to me. He'd been acting. Acting!

Stupid, stupid, stupid. You're pathetic, Anthony. Paolo

tried to warn you, but you wouldn't listen. You thought you knew everything. You thought Max was interested in you, but he wasn't. He wasn't!

At that moment, all he wanted to do was run away and hide. He wanted to scream; he wanted to cry; he wanted to feel sorry for himself, but he wasn't going to. Oh, no. No public displays of self-pity. No breakdowns. Now was the time for answers so he could put this whole horrible mess behind him. Later, when he was home alone, he could fall to pieces.

"A few minutes ago, you said you weren't into Paige," Anthony said. "That she was a friend. But when I asked you if I was a friend, you said I was more than that. What did you mean?"

"You're also my director. What did you think I meant?"

"I thought you were interested in me," Anthony said, deciding not to beat around the bush anymore. "You know. Like a boyfriend. I thought you were gay."

"Why would you think that?" Max asked, his voice puzzled. "I never said I was gay."

"And you never said you were straight, either!" Anthony snapped. "Pardon my confusion!" Anthony got up from the picnic blanket. "You must think I'm a joke, don't you?"

"I don't think you're a joke," Max said, as he got to his feet. "You made a mistake, that's all. It's no big deal."

Anthony ignored his words. "I'm the poor deluded gay guy who develops a crush on a straight guy, right?"

"I didn't mean to mislead you. I didn't even know I was misleading you! I thought you knew I was straight! Anthony, you're one of the best friends I've made since moving to New York."

"That's a laugh! Best friends tell each other things. You've never told me one personal thing about yourself. You hardly talk about your life in California and you never mentioned a boyfriend or a girlfriend."

"You never asked me!"

"You never gave me a chance! You want to know why? Because *you* never once asked *me* one personal thing about my life. You knew I was gay and you never asked me what it was like. You never asked me if I'd ever had a boyfriend or if there was anyone at school who I was interested in. You never asked me *anything*! You always kept your guard up and you always kept people at a distance. Me. Paige. Even Felix!"

"I didn't mean to do that. It's hard being the new kid."

"Am I supposed to feel sorry for you? How about feeling sorry for me? Do you think it's easy being gay?" Anthony demanded. "It's not! And it's not something that's easy to talk about. At least not at first. All those weeks when I was trying to figure out if you were gay or straight, I wondered if maybe I should just ask you, but I was afraid you wouldn't want to be friends with me anymore. That if you were straight, you'd be weirded out because I had feelings for you, and if you were gay, you wouldn't have feelings for me. I was in a lose-lose situation!"

"I never meant to hurt you."

"Well, guess what, Max? You did."

Max shoved his hands into the pockets of his pants. "Would it help if I said I was sorry? Because I am. Your friendship means a lot to me, Anthony. I hope we can still be friends. Can we?"

Anthony couldn't believe Max's words. That was a switch.

Max was supposed to be the one who didn't want to be friends anymore. He wasn't supposed to be wondering if Anthony no longer wanted to be friends with him.

Anthony didn't know how to respond to Max's question. How would he be able to face him knowing he'd made such a huge fool of himself? Would he ever be able to forget this horrible, embarrassing day? So much for his gaydar! One thing he did know, he was never going on a picnic again! Or putting mustard on a sandwich!

"I can't answer that question now," Anthony said. "Ask me again in a couple of weeks."

"I will," Max promised. "And if you still don't have an answer, I'll ask you again."

"I better go," Anthony sighed.

"Are you going to be okay?" Max asked, concern in his voice.

He was not going to cry! Maybe later, when he was at home. But not now, in front of Max!

"Sure, I'll be fine," he said, keeping his voice steady.

"We're still filming the movie next Thursday, right?"

The movie?! Oh, no. The movie!!!

"I still want to do it, Anthony. Do you?"

"Yes, I do," Anthony answered without hesitation. And he did. There was no way he was going to jeopardize his chances of getting into UCLA. Although, in preparation of the kiss, he was going to make sure he ate an onion and garlic sandwich for lunch that day. Maybe breakfast, too. "I'll call you the night before filming."

And then Anthony left Max in the park and headed to the Frosted Cupcake.

chapter twenty-three

*P*aige breezed into the Frosted Cupcake, where she found Anthony sitting at their usual couch. "I got your message and came as soon as I could. My phone was turned off during the show." She looked at the empty cupcake wrappers in front of Anthony. "How many have you eaten so far?"

"Two," Roger said, placing another chocolate cupcake in front of Anthony. "And he's been inhaling them, not eating them. He still won't tell me what's wrong. Maybe you can coax it out of him."

"Remember Max?" Paige asked.

Roger frowned. "Max?"

"Our crush? The guy in the photo we showed you."

"Oh, right. Him. The cutie."

"We finally got an answer to our question."

"Question?" Roger scratched the side of his head with his

pen. "Sorry, but I feel like I've stepped into the middle of a movie."

"'Is he or isn't he?'"

"Ah!" Roger said, his face lighting up with understanding as he gazed at Anthony. "He's straight?"

"Straight," Anthony said.

Paige sat next to Anthony on the couch while Roger went to take another order. "How are you holding up?"

"My life is over!" Anthony wailed, resting his head on Paige's shoulder. "I've struck out twice in the romance department this year. First with Ian and now with Max."

"If it's any consolation, I struck out with Max, too."

"But at least you had a fighting chance with him!"

"Did I?" Paige shook her head. "I don't think so. We never really knew Max, did we? Sure, he was fun to hang out with, but it was like he was keeping everyone at a distance. I'm not just talking about you and me. It's like he thought he was better than everyone else at Peppington Prep. Did you notice how he never belonged to any particular clique? He just coasted from one to another. And he was always throwing around his father's money. It was like he was trying to buy everyone's friendship instead of just being himself."

"He was the new kid," Anthony pointed out. "That's what new kids do. He was trying to fit in."

"Don't defend him! I was the new kid once, too, and you went out of your way to become friends with me. So did Colleen and Bianca and Rachel. We tried to do the same thing with Max and he wouldn't let us. Plus, he really wasn't such a catch."

"Then why were we drooling over him for so many weeks?"

"Temporary insanity?"

"Seriously."

"Okay, okay, we were blinded by his cuteness and he could be thoughtful on occasion. But he also had a lot of faults."

"Like?"

"I told you how competitive he was when we were playing Monopoly. It was only a game, but from the way he was playing, you would have thought it was for real money."

"Did I ever tell you he wore socks with holes in them?"

"No!"

"I always noticed in gym class when he was putting on his sneakers. His big toe would always stick out. And they reeked!"

"Oh my god! So that's where that odor was coming from!"

"What are you talking about?"

"When we were playing Trivial Pursuit on Saturday afternoon in the Hamptons, all of a sudden there was this horrible odor in the sun room. We thought maybe a skunk had passed and sprayed the side of the house—we had one of the windows open a crack—but it had to be Max's feet! He must have taken his shoes off under the table."

Anthony started laughing hysterically. "Maybe we should start calling him Stinky!"

"And did you ever notice how girly his handwriting was?"

"Yes! He definitely dotted with hearts!"

"That's debatable."

"Trust me, they were hearts."

"And he was moody."

"Moody?"

"You never noticed? Whenever he'd get mad or something was bothering him, he wouldn't tell you. He'd just sulk like a spoiled brat. Who needs that? If I wanted a spoiled brat, I'd baby-sit." Paige put a hand on Anthony's arm. "Feeling better?"

"Much now that you're here."

"Me, too."

In the message he'd left, Anthony had given Paige a recap of everything that had happened in the park, including Max's rejection of her as well. Misery loves company, right? Although Paige didn't look miserable at all. She looked happy. Very happy. Hmmm. Something was going on.

"How was the awards dinner?" he casually asked.

"It was fun."

"Fun? When I think of Paolo I don't think of the word 'fun.'"

"Well, it was. And it didn't cost us six thousand dollars. Were you crazy bidding that much for Max?"

Anthony shrugged. "Who can put a price on love?"

"In this case, we can!"

"Relax. Colleen's mother is paying for it."

"Thank God!"

Anthony squinted at Paige. "Is it my imagination, or are you glowing?"

Paige pulled out her compact and inspected her face. "Am I really glowing?"

Anthony gasped as he finally figured out what was going on. "Paige! Don't tell me my brother *kissed* you?"

Paige snapped her compact shut. "No, he didn't kiss me, but he did ask me out on a date!"

Anthony's eyes lit up. "He did?"

"Yes, he did. After I listened to the message you left about Max. And you know what? I'm glad he did! Who cares about Max? Yes, I'm disappointed that he wasn't interested in me, but even if we had dated, in the end things probably wouldn't have worked out."

"Why do you say that?"

"Think about it. Max wants to be actor. He was pretending with both of us and not letting either one of us see who he really was. For a relationship to work, you really have to know the person you're involved with. Otherwise it's never going to last."

"So you think Pow is boyfriend material?"

Paige mulled over Anthony's question. For years Paolo had always been Anthony's older brother. Until recently, she'd never thought of him as anything other than that. But in the last few days she'd discovered that *he* didn't think of her as Anthony's best friend. He thought of her just as Paige. Someone to laugh with. To argue with. To talk to. And maybe even more.

At that moment, Paige realized something. Sometimes what you're looking for is right under your nose and you don't even know it.

"I think Paolo is excellent boyfriend material," she said. "But ask me again after our first date."

"Oh my god!" Anthony gasped.

"What?"

"It just occurred to me that you could wind up being my future sister-in-law!"

Paige rolled her eyes. "You are *such* a drama queen."

"And on your wedding day, you wouldn't have to worry about me wanting to kiss your groom!"

Paige laughed. "Let's take things one date at a time." She gave Anthony a hug. "Have I told you lately that I'm so lucky you're my best friend?"

Anthony hugged Paige back. "And have I told you lately that I'm lucky you're mine? Who needs boyfriends when we have each other?"

Just then Roger arrived with two cups of hot chocolate, placing them on the table in front of the couch.

"We didn't order these," Anthony said.

"I know. Compliments of me. Having a broken heart sucks."

"Thanks, Roger," Paige said. "That's really thoughtful of you."

"Not a problem." Roger reached into the back pocket of his jeans and pulled out two concert tickets, holding them in front of Anthony's face. "Here's something else that might cheer you up. They're for this Friday night. Wanna go?"

Anthony's eyes widened with glee as he saw the name of the performer on the tickets. It was his favorite pop princess. "I love her! How did you get tickets? This show has been sold out for months!"

"I have my ways. So, you didn't answer my question. Wanna go?"

"It's sweet of you to try and make me feel better, Roger, but wouldn't you rather take one of your glamazons?" Anthony asked, biting into a cupcake. He glanced around the bakery and was shocked to discover no glamazons in sight. Huh. That was a first. "You're guaranteed a better time if you take one of them."

Roger gave him a confused look. "What's a glamazon?"

Anthony waved a hand while munching on a cupcake. "You know. One of your girlfriends. Tall, thin, leggy, big chest, long hair. The ones who look like they moonlight as supermodels."

Roger began laughing hysterically. "You thought those were my girlfriends? Are you serious?"

"Weren't they?"

Roger kept laughing. In fact, he was laughing so hard, his face started turning red. "No! I'm part of the tutoring program at my high school. Those glamazons are from our cheerleading squad. I was only helping them pull their grades up."

"They weren't your girlfriends?" Anthony asked, confusion in his voice.

Roger leaned over Anthony's hot chocolate and gave him an extra blast of whipped cream. "You and I are two of a kind," he whispered into Anthony's ear. "If you know what I mean."

Anthony started choking on his cupcake while an open-mouthed Paige started pounding him on the back.

"You're *gay*?" Anthony asked between coughs.

Roger nodded. "Yep. As gay as you are." He stuck the tickets back into his pocket. "Let me know by Friday if you want to go to the concert. You know where to find me. If you can't make it, we'll rent some scary DVDs. You said we were going to do that some night, remember?"

Roger then gave Anthony a wink before heading to another table.

"He's not straight," Anthony said to Paige in stunned disbelief. "He's gay. Roger is *gay*."

"Yes, I heard," Paige said. "I was sitting right here."

"I don't believe it. Roger is gay and he wants to go out with me." Anthony gasped. "Roger is interested in *me*. He wants to go out with me! All this time he's been right under my nose and I didn't have a clue! How could I have been so blind?"

"You jumped to a conclusion. Like you did with Max."

"Max?" Anthony asked. "Who's Max? I don't know anyone named Max. I only know the name Roger!"

"Does this mean you've got plans for Friday night? We were supposed to go to the movies, remember?"

"Get Paolo to take you. I've got a date with Roger!"

"I have to tell you something," Paige said to Anthony, taking a sip of her hot chocolate. "And I'm only telling you this because I love you, so listen closely, okay?"

"Yes?" Anthony asked, his eyes glued on Roger, as if he was afraid he might disappear. "What is it?"

"You really need to get your gaydar checked out!" Paige laughed. "For months you've had a hottie like Roger totally into you and you didn't even know it!"

"Okay, okay, you don't have to rub it in! So I'm not perfect."

"But Roger is," Paige said, watching him walk across the bakery. "He's so cute!"

Anthony licked a bit of frosting off his upper lip and grinned at Paige. "Isn't he?!"

acknowledgments

First, a huge thank you to Abigail McAden, who called, pitched me a two-sentence premise and then asked if I could come up with an outline. Abby, did I ever tell you I thought you were calling to ask me for the name of one of my authors to write this story? I'm so glad I was wrong and that you were calling to ask me!

An even bigger thank you to my fabulous editor, Lexa Hillyer. Thank you for your superb editorial letter and all your great suggestions. You've made this book the best that it can be.

Thanks are also due to my terrific agent, Evan Marshall, who I love gossiping with, and all my wonderful friends and co-workers: Tracy Bernstein (who loves to bash *Days of Our Lives* as much as I do. Will they ever bring back Steve and

Kayla?!), Libba Bray (yes, *that* Libba Bray, author of *A Great and Terrible Beauty* and *Rebel Angels*), Rosanna Chiofalo (who knows what it's like to be Italian!), Paul Dinas (I miss having you as my boss!), Neven Gravett (aka the Office Cupid), David Korabik (you know you're my best friend, right?), Kevin O'Brien (who loves good-bad movies as much as I do), Jim Pascale (my best friend from NYU), Elise Donner Smith (you will *always* be fabulous!), Aldo Palma (computer guru and my best friend from high school) and Justin Hocking, who helps me stay sane from 9 to 5 (and who I know will one day be writing an acknowledgments page of his own).

A big thank you, too, to Doug Mendini, for the champagne in P-Town and the Friday night margaritas in May 2005.